Advanced p

"The voice, writing, and atmosphere are absolutely stunning."
— **Damyanti Biswas, author of *You Beneath Your Skin***

"On a cold winter's night on the streets of the South Bronx, the white son of a billionaire is chained naked to an outdoor cage, where he is beaten and tattooed by onlookers. Following the stories of over a dozen characters—including a cop, a rapper, a tattoo artist, a homeless man, and a reporter among many others—the novel unravels the mystery of why the son of a billionaire has subjected himself to such violence. Equal parts Quentin Tarantino and Paul Beatty, *Blood at the Root* is a sharp-witted social satire that takes unflinching aim at race and class privilege in contemporary America. In a novel where countless small but forceful stories constitute the book's meaning, *Blood at the Root* reveals that it is ultimately the spectacle of racial violence that truly unifies us."
— **Justin Gifford, Associate Professor of English, University of Nevada, Reno; Author of *Pimping Fictions: African American Crime Literature and the Untold Story of Black Pulp Publishing* and *Street Poison: The Biography of Iceberg Slim***

"Totally engaging, full of vivid, varied characters"
— **José Sotolongo, author of *The Scented Chrysalis***

"Darkly fantastic explorations of race, class, and citizenship arrive dressed in a stark realism that forces us to recognize Darrell's world as our own. Darrell's prose compels us to turn the page, almost as anxious to see how and why these events unfold as we are to see just what will happen next. *Blood at the Root* is a book full of more questions than answers - and that is the point. Race, class, citizenship: these name the great questions of our age and *Blood at the Root* deepens them all. The novel is a powerful reminder that fiction still speaks its truth."
— **Donovan Irven, Associate Editor, *Analecta Hermeneutica*; Director of Philosophical Praxis, Filo Sofi Arts**

"Ciahnan Darrell's debut novel, *A Lifetime of Men* (2020), conveyed a strong sense of gender inequities in its gripping narrative of feisty women ensnared in the dark realities of social structures. *Blood at the Root* is similarly imbued with a sharp awareness of racial injustices and complexities. This timely and provocative novel poses incomplete and impossible questions, allowing the answers to dissolve, one into the other in a dialogical frame. Calling upon thirty-three distinct voices, Darrell explores the torsions of power and representation that shape race discourses in our society, offering neither resolution nor summary, but rather allowing these diverse voices to testify to the durable sway of racialized narratives. Audacious in its scope, meticulous in its construction, and relentless in its disavowal of its own authority, the novel is by turns shocking, insightful, offensive, humorous, and tender—an excellent catalyst for a visceral conversation."

— Amritjit Singh, Langston Hughes Professor Emeritus, Ohio University

Blood
at the
Root

Ciahnan Darrell

atmosphere press

To Rev. Chris Dorsey, Colten Hibbs, and Rory Johnson
for their wisdom, power, and generosity of spirit;
and to Jennifer and Grady Darrell, whom I love.

That whereof we cannot speak, thereof we must remain silent.

— **Ludwig Wittgenstein**

If certain things are described to you as being real they're real for you whether they're real or not.

— **James Baldwin**

J. CHRISTOPHER FAIRCHILD

It is four-thirty in the morning, not yet day but warming, the sky still mostly opaque, a phthalo green, now, as opposed to the onyx of true night. The boy is being led on a length of chain, handcuffed. He does not struggle. He does not speak. He is naked, shoeless; shards of glass cut into his feet as he walks, but he doesn't seem to notice, only continues walking, bleeding. It is hard to guess his age; his testicles have descended and he has a thatch of pubic hair, but there's no flesh beneath his epidermis, only bone reaching out through his skin, the ribs and sternum nearly free, the clavicle, skull, and vertebrae not far behind. The street is mostly deserted. The camera remains with the boy as he walks, so there is no way to tell where he is or who is on the other end of the chain. Two, three times, people appear behind him, their mouths open, frozen around words that won't come, their eyes gaping, suspicious. All are wearing thick jackets, winter hats, and gloves.

The structure appears like a leviathan, a hellfire-red, rolling steel scaffold eight feet high and six feet wide. The back of the man on the other end of the chain appears, followed by another man; both wear vestments: an alb, girdle, stole, and chasuble. One has braids that fall to his shoulders, the other's hair is cropped to his scalp. They undo the boy's chain and handcuff his wrists to horizontal slats on opposite ends of the scaffolding, then his ankles, and move off-camera.

The boy is shivering. His skin has taken on a purplish cast.

The man with short hair reappears and places a small table to one

3

side of the structure, and the man with braids places something on it too dark to see, and this is when even those who chose to watch the uncut version of the video reach for their trackpad, because the action dies for over an hour. The priests take up positions on either side of the boy, standing motionless, silent, and the camera doesn't pan or track, only stares into the darkness encompassing the two men and the boy between them. Light emerges from the womb of night slowly, releasing gradient and line, detail, breath by skein, the advent of color.

One of the priests is Caucasian and one is African American, and both wear masks that cover their eyes and the upper slope of their cheekbones. The Black man's mask is ivory, the white man's onyx; both are hand-carved and polished to a sheen. The men's vestments are identical.

Light flashes off a small puddle between them—the boy's urine, passed under cover of night.

People come. At first, there are very few, and they are very cautious; we don't see them, but the camera seizes upon their footsteps and voices, their breathing. We see a hand take the object from the table, hear a click and a loud electric whine. The noise stops, but the object isn't returned, and we wait for the priests to object, but they don't, only reach for a replacement.

The camera stares.

There are new voices, loud voices, and fresh footfall.

"Yo, man, what the hell you doing? What is this?"

"An offering," says one priest.

"Foolishness," says the other.

"What?"

"This man wishes to atone for his sins and those of his forefathers."

"This man is merely compounding them."

"Four fathers? What the hell you talking about?"

"He offers you his body and voice."

"His body?"

"He offers nothing."

"Da fuck do I want with his body?"

"It is what he takes from you, what his forefathers took from your forefathers."

"Took from me?"

"I warn you, Friend, he only seeks to relieve himself of the guilt he feels."

"I ain't never seen this cracker before in my life."

Time.

The white priest scratches his nose, checks his watch. The boy's eyes are glassy, unfocused; his head lolls left, right, falls, jerks upright.

The day swells, the light growing increasingly intense, blinding the camera.

Time.

An hour more; people move around the periphery, but no one touches the object on the table, no one steps into the frame. The boy is awake if not alert, staring at the broken asphalt in front of him. The priests step off-camera, resume their places immediately, different, somehow—one shorter, the other taller, maybe.

The boy collapses, his knees corkscrewing out from under him. He falls forward, jerked backward at the limit of the handcuffs, dangles.

"Shit!" The Black priest rushes to the boy, tries to hold him up. "Help me get him down," he says. "We need to get him to a hospital!"

"No," the white priest says. His voice is different than before, higher.

"What do you mean, no? He's going to die!"

"He isn't."

"So now you're a doctor?"

"No, I'm seven hundred bucks short of making rent."

"I'm calling!"

"The fuck you are!"

The Black priest reaches into his pocket for his phone, but the white priest grabs his wrist and twists it up behind his back. "Six hours," he says.

"Let go!" the man flails, trying to jerk himself free.

"Take it easy, bro. Okay? Take a deep breath."

"Fuck you! Let me go!"

"All we have to do is stand here for six hours, then we get paid."

"He's going to die!"

"He's not going to die."

"Look at him!"

The boy is in a fugue state, half-hanging and half-standing, caught in a torsion of spasms that send him twisting one way, then the other, like a marionette hanging from its strings.

"He wanted this, remember? He hired us to do this. He's a sick fucking bastard, but that's not our problem. Our problem is rent. Rent and food. Now, I'm going to let you go, and I need you to be cool. Can you do that?"

The Black priest nods.

"Good."

A detente.

Time.

Light and wind; trash blowing through the camera frame periodically: a wrapper from McDonald's, an advertisement from *The Post*, ticket stubs, and a plastic bottle rolling the length of the alley until it hits the Black priest's foot and he kicks it away.

We don't know this, but it's Saturday morning, and even if much of the city didn't make it home from their post-after-party breakfasts until seven or eight, it's still New York; the ambient noise, constant, a susurrus of conversation, traffic, footfall, and wind.

It is just shy of eleven when the next person comes on camera, virility emanating from his pores, rising with his breath. He is twenty-five or twenty-six, walking with two women, his chest and jaw thrust at the world like a blade as his muscles threaten to burst from his tank top, which is visible because he's unzipped his jacket to his navel despite the cold. His hair is done in tight rows.

"Fuck is this?" he asks, separating from the women, directly in front of the camera.

The priests tell him, one then the other, following the script.

"Whatever you say, man." He gestures at the object on the table. "That an iron, for, like, tattoos and shit?"

"It is," the Black priest answers.

The man takes the iron from the table, handles it, grins. "Don't see many marshmallows around here."

The priests are silent.

"You lost, Marshmallow?" the man asks the white priest, sunlight dancing off the diamonds in his ears. "And you." He turns to the Black priest. "How stupid is you, nigger? How stupid you have to be to be hanging out with Marshmallow and his butt-ass-naked honky friend in Mott Haven?"

"Come on, D," one of the women calls, "let's get out of here."

D ignores her.

The white priest says his line and the Black priest follows with his.

"What the fuck are you talking about?"

D moves closer to the priests, muscles taut, teeth bared. A shard of light leaps from the tattoo gun. D clicks it on, unleashing a pulsating electric shriek.

"What I do know is your friend's about to get a tattoo."

The white priest nods.

"What?"

"It is foolishness." The Black priest's voice is barely audible as he speaks.

"Fuck did Uncle Tom just say to me?"

"He is here to atone for his sins" —the white priest's voice cracks beneath his mask— "and those of his forefathers."

"Fuck his forefathers."

The man takes the gun from the table, grabs a fistful of the boy's hair, and yanks backward, exposing his forehead and throat.

"You pussies ain't even gonna try to stop me, is you?"

"Why would we?" asks the white priest. "This is why we're here."

Metal; motor; time.

The man finishes, drops the gun on the table without turning it off, squints at the priests, spits, and turns to go without a word.

"Shit," says the white priest.

The Black priest doesn't respond, reaches for the tattoo gun, and turns it off.

"What's it say?"

The boy is semi-conscious, barely able to stand. He's not supposed to talk, but we don't know that, nor are we aware that he hasn't eaten in twenty-two days, or slept for three. All we know is that he's naked, emaciated, and cold.

And that this is the first tattoo.

The white priest tries to read it, fails. "I can't make it out," he says. "There's too much blood."

"It says, 'This what happens to cracker-ass, honky, marshmallow motherfuckers who come to the Mott with their bitch-ass, bonky, oreo friends.'"

The white priest squinted. "You can get all that?"

"I watched him write it."

THE GIGGLE HOUSE

Alright, alright, I get it—I'm funny as fuck. Thank you, thank you very much—alright! Listen, people, it's time to cut that applause shit and get down to it. This stuff is no joke, and we don't have a lot of time, so a brief shout out to The Giggle House—thank you for inviting me—and it's time to get real.

DESTA

Desta's momma had to work because her daddy couldn't. He hadn't worked a day in Desta's remembered life, and couldn't even take care of himself, so someone had to stay home with him, and because Desta was slow, that somebody was her, and she had to stop going to school.

That was in the fifth grade.

Desta's brother's name was Denis but they called him DJ. DJ was good in school and Momma and Daddy was real proud of him. He went to three different schools and he did so good he got to go to a special school Desta couldn't remember, and he did good there, too, so he got to go to a school where they taught doctoring.

Then the police came and said DJ done bad and was in trouble and Momma had to get him out of jail, and after that, he had to stop doctoring school.

It happened again two or three more times and Momma said he was real sick and couldn't come home no more.

He in jail? Desta asked, and Momma shook her head.

They keeping him in some kind of hospital.

Because he sick?

Momma nodded.

Did he take a pill? You give me a pill when I'm sick and it makes me better.

It's a different kind of sick, Momma said.

That was a while ago.

Daddy died after the police decided to keep DJ and Momma wasn't Momma after that. She was like she was dead even though she was moving.

Then one day, Momma didn't wake up, and Desta went into her room and found she wasn't breathing, and since Desta didn't know what to do she didn't do anything. When Momma started to smell after a few days, Desta still didn't know what to do and the smell got so bad, a neighbor called the police and the police came and took Momma away.

Two people came with the police that wasn't police but was still some way important. They asked how old she was so she said sixteen and they wanted to know where she went to school, so Desta told them she didn't go and they asked why and when she told them they got quiet and frowning and asked if she had any other family.

She said no and they said she had to go live somewhere else and she said she didn't want to but they didn't listen.

The places they made her stay were bad and dirty and mean and she didn't like them.

She saw DJ once from the bus she and the woman whose house she lived in took to the grocery store. After that, she would sneak out of the house and go looking for him. She didn't find him most times and when she did he looked like he wasn't eating or taking no showers.

Momma said you had to eat so you don't disappear.

Maybe the important people made him live not at home too and he didn't like it neither and was trying to disappear so they couldn't make him.

DJ never answered when she spoke to him and it made her sad. He pretended like he didn't know her even though he was her brother.

But she still liked seeing him.

One time Desta saw him when she was with the woman. Desta waved and said hello and the woman whose house she was staying in told her not to speak to street people and Desta said but DJ my brother and the woman looked at her and shook her head.

Poor thing, the woman said, which didn't make no sense because DJ was the one was dirty and ashy and wearing nasty clothes.

Desta was fine.

Right as rain.

Daddy used to say that.

A white woman visited her at the woman's house once a week and kept saying she wanted to get reading lessons for Desta and would Desta like that and Desta kept saying yes but the woman couldn't figure how to do it which confused Desta.

There was lots of schools.

All she had to do was pick.

Two other girls stayed in the house with her and the woman. Desta didn't say nothing to them because they made fun of her whenever she did and said retard and stupid and she looked funny.

Desta didn't look funny.

There was a mirror in the bathroom and she'd looked to see.

And how she supposed to be smart if she couldn't go to school?

Momma said she wasn't dumb. Things just took her awhile.

Momma said that was fine because she wasn't never gonna have no job or no man to cook for.

Last time Desta saw DJ he was near the tracks that go under St. Ann's Avenue. Sometimes she'd sneak out and try to find him. People said you shouldn't never walk in Mott Haven at night like they was afraid of something, but Desta didn't know what.

She liked walking at night because it was quiet and no one bothered her the way those girls did in the day.

They was real mean.

One time they saw her go out and the next day they had a boy with them and said they'd tell the woman what she done unless she lifted up her dress and let the boy touch her.

She didn't want to get in trouble so she did, but she didn't like it because the boy was hard and made her bleed and the girls called her slut and ho after, which wasn't fair because they was the ones made her do it.

One night Desta went out looking for DJ and found a white boy instead. He was tied up to some kind of cage thing in an alley which didn't make no sense. And she didn't mean to but she saw his thing, which she knew was bad because Momma said no man should ever show a woman his thing and no good woman should ever look at it.

She'd closed her eyes when that boy was touching her so she wouldn't see nothing she shouldn't.

Momma said you couldn't touch yourself certain places because they was private and if you couldn't touch them Desta figured you shouldn't be showing them to no one either.

She wasn't for sure about it though because Momma didn't pay her own word no mind when it came to privates and touching. Desta used to hear noises at night, and a couple times she'd gone down the hall to see what they was and seen Momma doing stuff to those parts with men that wasn't Daddy.

She asked Momma about it and Momma just looked at her and sighed and said something about Jons and Bills which Desta thought meant that it was okay to do stuff with a man's thing if his name Jon or Bill, which didn't make no sense neither.

But Momma knowed stuff because she was older than Desta so Desta just figured that rules about Jons and Bills and their things was another something it would take her longer to figure out.

The alley the white boy was hanging in was only a couple blocks from the place she'd last seen DJ. She figured maybe she'd see him again if she waited long enough and since other people was all there staring at the white boy, she thought maybe he was one of those Jons or Bills and it must be okay if everyone else was seeing his thing, so she hid beside one of the trash barrels with a fire in it and tried to get warm.

Two weird-looking guys in masks watched people do things to the white boy until a man and woman showed up and waved guns and told them to get gone. Then they took loud pens out of their pockets and started drawing on the white boy.

She hadn't seen many white people up close and none that had blue eyes so she hoped the boy would wake up and open his eyes and they'd be blue, but he never did.

Blue was her second favoritest color.

When Daddy was alive he said that white people wasn't no good and was mean and bad, but this one didn't seem mean or bad. Just cold. He kept shaking and shaking and didn't nobody bring him nothing to warm him up and at first she thought they was mean but then she realized she was wearing gloves and a hat and a scarf and a sweatshirt and a coat and hadn't given the white boy nothing neither and she couldn't figure whether she was mean too or if it was okay because she was still cold even with all her clothes on.

She inched closer to the fire barrel near where the boy was hanging. Up close she saw he had hair that was thin and straight and near white—yellow and white at the same time, like some of the thread Momma used to put buttons on the clothes people brought her.

Desta could see the boy's veins through his skin and wanted to touch him to see if his skin felt different like it looked, but then she saw Maurice and knowed that if he saw her he'd make her go home because he knowed Momma when she was alive and that Momma wouldn't have wanted Desta out this late.

Desta made herself small behind the barrel and stayed close to it to get warm but not so close it burnt her and watched the boy until a man she didn't know started pestering her.

Little girl, he said. Little girl. He was laughing and poking and putting his hands where the other boy had. She slapped them but he kept putting them back and laughing and then he grabbed her hard and she yelled and Maurice jerked his head toward the sound and saw her and growled at her to go home and yanked the man off his feet by his hair and started beating on him.

Desta ran until she couldn't breathe and then she had to stop and she looked up and saw that she was close to where she was staying and she was cold but not tired and she wanted to see her brother, so she walked real slow and counted how many different things she could see to give her brother time.

But DJ never came and Desta's hands and feet got to hurting real bad so she climbed through the window back into her room.

She missed her brother and started to get sad but then she thought how pretty the light from the streetlights was shining off the broken bottles on the sidewalk and in the street and how the shoes hanging from the power lines made her think of angels running in the sky.

She took off her gloves and boots and hat and scarf and set them on her dresser and she took her coat off and, as she hung it on the hook on the back of her bedroom door, she wondered what Maurice had done to that man that grabbed her.

She kept her socks on but got out of her clothes and put on pajamas and got in bed and pulled the covers up tight.

Daddy didn't like white people but she thought that maybe if he'd seen that boy and talked with him some he might have liked him because the boy didn't look like he wanted to do nothing bad to no one.

Sleep was coming on quick but Momma said you should pray before you went to bed and so even though she'd prayed when she went to bed the first time she thought she'd better do it again. She said everything she always did, asked God to watch over the woman who owned the house and to make her smarter so the other girls wouldn't make fun of her and to send DJ to see her. And she asked him to take care of the white boy too and make sure he didn't get too cold.

THE GIGGLE HOUSE

Y'all hear about the new drug they coming out with? Yeah? It's a dick pill. They calling it "Black," guaranteed to double your dong in a New York minute.

Now before you wypipo hiding in the corner get too excited, you should know that it has some pretty serious side effects: cab drivers, employers, and loan providers won't be able to see you no more, cops in your vicinity are going to hallucinate automatic weapons, and hot damn if you won't be drawn to Tyler Perry movies, drinking water at room temperature, and baby BOUGIE tees like a moth to a motherfucking flame.

THE TREE

It is the beginning of the second night, the second of three—four-thirty, or five o'clock, the sun casting its last fits of light.

Five or six people are camped in the alley while the boy bleeds, derelicts in decaying clothes smeared with filth, all of them out of their damn minds, mad or otherwise, getting their drunk on, their rock, their high. Every so often, one of them glances up, but his eyes dart away from the boy even before they alight, as if his pipe, his pin, his rock, his blunt would up and vanish apart from the weight of his eyes. They're waiting for something, maybe, gauzy-headed and brick-tongued, the agitated and the floating, the high and the low.

The tattoo artists work without looking up. The man is wearing a knit hat and at least two layers beneath a hooded sweatshirt shimmering in the camera light; there are teardrops falling over his coal-Black skin, tattoos in Spanish and English and Latin, and a snub-nosed .45 tucked in his back pocket. Muscle stands sentry at the perimeter of the alley, strapped and flying Brims' colors. The other artist is a chicana, maybe, some kind of light-skinned mujer; she's wearing jeans, a flannel shirt, thermal underwear, a scarlet bandana that keeps her hair out of her eyes, and a scar that looks earned, a razored crease curling from her lip to her ear.

Tom Shipp dangles just beneath the boy's left armpit; Abram Smith's a little higher up. The gray work is stunning, brings death to life, mangled flesh and viscera, limbs and wreck-necked bodies soldered into a harrowing gnarl. The boy is waking now, moaning.

The woman cuts the power to her iron and fishes two pills from a bottle in her pocket, pries the boy's mouth open, and pushes them in. She shoves a water bottle between his teeth, holds his mouth shut, clamps down on his nose until he swallows, checks his throat, and returns to work.

The corpses they put on the boy are bleeding him dry, siphoning his flesh into their own distended bodies, but The Tree—the woman is finishing it now—The Tree is an allegory, a god gorging on the boy's spine, driving rods into his bones, carving a trough down his shoulder and into his armpit, then casting his life-sucked carcass aside and turning on the artist, wrenching her to the bidding of Its serrated roots as with so many others, mile after mile in Texas, from Gainesville to Waco and onward, in Marion, Indiana and Duluth, Minnesota, outside the Rex Theater in Leland, Mississippi, strange fruit thrown and flowering at every stop, sweet and dripping and metastatic—in Bainbridge, Georgia, the hardwood and whispering leaves bold and lush as the roots below gorged on screw-necked bodies and salt-metal blood and the excrement voided as the twitching dead were sacrificed and borne into the air, and The Tree tumescent, ejaculating into the hoary earth and whelping wraiths, vicious, feral creatures bound to torment and shrieking agony as their blood turned to ash in their veins and flesh and tallow ran liquescent in the anguish of interminable fire as they killed and spat and sucked and were not slaked, rapacious legions of abominations churning through soil and rock and time as the '30s became the '40s and '50s and '60s, scything through Walton County, Georgia, and Money, Mississippi, the stench of rotting flesh pulsating from their lipless mouths, and the revulsion, dazzling raped and glut and savaged—seizing bodies and hauling them into the earth to lay before The Tree in a lightless pit, flesh for The Tree to suck and sup and transmute into the miasmic perfume that wafts from Its leaves, calling to all who might walk and breathe and hate as necrotic blood falls along the crenelletions in Its bark like sweat beneath an eternal sun.

THE GIGGLE HOUSE

That's right, wypipo—I may not be able to see you through these stage lights, but the place smells like wet dog, so I know you're here, plus there's thirty Priuses parked in the valet.

I have no idea what the hell you're doing at a show called "Surviving Black." You're not even allowed to laugh at most of the jokes.

I'm serious. You laugh, and Oscar's going to run you—I ain't playing.

You're still fucking laughing.

Wypipo amazing.

DANTE

"He said what?" Fat Mike crowed. "Oh, shit, oh shit! Goat done say Dante a bitchmade Earl! He bringin' maximum disrespect, nigga—MAXIMUM! That's some motherfucking, dope-ass, bodybag material!

"Dante! Dante! You look a little shook, nigga—you gonna be okay? You lookin' a little exposed, like you might could be about to choke. Say it ain't so, youngin. Tell me you ain't about to bitch the fuck out."

He knew he shouldn't buck, needed to reel it in. But fuck, this wasn't no URL—just a small room in the back of an old warehouse with a bullshit stage and a bullshit sound system where local rappers battled for bullshit prize money on Friday and Saturday nights.

It wasn't much better than a cipher, really, hardly even a PG, because ain't no more than a handful of people around to see what went down—and that bitch-nigger host who ran the battles hadn't mattered in a minute, not since he got shit-canned from his radio show.

Fuck him, Dante thought. And fuck his mother.

He glared at his opponent, working out his angle as the host tried to hype the crowd. A tall-ass, albino-nigger that looked like a Q-tip.

Fuck him.

Dante called heads, lost the flip.

Q-tip pointed at him.

Now the host was in his face, taunting him, "What'll it be, Dante? You gonna battle, or piss yourself? It look like you about to piss yourself."

20

Dante took a step closer to the man so the mic'd catch his words. "First, I'm a KO this bitch, then I'm gonna fuck your mother in the alley, and come back 'round and clip the next bitch you put in front of me. We'll talk after, you tired old haz-been, stank-ass, dime-store nigger."

The audience roared.

"Tough talk for a nigga whose balls haven't dropped."

"You keep my balls outta your mouth, nigger." Dante ripped the mic out of his hand. "And get the fuck out of my way."

He worked the saliva around his mouth with his tongue.

The lighting in the room was shit, the crowd a shadow.

The mic cracked in his hand.

Fuck it.

No windows, sawdust beneath his feet, and a room full of faggot-niggers smelled like piss and malt liquor.

His pulse thundered in his ears.

The host cued the DJ.

The beat dropped.

Alright...Alright...Mic check, one, two, one two...

Fuck the world.

Life iz a battle, nigga & I'm going out rich
Doin' lyrical murder, ballz deep in yo bitch
Bodies b dropping and it only g'tting' hotter
Cuz Ima 'bout to throw down like Afrika Bambaataa

They call me Jack fucking Ripper cuz I'm boss with a
    blade
Better run, poser, cuz you bout to get flayed
You playin' like u here 2 battle, but u need to a doctor
Cuz u came in here like a lamb 2 da slaughter

Kilos, chrome, & bitches, u b using the right words
But u writin' 'em on a laptop in yo mama' house in da
    'burbs

Ain't nothing real 'bout you, nigga, so tru G's b ownin'
    ya
Yo' wack rhymes is booty & yo' bling's cubic zirconia

Look at that bitch, he make Ambian obsolete
Don't have shit to say once da DJ drop a beat
Ain't no bullets in hiz piece, cuz buster ain't no gangsta
Just makin' shit up like the original wangsta

Let's just say what everybody know
U biting big dicks, cuz u like da taste when they blow
You lethal boring, nigga, your condition is critical
But don't worry, u gonna live, cuz my intervention b
    biblical

I murdered this man, now Ima give him back his life
Cuz Niggas ain't b needin' any more strife
Dr. Dre, ain't lyin': bullets iz flyin' and brothers iz dyin'
Pappa in the pen & momma iz cryin'

2Pac b right & Slick Rick & Andre
Nas, Common, Rhymefest, & mother-fucking Kanye
Tru niggaz hustle & perpetrate heists
But they ain't takin' from each other, they ripping from
    whites

If u a tru nigga, u don't kill no brother
Wake the fuck up—the cops got that shit covered
If we ain't together, then we're fallin' apart
Black America: GSW, 2 pills in da heart

Yesterday I needed scratch so I vicked a man, he
Wore high heels and a dress, guess he waz a tranny
Wallet, watch, & phone, I told him 2 run 'em
No one had 2 bleed, but the bitch bucked, so I stuck him

I ran a few blocks, came on some niggas in a rage
Beating the shit outta a honky in a cage
His dick b jus' hangin' there 2 tiny 2 screw

22

And seein' him, nigga, remind me of u

Stuck, cut & bounced left the tranny in the street
U do what u have 2 cuz a brother gotta eat
Life hard, so we gotta b harder
So get stony, homie, and keep away from King Arthur.

The beat died. Dante dropped the mic where he stood and walked off stage.

Let that faggot pick it up.

A few men chucked him on the shoulder as he walked by, but he didn't stop, punched through the front door and hit up a bodega, twenty bucks for a 40 and a dime of dank-ass sticky.

Two battles down, one to go.

He rolled a J, tucked it behind his ear.

Ain't none of these bitches can touch me.

"You gonna share the wealth, young buck?"

Old man was pointing at his Chiba.

"This ain't no cyph, nigger."

"Well, fuck you then."

Fuck me? Naw, old man, you done fucking. You been done fucking for a long motherfucking time.

THE GIGGLE HOUSE

Who else we got here tonight? I see a bunch of brothers and sisters, hermanos y hermanas—I know my people've had beef with your people, pero the enemy of my enemy, right? Solidaridad—tenemos que mantenernos unidos.

Laquanda's an eighty-seven-year-old, sword-swallowing lesbian from Detroit, José is a seventeen-year-old digital overlord from Oaxaca. She loves Sudoku; his momma once drilled him with a shoe at thirty yards—what brought them together?

Wypipo.

ARIANA

There were tears in Ariana's eyes as she walked; some belonged to the cold, and some to the gash on her face, but most were Javy's.

He lay in a bed in the ICU at Lincoln Hospital, comatose. She'd been at his bedside holding his hand when his girlfriend arrived, knocked her to the ground, and beat her with a metal bedpan until two orderlies pulled her off.

"Fucking puta," the woman spat at Ariana, "you ain't nobody's cousin, I don't give a damn what Javy say."

It was true. She wasn't.

She was bleeding tears into a metal wind with three stitches in her eyebrow. She'd walked fifteen blocks from the hospital to her apartment at 137th and Brook, trying to clear her head, doubled back despite the cold, moving north with no destination in mind, away from the decaying, chapuza studio she shared with two chicanas, needing to move and to feel herself doing it, for the twist and rip induced by twelve straight hours of tattooing to blot out all thought.

She had grown up amongst the wealthiest habaneros, wanting for nothing, came of age in the ballroom of the Hotel Nacional, wearing a dress designed by Rei Kawakubo; people talked about her quinceañera for months, about her gown, the food, the elegance of the couples dancing around her, the brilliance of the diamonds she wore in her ears and around her neck, exceeded only by the startling perfection of the waltz she danced in the epicenter of the ballroom, five hundred eyes watching: celebrities, dignitaries, diplomats, family.

Fidel had declined her father's invitation with apologies, and sent Raul in his stead.

She was beautiful, would have been even without the gown and the jewelry and the hours spent on her hair and makeup. Her father doted on her and her mother, surprised them with little gifts for no reason, kissed them frequently. Los amo, mis corazones, he'd say. And her mother loved her father back, and loved her and her brother and sister, too, and cared enough to teach them about the world, to make sure Ariana and her siblings knew how the rest of the country lived, including los vagabundos y los indigentes. Her mother took her to a soup kitchen on the outskirts of La Habana one night a week, and they helped serve food and pour drinks, and cleaned up after the desamparados had gone and the doors were locked.

Lo más importante, her mother said, was to know that their fortune was a matter of luck, rather than merit, and to strive to be as good as they were lucky.

So she'd known about the needy, but nothing of the predatory. She listened to her mother and made herself into light and joy and kindness, but was told nothing of politics, was never warned of the tectonic plates shifting beneath her family's feet.

She adored everyone, and believed that everyone adored her, and then, a week before she turned twenty-one, her father traded her to the Minister of the Interior, an obese man forty-three years her senior, renowned for the perversity of his appetites.

Her father traded her for her mother and sister and little brother—for their lives, and probably his own.

How could she be angry?

The Minister of the Interior had been in a limousine driving down Calle Empedrado as Ariana was leaving La Catedral de la Virgen María. She saw his car stop and thought nothing of it, not even after a man got out and walked straight towards her. He couldn't have been more than twenty-two or twenty-three; a tiny crust of blood leftover from a pimple he'd popped that morning clung to his chin. She was so naive, then; she'd been surprised when the man introduced himself as Minister Cabra's assistant and asked for her name and residence, but hadn't sensed any danger.

Twenty-four hours later, her mother was locked in an upstairs bathroom, and Ariana was wearing the dress the Minister had sent and ducking into his limo as her father stood in the door, ashen, watching the little girl he loved and had sold begin her journey to the abattoir.

And then she was in the Minister's apartment: the living room, the kitchen, and the dining room, and she forced herself to eat from the succession of plates and sip from the succession of glasses that the servants put before her and whisked away. Cabra told her that in a month's time, she would have the privilege of marrying him, and she still didn't get it.

"Excuse me?" she asked.

"I'll be taking you as my bride."

"You're joking," she said.

"I never joke."

"But you must be mistaken."

Equivocado. The word sucked the light from his eyes, the color from his face.

"What did you just say?"

Malice burst from his pores, and his breath turned thick and vicious, and only then did she begin to grasp the terror of her situation, but still, she couldn't stop herself from shaking her head, couldn't prevent the 'no' from bursting from her lips.

"¡Puta sucia!" Cabra snarled. "¡Sata!"

But the words didn't land. She was paralyzed, watching the knife in his hand, so she didn't move when he lunged at her, but the man was short and short-armed, and his prodigious gut hit the table, driving the air from his lungs and attenuating his reach and the arch of his slash, and the sensation of his saliva hitting her face made her turn away so that only the point of the knife penetrated her flesh, entering beside her lip and cutting its way to her ear. She felt the blood blossom on her face as he came around the table, grabbed a fistful of her hair, and yanked her upward. He kicked the chair out from under her, only to realize he couldn't maintain her weight, and let her fall.

"¡Mojaneta!"

She didn't try to flee or move or protect herself as he advanced, glowering down at her as he sucked and wheezed.

The knife, forgotten as he braced himself against his corpulence, gleamed and threw light beneath the chandelier.

She felt the blood sliding down her cheek, over her jaw, onto her neck.

Cabra had given her less than twenty-four hours to leave the country. He'd scribbled an address on a notecard and flicked it at her feet, told her to be there at midnight.

If she weren't, he'd have her family killed.

If she contacted anyone at any point, now or in the future, told anyone she'd gone to America, he'd have her family killed.

If she tried to withdraw any money from her bank account, he'd have her family killed.

"And Tuerca," he'd sneered, "I won't do it quickly."

And just like that, Ariana Ireneo Lorca Peláez was erased from the face of the earth.

She met Javy on the boat. She'd had nothing but the dress and the high heels she was wearing, and all he'd had was a small canteen, a compass, and a switchblade. They'd made the voyage, and stuck together afterward, cobbling together a life in a detached garage behind an old widower's house on the outskirts of Miami. Ariana was three years older than Javy, smarter and more practical. Javy's father had been associated with several of Cuba's opposition groups, with Yo No Coopero Con La Dictadura, and with others that had no qualms about killing. He was among those arrested during the Black Spring, and Javy hadn't heard from him since. He and his father had been ducking the authorities for as long as he could remember, so Javy had never been to school, but his father had been a doctoral student before he became a dissident, a poet, and a philosopher, and saw to his son's education as best he could, improvising a curriculum he hoped would facilitate both survival and the life of the mind. Javy never developed an interest in reading or showed an aptitude for math, but he could fieldstrip and clean a Kalashnikov, handle himself in a fight, and gerrymander a bomb from household ingredients. He knew Morse code and spoke fluent English, Spanish, and Haitian French.

Ariana was a brooder, a planner, and a meticulous accountant, while Javy neither planned nor worried. He greeted all that befell him with a grin and a silver tongue, and ingratiated himself to everyone he met. He got a job on a landscaping crew, and she worked as a maid at a motel that rented by the hour, and since they both received an indocumentado's wages, there were days when they went hungry, and months in which they couldn't make the rent, and on those days and months it was Javy that kept them going, Javy that talked the landlord into giving them a few extra days, or letting him cover the difference between what they owed and what they could pay by doing work around the landlord's house—fixing the porch, mending the screen, and repairing the roof or the car or the washing machine. And when they stopped going hungry, it was because Javy talked the owners of the local grocery stores and butchers and restaurants into letting him buy the food they couldn't sell for a price only slightly greater than nothing. Ariana cut coupons for the items he couldn't bargain down, and they were able to save a little money, and even began to imagine going to see an immigration lawyer and applying for political asylum.

They'd slept in the same bed for the first few months, dressed, with their backs to each other, on either side of a curtain Javy had hung so she could have some privacy. She smiled remembering Javy, a young seventeen, interested and terrified and earnestly trying to keep his hands and his eyes to himself, to hide his arousal as they lay in bed, pressed against each other, trying simultaneously to sleep and maintain a semblance of propriety without falling out of the twin-sized bed.

It took her two and a half years to decide she wanted him, and less than ten minutes to claim him.

It was late at night, after ten by the time Javy got dropped off. Brakes shrieked, a door slammed, and then the passenger door ground open and wailed shut and the truck coughed and drove off. She knew that he'd come through the side door carrying the aqua blue polo shirt he had to wear for work, and that the contrast between his skin and the white undershirt he wore would be atomic.

She let him come in and shower, shed the day's exertions, the scabs of salt that welled up in the course of fourteen mindless hours toiling beneath a relentless sun, blasted from his body by shards of tepid water and knocked to the concrete floor to meander around the drain before slinking down into the pipes and out of sight. She was old-fashioned enough that she wanted him to make the first move, impatient enough that she didn't want to wait any longer, so certain of who he was and who she was and that they would work that she didn't want to place *them* on the far side of the weeks and months it would take to peel away the layers of reticence, timidity, and decorum that had allowed them to live together chastely.

"Javy," she said, but with tone, an inflection that said everything had changed. She didn't dress up or down or try to sex things up, just said, "Es la hora," and he said, "¿La hora?" and she nodded and touched his arm.

He'd smiled at gangsters, people threatening to report them to INS, landlords, and repo men, and talked them down without a stutter, but he could barely breathe as she approached him.

She didn't let herself remember this often, anymore, couldn't, not with things the way they were. But she did now, and by the time she'd finished, her heart was racing, and she looked up and saw a sign for Hastings-on-Hudson, saw that she had put Bronx and Yonkers behind her, looked down at her watch and saw that she'd been walking for nearly five hours.

They'd had two years together, afterward, and she could still see him standing in the street outside Carlito's Lounge calling out *piropos* as if he'd never seen her before and whistling her so that she wanted to slap him. But she never did, because of the way he looked at her, and the tightness in her chest, and the way she felt like she was sixteen again and giddy when he held her hand.

But then he'd gone, and he was still gone, even if she saw him now and again, and she told herself that it hadn't really been the way she remembered it, that she and Javy had only ever been just another couple, and she hoped that if she said it enough times, she'd start to believe it.

Then he'd come home early one night. She'd been in the bathroom and didn't hear the door open. "¿Mi amor?" he'd said in the silly, singsong voice he only ever used when he was teasing her. "¿Dónde estás, mi amor?"

"Momentito," she'd said.

"Tengo una gran sorpresa," he'd said.

She came out.

His hands were empty.

She shook her head, confused. "¿Qué sorpresa? ¿Dónde?"

Javy just grinned.

The landscaping crew he worked on had been on their lunch break. The couple that owned the house were nice; the woman arrived from Cuba when she was eighteen, an indocumentada. They brought the workers lemonade and let them eat on the patio furniture in the shade of umbrellas rather than making them eat in the back of their truck.

The husband had a drawing pad in front of him when the crew sat down. Javy watched the man out of the corner of his eye, saw him sketch a line, erase it almost immediately, try another, erase it, rip the paper from the pad and crumple it up in a ball and continue on like that for almost twenty minutes, until it seemed he was about to snap his pencil in two and chuck the pad into the pool.

"Artist?" Javy asked.

The man wasn't much older than he was, ten, fifteen years tops. He nodded. "Tattoos. Been trying to design a sleeve for one of my clients for weeks"—he shook his head—"don't have shit to show for it."

"Can I look?"

"You an artist?"

Javy shrugged. "Not really. I draw some."

His sketchbook had been the one thing Javy had kept from her. She'd go to bed and he'd stay up drawing. He was always beside her when she woke, the sketchpad always hidden away.

"¿Qué sorpresa?"

"Tengo un nuevo trabajo," he said, playing coy.

"¿Más dinero?"

He nodded. "Más dinero, menos horas..."

"¿Y es legal?"

"Nada de lo que hacemos es legal en este momento, mi amor, pero pronto..."

"¿Pronto...?"

Javy had designed the man's sleeve while the rest of the crew finished the job, and the man hired him on the spot, only $10 an hour to start, but if everything worked out, he'd be tattooing at the hottest shop in Miami within eighteen months, making $150-$200 an hour.

"Two hundred dollars an hour?"

Javy nodded.

"¿Doscientos dólares?"

"Sí."

"¿Por hora?"

"Sí."

Ariana leapt into his arms.

There were melons and old tattoo magazines everywhere for the next five months. The tattoo shop couldn't give him enough hours to live off at an apprentice's wages, so he'd had to keep his landscaping job at first. His crew boss let him work partial days, odd hours, from five-thirty in the morning to four-thirty in the afternoon, six days a week, then he'd go to the tattoo shop from five o'clock until midnight. And in the few hours in which he was at home and wasn't sleeping, he'd be sitting at their table tattooing melons for practice, and because they couldn't afford to throw food away, they ate them afterward.

She couldn't even look at a melon without gagging, now, but it had paid off. Javy's boss said he'd never seen anyone get so good, so quick, and let him start taking customers unsupervised. He did his own designs and did them well, and the money started coming in.

Javy said she worked too hard and made her quit one of her jobs, and then she admitted that she'd had art lessons her whole life and asked, if she started drawing again, did he think his boss would consider taking her on?

Javy thought so, and surprised her one day with a new sketch pad and set of pencils, and a couple weeks later, a flamante iron, a custom rotary tattoo machine he'd helped design and had made for her. And so she quit another job, and after six or seven months and four or five hundred more melons, Javy brought her into the shop and had her show his boss what she could do, and he hired her on the spot, just as he had with Javy.

They went to see an immigration lawyer on a Wednesday afternoon, found out they couldn't apply for refugee status, only for asylum, and filled a USCIS I-589.

And that was the beginning of the end.

Neither of them had any of the required documents, which their lawyer said would make things harder, but not impossible. At the meeting's end, they shook his hand and left feeling hopeful, even confident, and they went to Sergio's, the place they'd gone to celebrate Javy's first week earning real money, the first restaurant they'd ever eaten at in America.

Three months later, Javy was gone.

The asylum office approved her case and denied Javy's, and after that, the Immigration Court judge rejected his claim for asylum, and their lawyer filed with the Board of Immigration Appeals, which also declined to grant his petition. They were leaving the courthouse when their lawyer asked for a moment alone with Javy.

When she woke up the next morning, he was gone.

She figured it out, eventually, that their lawyer had told Javy he'd endanger her asylum if he stayed with her, that she'd never be granted LPR if the court became aware she was associated with an illegal whose father was a terrorist. The fact that Javy's father had fought against Castro wouldn't have mattered.

The system was the system.

She looked up from her memories and found herself on Warburton Avenue in Hastings-on-Hudson, staring at a scarlet and gold awning and a sorrowful tree, scrawny and naked in the winter cold.

She'd stayed at the tattoo shop long enough for her paperwork to go through and to finish her apprenticeship, hoping every day for a postcard or letter, but none came. She started doing guest gigs at various shops, three to six weeks in Richmond, New Orleans, Memphis, and so on, and it was only after more than a year on the road that she admitted to herself that she was looking for Javy.

Three years later, she found him, working at a shop in the Bronx.

He had two kids.

She hadn't seen that coming.

The sign on the awning behind the tree read 'Antoinette's Patisserie,' and she realized that she'd been here once before, with Javy. They'd met some cracked-out white boy who looked like he hadn't eaten or slept or showered in weeks.

Blanco had paid them ten grand each to tattoo two dead Black guys on his back.

Javy had talked a mile a minute the whole way back. He was done, he said. Terminado. He'd worked it out with El Rey: for ten stacks, he could leave the Brims, no hard feelings, no strings. Solamente, adios. Rey said Javy didn't even have to hold product for them anymore. No badrock, no bammy, no boom.

Nada.

Nunca más.

Ariana had had to avoid Javy for three days after she first found him. His happiness was like memory heroin, brought her right there: back in his arms, full of him, inhaling him, tasting him.

It made her remember that there was no resisting his joy. It swept you up until you were so happy you couldn't remember sorrow or what it was like to hurt.

She hated him for what he'd done, for not giving her a choice. If he'd come to her and said, do you want me or LPR, she wouldn't have hesitated—she'd have hit him as hard as she could, and then kissed him and held an ice pack to his split lip.

Tú, idiota. No es ni siquiera una pregunta.

But he hadn't asked. And now he had a family, and she didn't want to mess that up.

She knew nothing of gangs. Only what Javy had said since she tracked him down, which wasn't much: he took a greyhound to NYC after Miami, didn't know anyone, couldn't get work, got his girlfriend pregnant, and fell into a gang. Now he wanted out, había sido un puto for ever getting involved.

He never said what she was thinking, que la vida es una puta para un ilegal.

And she knew it wasn't guilt that kept him from saying it, but the fact that he didn't feel that way, that it never would have occurred to him to resent her because she got in, because her petition was granted and his wasn't.

She'd seen the men following them as they walked to the subway after finishing the tattoo, the same guys that had stood lookout for them while they worked. "Javy," she said, "those guys behind us."

He turned.

"¡CORRE!"

She hesitated.

"¡Ahorita!" He shoved her. "¡Vete!"

She ran, heard the shots, didn't look back.

"Miss? Miss? Are you okay?"

The woman touched her, and she jumped, realized she was standing in a coffee shop.

"P..." she stammered. "Per...Lo..."

The woman was nearly seventy, her skin translucent and sagging. "Are you okay, honey?"

"Yes," Ariana managed. "Sorry."

"Are you sure?" the woman asked.

Ariana assured her she was, ordered a hot chocolate, waited for it, then chose a table in the corner. Not five minutes later, a couple placed an order and sat at the table across from her own. They wore snowflake-dappled hats and scarves wrapped tightly around their necks, and they were holding hands despite the thick gloves they were too cold to take off. Ariana cupped her hands around her drink and watched them out of the corner of her eye. Their food came, and they started to unwrap their winter armor, laughing at themselves as they did so, and finally they were more human than Gortex, pale of face and red of cheek, with brilliant white teeth, both of them glowing. It took her fifteen or twenty minutes to realize that neither of them was anything one might call beautiful, and that she'd only thought they were because they were in love.

She folded into herself and lay her head and arms on the table so that no one would see her crying.

THE GIGGLE HOUSE

Anyone here of Middle Eastern descent? Okay, a couple of you—could you stand up, please? Thank you. These people are not buying another drink the whole damn night, do you hear me? I'm talking to all y'all tight-ass, non-tipping, complain-to-the manager-trying-to-get-your-meal-comped brothers—I'm looking at you, Tyrone, but the rest of you know who you are.

You and I are going to be picking up their tab, and we're going to do it with some goddamn brio, because thanks to them, for the first time in the history of our country, the cops have people they like fucking with almost as much as they like fucking with Black folk.

Middle Eastern is the new Black.

VOICES

He was sitting.

His back was against a dumpster.

His legs stretched out in front of him.

He had half a pack of cigarettes in his jacket pocket.

The voices were quarreling, and he was yelling back, though under his breath, so that the people walking by heard only a stream of barks and growls.

He had a Styrofoam cup he'd gotten three weeks ago at a soup kitchen.

It had coffee in it when he got it, but now there was money, a couple dollars in change.

He had a Walkman he'd bought at a Goodwill. He turned it up all the way to drown out the voices, still couldn't keep himself from screaming obscenities through his teeth.

The noise was good, death-metal driving steel pikes through his ears and brain and teeth until it hurt so bad it brought him some of the way back to the streets and stares and endless assault of people.

Some people threw money at him, most hurried past. Others stopped to kick him or throw their cigarettes or empty bottles at him. The ones that used his body to stub out their cigarettes brought him close to sensate, the mind-piercing, cauterizing char unleashing the smell of burnt flesh like fingers shoved two-joints deep up each nostril, yanking him to presence.

At his worst, he had no thoughts, nothing but the howling terror of metal voices carving up his insides, demanding viscera, bowels, malice, such that all that would remain after he was done with his victims would be a meat suit and a few soulless organs waiting to end.

But only if he gave in.

He drank when he could, malt liquor or skunked beer or ethyl alcohol until he Blacked out. He smoked or ate or snorted or shot whatever drugs he came across with communal pins or razor blades or jagged-edged light bulbs turned crack pipes, bent on annihilation, if possible, oblivion at a minimum.

Then, sometimes, things went quiet.

The quiet spells were the hardest. Without warning, something in him shifted, and suddenly the voices were nowhere, and he heard the wind, traffic, ribbons of conversation. He became aware that the things he saw in his mind's eye were only echoes, the reverberations of someone else's deeds.

They recurred.

When the voices stopped, he remembered a wife and a child: watching them sleep; holding a gentle hand to his daughter's cheek as she took slow, unburdened breaths; brushing a lock of hair off her face and tucking it behind her ear; kissing his wife.

He remembered hearing the voices for the first time, mere murmurs, then, a susurrus he could ride into slumber. He remembered them growing louder, vicious, commanding violence.

He remembered when they began to speak in images as well as words, the half-speed silver-lit films that were, at first, content to terrorize him, and, later, drove him to a place where he couldn't be sure what he had and hadn't done, or to whom, where his daughter's reeking blood shimmered in the streetlights and fell from his teeth, over his lips, and down his neck. He remembered the voices cooing:

...not giving in...	*nowsey, nowsey, nowsey*	*already happened...*
		...the blasts of—kiddie
already—knife-		*chunk-fleshripping*
fucked—	*mother-sticker*	*through, face-rape, the*
		blood dripping rip-
EVILShit Eat—	*!GLUT!!!*	*throat*
YUM!...		*child throat*

He remembered that he left his family.

And that he could have fought harder, done more, tried new medication, electroconvulsive therapy, cognitive-behavioral...

He didn't, though. He had visions of his wife draping an afghan over his insensate form, stealing away to their bedroom or the bathroom and doing what he no longer could, slowly replacing him with a battery-operated, mail-order marriage-wrecker; he saw his daughter's concern turning into embarrassment, into resentment, contempt.

He saw her lying to her friends and making excuses as to why they couldn't come over.

He couldn't do it, couldn't bring himself to play the little Dutch boy plugging a hemorrhaging dike with his fingers. So he left. He went to an ATM, got cash, bought boots, a jacket, and a hat at a sporting goods store, and then went to the bus station where he bought a one-way ticket to New York City. He cut up his credit cards on the way there.

He lived on the streets, slept in alleys. The voices got so loud and their commands so specific and cruel and repugnant that he would start rhythmically slamming his head against the nearest wall or building or dumpster until he lost consciousness.

He started praying for death after he woke up in the Psych ER for the second time, found himself strapped to a bed, immobilized, and spent the next thirty days in a similar fashion, narcotized, carted from room to room.

The doctors asked him if the voices were gone, and he said yes, but they weren't, only hiding.

The truth was beyond him—every stray thought died even before it could arrange itself into something retrievable—so he couldn't have told it.

He was a body shelved and shackled, a maker of feces and urine, mucus and spit. Sometimes he was changed or wiped or bathed, but those that did so came from nowhere and didn't exist in the intervals between their visits, and he had no sense of them even when they were there.

He was mesmerized by the contrast between him and them; he had no concepts, no ideas or thoughts, only a diaphanous *me* or *I,* and a *not me, not I* to stand in for *they* and *them*, and discontinuous sensation, flares of contrast.

And then he was back on the street, with no plan or

understanding of why he'd been released or how long he'd been in lockdown, or what he was supposed to do with the prescriptions that had appeared in his pocket.

The narcotics and antipsychotics and mood stabilizers were wearing off, and the voices in his head hotting up like frenzied garrotters and lynch-men working themselves up to a frothing rave, chanting in half-breaths as they gnashed their teeth, vile promises rising like pestilence in sprays of blood and spewing presentiments of carnage and agony as they churned.

How much time did he have?

He had no money.

He tried to think, but his mind was grating against itself, blinded by a shattering of insensate vollies that were fill and flush and static.

He was Black, and they'd been white.

He was dark, they were light.

The voices were so red they were Black.

Black was dark, dark was evil.

Light was good.

He walked and walked and walked.

The voices got angrier.

No music.

Where was his Walkman?

Gone.

Where was his Walkman?

Still gone.

Or in the plastic bag hanging from his wrist?

Batteries?

Dead.

He reached an alley, peered into it.

There was a boy hanging from chains.

hurtRape flay	*Kill*	B
T e A r	*bone cut crush fuck*	L
	Rip	oo
flessssshhhhhhh	*dick cock junk sever*	D

He shook his head. Tore at his beard.

It was cold. The boy was naked. This wasn't real.

Bottle dumpster	*Carve!UP!*	*Smeeeeearrrrrrrr*
sodomy	*fleshchunktear*	*fecessmearfecesfeces*
shred bleed.cum	*fromfromfromfrom*	*Urinate shatter face*
snot	*bodyface*	
swallow filth		

Take belt! OFF! eat	*Choke ass-fuck-rip!!*	*Anus-bottle shriek!*
him!	*With teeth! him!*	*Ripthroat!*
Buckle...flesh from	*Piss-drink!*	*Drink!*
face		
Bloody maw!		

He was staggering as he entered the alley, shrieking as the voices and images screwed together in a shattering metal weave.

No. No. No. No.

The boy's eye flickered open. He was shivering, lifted his head.

There were priests on either side of him.

They were wearing masks.

The sun was glaring off the boy...

So white...

Burning his eyes...

Tear them from his head...

His steps quickened. He felt himself undoing his belt.

Yes! Yes! Yes! Lust	*Wrap end, fist-*	*Harder! Two*
fuck!	*leather*	*mouths!*
Hate kill—carve flesh	*tight hand-*	*Filth! Eat filth!...!*
from! Make himeat	*noose—THRUST*	*Mind.*
face eat! Not real. Not	*FUCK!*	*In mind.*
real. Better. Not	*don't...*	*Drink drunk , lap*
you'll...	*Not...*	
better.		*violation*

He let the buckle drop, reached back, swung as hard as he could.

Hate!—The first clarity...in weeks, months...

The belt buckle tore a jagged chunk from the boy's chest.

Yes! Yes! Yes! Yes!	*Yes! Yes! Yes! Yes!*	*Yes! Yes! Yes! Yes!*
Yes! Yes! Yes! Yes!	*Yes! Yes! Yes! Yes!*	*Yes! Yes! Yes! Yes!*
Yes! Yes! Yes! Yes!	*Yes! Yes! Yes! Yes!*	*Yes! Yes! Yes! Yes!*
Yes! Yes! Yes! Yes!	*Yes! Yes! Yes! Yes!*	*Yes! Yes! Yes! Yes!*
Yes! Yes! Yes! Yes!	*Yes! Yes! Yes! Yes!*	*Yes! Yes! Yes! Yes!*
Yes! Yes! Yes! Yes!	*Yes! Yes! Yes! Yes!*	*Yes! Yes! Yes! Yes!*

He cocked his arm back again, ripped the belt buckle forward and down again, hit the boy's neck.

It felt right.

He reached back.

The boy deserved this.

He reached back.

He didn't know why, but it needed to happen.

He reached back.

He felt it in every cell.

He reached back—

"Enough!"

He dropped, cracking his orbital bone against the pavement, convulsing as ten thousand volts ripped through his body, vomiting as another ten followed.

Fading.

Urine pooling.

He saw them, but they were fading.

Was he? Barely...

They were speaking...

Words?

"...offering..."

His.

A boot.

"...compounding..."

Footsteps...back.

"...eternal."

Eternal.

Eternal eternal eternal eternal eternal eternal eternal eternal.

Eter. Eter. Eter. Eter. Eter. Eter. Eter. Eter. Eter. Eter. Eter.

Et. Et. Et. Et. Et. Et. Et. Et. Et. Et.

E. E. E. E. E. E. E. E.

E. E. E. E.

E. E.

E.

THE GIGGLE HOUSE

Any Asians here tonight? I see one, two—a handful of you. Good. All y'all, look around. Make one of these people your friend. Buy him beer, sake, Pokemon—whatever it takes to get him to teach you his ways, because Mr. Suzuki and his folk went from internment camps to honorary white people in less than fifty years.

That is some bad-ass, Jedi mind trick shit.

G.O.

"Damn!"

"What is it, G.O.?"

G.O. was walking between two women, an arm around each. He took three steps into the street, squinting. "I know that ain't Sputum Dokes."

The man walking the other way stopped. "G.O.?"

"Hell yeah!" He looked left and right, and strutted across the street "What up, what up?"

They did daps. G.O. motioned for the women to follow.

"Aiesha, Teja, this my boy, Sputum. Sputum, Aiesha and Teja."

"What he call you?"

"Never mind him—G.O. think he funny, but he ain't. Name's Bay."

Teja made a face. "Like Rustin?"

"Yeah—how you know about Bayard Rustin?"

"What, I'm hood, so I gotta be dumb?"

"Easy, girl!" G.O. put a hand on her shoulder. "No need to trip—Sputum's hood, too. We came up together over in Patterson."

Bay smiled. "Morris and 139th."

"You know," G.O. pointed from Bay to Teja and back, "you and Teja got that same vibe going on: too much reading, not enough fucking and weed."

Bay rolled his eyes. "There you go again. I ain't seen you in years, and you already fading me."

"It has been a minute since we kicked it."

44

"Almost six years," Bay agreed. "What you been up to?"

"Same old, same old." G.O. stacked some signs. "Just tryin' to get mine."

Bay nodded.

"What you been doing with yo'self?"

"School, mostly."

"Going on six years? You finna be a doctor or some shit?"

"Something like that. A psychologist." Bay risked a wink at Teja.

"A shrink?"

Bay nodded.

"Well, look at you...all fancy and shit—just don't let it go to your head like Teja here. She think she all that just cuz she go to Concordia, now."

"It's Columbia. Columbia University, you ignorant slob."

His eyes cranked to slits. "What you say?"

Her face went rigid as her pupils gaped and her lip began to tremble. She shook her head.

G.O.'s voice was a low growl, his syllables barbed. "What the fuck you just say to me, Teja?"

"N-Nothing," she stammered. "I'm sorry—I was just playing."

"The fuck you were." He moved forward until there was no space left between them, all six feet and four inches and two-hundred and eighty pounds right up in her face.

"Come on, man—" Bay tried.

G.O. silenced him with a finger.

"I'm gonna let this one go, because there ain't no one here but us and Sputum, and he down, so I know he won't say shit, but you pull that shit in front of any of my crew, and I'm gonna put you in check." He lifted his sweatshirt, exposing the Glock tucked in his waistband. "For good. You get me?"

She nodded, choked, managed to cough out the word. "Yes."

"Good. Now stand over there," he gestured with his chin, "and shut the fuck up 'til I tell you otherwise."

G.O. turned back to Bay. "I know you don't like the hard shit, but that's business—it's twenty-four-seven, you know? You slack for a minute, drop your guard, and you get assed out."

"Sure, G.O.," Bay said quickly. "You right."

"So what bring you back?"

"Back?"

"To Mott."

"Lamar."

"Lamar? Skinny ass foul-smelling nigger used to follow Seale everywhere?"

Bay nodded. "Funeral's tomorrow."

"How?"

"Shot."

"Aw shit! Yeah, I heard something about that, come to think—cops involved or something."

"My girl Tammekah say she saw the whole thing," said Aiesha.

The men turned. The girls were leaning up against a vacant, smoking.

"Tammekah say there was a doctor or something that was right there, and he was doing CPR, but the cops ripped him off and cuffed him."

Bay winced. "It was Seale."

"No shit. Seale a doctor now?"

Bay nodded.

"You know the police be hating on niggas when they bust a brother for trying to save a nigga's life."

"Well," Bay said, "I should be—"

"What?" G.O. interrupted. "Tired of the old hood already? Don't like my company?"

"My mom—"

"Is at Bingo, along with every other mom that go to Redeemer."

"I—"

"Okay, okay. Ain't no need to be faking jacks with me, player. We cool. I get it. You out, don't want no part of the life. OG's like me make you nervous."

"It ain't like that."

"No?"

"No."

"How is it, then?"

Bay was silent.

G.O. arched an eyebrow. "I'm waiting."

Bay turned to the women. "Sputum's a good name, right?"

"There it is!" G.O. threw his hands in the air. "There it is! Now you just announcing you full of shit."

"It sound tough, though," Bay asked, "right?"

Aiesha shrugged. "I guess."

"Teja?"

Teja waited for G.O. to nod before she answered. "It sound nasty to me. How you going to let people call you snot?"

"What?" Aiesha said. "Gross! Your name Snot? What the hell wrong with your parents?"

"That the name he gave the cops," G.O. snickered.

"What cops?" Teja asked.

"We was in ninth grade," G.O. said, "and I was flunking math, history, too, so they made Sputum here help me with my homework.

"Most days I only put up with that homework shit for an hour or so before I said fuck it and bounced, but I'd been involved with some extra-curricular activities of the non-legal variety over the weekend, so I was all about studying come Monday. We stayed late—I mean, late, late, like the janitor had to kick us out so he could lock up and go home, kind of late. Anyway, we both lived in Patterson, so we walking home together, and all the sudden 5-0 come out of nowhere, drive their cruiser up on the sidewalk, and block our way."

"So track star here bolts," Bay said.

G.O. grinned, winked at the girls. "I'd been running from the cops for a long while by the time we hit high school, know what I'm saying? I wasn't waiting around for no police to jack me up."

"But I froze."

"And since officer all-you-can-eat and his partner didn't chase me no more than half a block, I was able to circle back around in time to see them put homeboy here up against a wall."

"Cops start telling me how much trouble I'm in, how I'll be going to juvie" —Bay was shaking his head— "telling me what happen to little punks like me there."

"Cops be saying he going to get his shit pushed in and Sputum don't even blink." G.O. cackled. "Just stands there like a boss!"

Bay laughed.

The women listened coolly, noncommittal.

"One of the cops go, 'What's your name, you little shit?' But Sputum don't say nothing, so they start giving little love taps, gut shots, and throat taps with their nightclubs, a couple in the nuts, nothing that'll leave no mark, but enough to tune him up some. They keep knocking him down, but homeboy just keep picking himself the fuck back up and looking at them like, 'What?' and they really starting to sweat by then, which pissed them right the fuck off, and one of them was wheezing like he been running for miles, and finally—"

Bay cut in. "Cop tells me he going to ask me one more time, and if I don't answer, he going to shove his club up my ass and take me straight to lock up so the inmates can fuck me with it."

"So homie say 'Sputum Excreta! My name Sputum Excreta!' And I'm like, where the fuck that come from? And the officers are—I shit you not—writing it the fuck down on their clipboards when a shots-fired comes over the radio, and they jump in the cruiser and bounce."

"No way," said Aiesha. "You for real?"

Bay nodded. "Good times, right?"

"For the next four years," G.O. added, "everyone call him Sputum."

"It's still gross," Aiesha said. "But a little funny, too, I guess."

"The only fight the man ever got in was the week before he graduated high school," G.O. said. "People making a big deal out of the fact that he one of, like, five or ten in our class going to college, and he just play it off, say he just happy no one will ever call him Sputum again, and some local nigger say he going to make sure that shit sticks, that he going to go up to campus and tell everyone, and Sputum say you better not, and nigger say what you going to do about it, and Sputum be like, BOLO, mother-fucker"—G.O. slammed his forearm against his palm— "and drop him."

"Not my proudest moment."

"Fuck that!" G.O. waved Bay off. "Fuck that forever. Sometimes you got to go! Someone step to you, you gotta bust, do him before he do you, because if word get out that you someone can be done, the whole world going to line up to fuck you."

"True that," Aiesha nodded. "Ain't no one going to hand you nothing."

"Now wait," Teja said, a smirk spreading across her face. "I seem to remember a certain girl flashing her tits to someone the other night, no charge."

"What's this?" G.O. glared at Aiesha.

"Girl, I don't know what you talking about! She a liar, G.O."

"You don't remember going from the club to the crib and coming across a white boy strung up like a southern nigger?"

"Oh, shit!" She covered her mouth. "It was nothing, G.O., I was laced, and he was naked and chained up and shit, and people was all tattooing on him and beating on him, and then this one brother started pissing on him, and I just—I felt bad."

"So you showed him your titties?"

She nodded. "Well, only one..." Her voice trailed off.

No one spoke for a while.

G.O. turned to Aiesha. "That really happen?"

"Showing my titty, or the naked white boy?"

"Both."

She nodded. "There a video of the white boy online."

G.O. stared at her for a while, then turned away, silent.

"I guess," he said finally, looking at Bay, "I guess, if I'm chained up outside ass-naked in February, and people doing that shit to me...titty about the only thing that might help, don't you think?"

THE GIGGLE HOUSE

The first thing we got to talk about when we talking about surviving Black, is the 5-o.

For the wypipo in the room, the 5-o is the police.

Now, all y'all know the single greatest threat to African-Americans is posed by the ass-whoopings our mommas and daddies give us, but the 5-o come a close second, so whether you an OG, BAMF, or a DKNY, if you don't want to get KO'd by the 5-o, BOHICA, you got to keep yo shit on the QT, cuz it don't matter if you 1337, or legal, goodieMob. Black = NSFL.

MERCEDES

Mercedes sat quietly in the chair, playing with the doll Abuela had made her. Papi had been asleep for three days. The machines attached to him made noises: beeps and whirs and whooshing sounds.

She wished he'd wake up so they could go home. She was hungry, and the room smelled bad—not as bad as some of the rooms she walked past to go to the potty, but weird.

She wanted tamales and arroz, and the can of coconut water she got after church if she was good.

She was wearing the clothes she'd had on when her Mami pulled her out of bed, a hand-me-down sweatshirt and Dora the Explorer pajama pants and socks that didn't go together.

Someone had put a blanket over her while she was sleeping, so she had that, too.

Mami and Papi and Tía and Abuela made her take a shower every night before bed at home because they said it was sucio to go even a day without one, but it had been three days since she'd had a shower, and no one had said anything.

At least no one was screaming here.

People had been screaming in the first room they'd been in. Mami had been crying, and the woman at the desk had told them to wait, and the only chairs were next to people who were yelling at each other, screaming malas palabras.

Mercedes knew not to say malas palabras.

Once, she asked Abuela what maldita puta meant, and Abuela's eyes got big and her face turned red, and she'd started calling out to Mami, who ran into the room yelling, ¿Qué? ¿Qué pasó? and her abuela said, Tu hija dijo maldita puta, and then her mother got muy enojada, and Mercedes got azotada en las nalgas desnudas.

She squirmed, remembering.

Mami had tried to make her say where she'd heard the words, ¿Dónde?

SMACK!

At school!

¿Quién?

The girl was silent.

¿QUIÉN?

I forget.

SMACK!

¿QUIÉN?

¡NO SÉ!

SMACK!

¡NO SÉ! ¡NO SÉ!

But she knew.

Papi said them after Mami's dog hizo caca in the kitchen, and he stepped in it.

She didn't say so because Papi said they had to stick together, that Mami got a little loca at times, because she loved them so much.

Mami had fallen asleep in a chair beside Papi's bed; Mercedes watched her sleep for a while, watched the hair hanging over her mouth bend and sway as she breathed.

Mami got mad at Papi a lot at home, but she hadn't been mad at him once since they were here.

Maybe she should just sleep all day, too, Mercedes thought, then she wouldn't be in trouble all the time like she had been since she started school.

She tried to be good at school, but it was hard.

¿Quieres terminar como tu padre y yo, her mother would yell, estúpidos y pobres?

Mercedes didn't think her parents were dumb.

And Papi had a roll of money with him every night when he got home from work.

She was getting bored with her doll.

A nurse came in and asked if she could get her anything. Mercedes checked to make sure her mother was still sleeping, and then asked for Jell-O and a ginger ale, because her mother wouldn't buy them.

The woman came back with the soda and Jell-O and a straw and a funny-looking spoon, and the girl remembered to thank her and felt proud until the woman said de nada, and Mercedes realized she'd said gracias instead of thank you.

You have to talk English to white people, her mother said, or they get mad because they think you are saying stuff about them.

Most of the time Mami was.

Mercedes looked at Papi.

She was glad Mami was asleep. She'd been acting weird. She kept saying Papi was going to be fine, even though no one was asking.

Él estará bien, Mami said.

Yo sé, she answered, but Mami didn't hear her.

Estará bien, Mami said again.

Yo sé, Mami, she said.

Estará bien, her mother rocked. Estará bien. Estará bien. Estará bien.

Mercedes set her doll aside and was sad she didn't have any crayons or colored pencils. If she had those, and some paper, Papi would draw her a princess or a butterfly or a My Little Pony, and then she could color them in or practice drawing one of her own.

But Papi was asleep.

She hoped he'd wake up soon. She was never bored when Papi was awake. He would tell her jokes and tickle her and make her laugh.

Sometimes Mami would be yelling at her for not listening to her teacher, and Papi would start making faces and acting gracioso, and she would try to listen and not to laugh, but always ended up laughing, and then Mami would start yelling at him and forget that she was mad at her.

Sometimes Papi would take her places, too, to the park or for ice cream. Once he even took her to Coney Island and got her cotton candy. He let her watch the rides for a while. She wasn't supposed to tell Mami about those things because Mami would get preocupada por el dinero.

Mami got preocupada about a lot of things.

Papi said that was her job, but when Mercedes asked him if Mami got paid, he laughed and told her that he paid Mami in love, and she didn't know what that meant.

Sometimes Tía Mía needed Mami's help at the store, and then she got to go to Papi's work with him and sit in the back and drink soda and laugh at Uncle Hector's jokes while Papi drew on people.

Uncle Hector wasn't really her Tío, and Mami didn't like him. She heard Mami tell Papi he wasn't allowed to bring her around Uncle Hector, and a different time Mami told her to call her right away if Papi ever left her alone with him.

Mercedes didn't understand her Mami sometimes. Hector was nice and smiled and brought her candy bars or bubble gum sometimes when he made his deliveries to Papi's shop.

The deliveries were another thing she didn't understand. Papi never touched the packages or opened them. Uncle Hector brought them, and someone else picked them up.

She didn't know what was in them, only that they were serious. Papi never yelled or spanked or got mad at her, but the time he caught her playing with one of the packages he spanked her so hard and so long that her nalgas turned colors and it hurt to sit for days.

No los toques, Mercedes, he pointed. Nunca. Entiendes? Por ninguna razón.

Entiendo, Papi.

Prométemelo.

Te lo prometo, Papi.

Papi didn't stay mad long. Soon he was smiling, his teeth like bright stars.

Mercedes had never seen anyone Blacker than her Papi. He was proud of it.

Soy más negro que la noche, y aún más misterioso, he told Mami over and over, and even though she didn't know what it meant, Mercedes liked that he said it.

She checked again to make sure Mami was asleep, then climbed down from her chair and walked to Papi's bedside.

He'd been shot, though she didn't really know what that meant, just that some people died when it happened. Two girls in her school had family that got shot, un primo y un hermano.

The primo died.

She wanted to hold Papi's hand, but she was scared of the tubes sticking out of him.

All the bandages were on his right side, though, so if she was muy cuidadosa, she could climb into bed with him on the left.

She checked Mami again, then struggled up over the railing.

She nestled against Papi and thought of the dead primo again.

She wasn't worried for Papi, though.

He'd told her he couldn't die on the way home from the primo's funeral.

¿Cómo podría yo morir, chistosa? he asked. No es posible. Soy el hombre más afortunado del mundo. De otro modo ¿cómo podría un tipo como yo tener una hija como tú?

She felt her eyes closing, the warmth of her father's body.

Todo va a salir bien, hija, he always said, te lo prometo—mejor que bien.

THE GIGGLE HOUSE

First thing with the 5-0: don't be running where they can see you. In fact, Black folk should never run outside a sports-related context in which wypipo have monetized our exertions.

For those of you who rode the short bus to the club: Black folk like neon and cameltoe just fine, we're just not down with getting shot.

5-0 sees a brother running, he thinks there's a reason, and out comes the steel.

So no running, my brothers and sisters. Dear God, no running.

ALLISON

List of 60 Coping Strategies for Hallucinations.
Number One: Humming.

Fucking awesome. Why hadn't she thought of that before? Aidan, she could have said, all you have to do to stop the homicidal voices is hum to them.

Dismiss the voices, she read. *Remind yourself that no one else can hear them.*

Even better. Hey, babe, she should have said, in case you forgot that you're clinically psychotic, I just wanted to remind you that the voices aren't real, and that you're the only person in the whole wide fucking world who can hear them.

Prayer, she read.

Oh, God.

Take a warm bath.

Ooh! she thought, will it still work if it has bubbles in it?

Use guided imagery to practice coping with the voices differently.

That was a true winner.

Listen up, Aidan, she'd say, you're thinking of this all wrong. You're not crazy, it's just that there's a fifth dimension beyond that which is known to man, and you just happen to have the super special ability to get dropped there without warning so you can hear all the fucked-up things the voices scream at each other.

Roleplay for and against the voices.

Holy. Fucking. Crap.

Satan is commanding you to filet your girlfriend with a carving knife, but Jesus says you should slit your wrists to keep yourself from hurting anyone. Act out both sides: which do you think is better advice?

Allison resisted the urge to shred the paper.

This was her life, lately, rushing from auditions to meet Aidan at their apartment so they could go to yet another doctor's appointment and be given more asinine handouts.

Aidan was supposed to be the breadwinner, freeing her to conquer stage and screen, to smile on her way to fame, fortune, and adulation.

Aidan, who had degrees from two Ivy League institutions, a great face, and a body that turned heads.

Aidan, who'd had that it-factor, that *je ne sais quoi* that made every room he entered his.

Had.

Past tense.

As in, not anymore.

Or not reliably.

And that was a problem. A big problem, because that had been their thing: they didn't want kids or dogs or a white house or a picket fence; they wanted high-powered, high-speed, high-glamour lives and careers with nothing holding them back, no obligations, complications, pets, or children. They were definitely into each other, and the sex was amazing, but the most important thing was that they were both committed to grabbing life by the throat and doing whatever it took to make the world their bitch.

She didn't fully understand what he did, but she knew it involved the development and implementation of application systems for fiduciary agents responsible for tracking and analyzing international markets.

He was going to make Steve Jobs and Mark Zuckerberg look ordinary.

She was going to be bigger than Scarlett Johansson.

And they'd been doing so well. She'd been getting more and more callbacks, had started landing speaking roles, and he'd been working as a consultant and taking meetings with Fortune 500 companies.

They were starting to get invited to the parties people really wanted to go to.

And then he'd fucked it all up.

First, he started flaking on her, making plans and then standing her up; staying out all night, then waking her up at three or four in the morning when he finally came home so he could babble on in an incoherent frenzy.

Then he'd fucked up at work, started acting insane in meetings and hemorrhaging clients.

He started doing coke and ecstasy, got hammered four nights a week, five.

At first, she was just pissed, figured he was getting cold feet or had met someone else, but then he started disappearing for days at a time, and she started to get calls from their friends.

Is Aidan alright? I saw him at X, and he was really messed up...

Did you and Aidan break up? He looked like shit at the club yesterday.

His clothes are all nasty...

He doesn't seem to know where he is...

You need to get here now...

He just attacked someone...

Then she got the call from the Psych ER.

"Allison Blake?"

"Speaking."

"My name is Angelica. I'm calling from the Psychiatric Emergency Room at Lenox Hill Hospital. Do you know an Aidan Levin?"

"He's my boyfriend."

"We admitted him a few hours ago, and right now he's sedated, but you'll want to get here as soon as you can."

"Oh my god! What happened? Is he okay?"

"I'm sorry, Ms. Blake, but you'll have to ask the doctor."

"Do you know what happened?"

"His chart says he was in an altercation. That's all I know. What medication is Mr. Levin on, Ms. Blake?"

"He's not on any."

"No medication?"

"No...he...uhh, they're still evaluating him, so no, not yet."

"Thank you. I'll inform the doctor."

That was months ago. Neither the owner of the bar nor the men he attacked pressed charges, but things hadn't gotten any better. The doctors couldn't agree on the cause of his psychosis. One said schizoaffective disorder, another said bipolar, yet another said borderline personality disorder; the meds made him comatose, or impotent. Some exacerbated his depression; others triggered his mania. They finally found a medication protocol that worked, but it caused such crushing migraines that Aidan took to carrying a wastebasket around the apartment so he wouldn't vomit on the carpet, and so the search continued.

It was crushing watching him struggle to ride out the intervals between his periods of exhaustion and/or narcotic-induced unconsciousness, to watch their dreams wither before her eyes.

And the worst part was how alone she felt, the way in which it was almost worse for her than for him because he was so consumed by his struggles that he couldn't see how awful it all was for her. The life they'd worked so hard for, the one they'd been so close to, was gone.

Their future was gone.

Gone.

They'd spent the last of their savings and maxed out all of their credit cards to pay for Aidan's might-or-might-not-work-medication. They were exhausted, broke, and hopeless.

Then Fairchild saved them.

All of their "friends" had disappeared since Aidan wigged out, except for one, a guy Allison had thought of as an asshole since he hit on her at a company party once, not ten feet from Aidan. But the asshole was the only one who ever reached out, now, and he was the one who had pointed Chris in Aidan's direction.

She'd never heard of Chris Fairchild or his work, but he'd said he was a performance artist, and needed someone to handle the tech for his next piece. He wanted Aidan to buy the best gear available and run it. The pay would be $20,000 for a job that wouldn't take more than a few weeks, between filming and editing, and Aidan could keep the tech when he was done.

She'd said yes on Aidan's behalf on the spot, and somehow Aidan had managed to pull it off.

Shooting the footage had taken three days, and he'd had to be on-site the whole time. She didn't see him once that weekend.

He came back on the fourth day, unshaved and greasy, walked straight to their liquor cabinet without a word, grabbed the handle of Jack Daniels, and closed himself in the bathroom. She waited until she heard the shower cut on before she let herself cry.

The seventy-two hours he'd been gone had been the best she'd had in the past six months.

Her friends, her therapist, everyone assured her that wanting to leave him didn't—wouldn't—make her a horrible person. They weren't married, and playing nursemaid had never been part of their deal.

She knew he'd bought an engagement ring a few weeks before things started getting bad, and that it had been in his sock drawer ever since.

She flinched every time he opened the drawer, every time he reached into his jacket pocket. He'd bent down to tie her shoe, once, and she'd thrown up a little in her mouth. Still, part of her wondered why he hadn't asked.

Was he waiting until he got better?

Or was it that he knew she would say no, and that would be the end?

It took him three days to put the final product together, to select the footage and get it edited and clean. He said almost nothing during that time, nothing beyond *thank you* if she brought him something, or *no, thank you* if she asked him if he wanted anything, and *have fun* if she said she was going out.

Chris had been nice enough, but there was something about him and the project that creeped her out, so she hadn't asked Aidan about it, but then Aidan was finished and sitting in the living room with her, still mute, so she brought it up just so they'd be talking again, and things wouldn't be so tense.

She regretted it immediately.

"Naked? In South Bronx? In February?" she asked, incredulous.

He nodded.

"That's terrible."

"Yeah. People did some really messed-up things."

"And he let them?"

"He was in chains. Unconscious for lots of it."

"They tattooed him?"

"Yes."

"What did they do? Was it awful?"

"Some of it."

"But not all?"

He shook his head. "No, not all."

"People are horrible."

He nodded. "Chris told me it might get bad, made him promise not to intervene no matter what, but...he was in pretty rough shape by the end."

"I don't want to hear any more."

"Watching those people beat the shit out of him as he hung there, bleeding...those people were so angry they weren't even human."

"Enough! Fucking stop it! Goddammit, Aidan, I said I'm done!"

He put his hands up. "Me, too. Sorry."

She nodded.

They looked away from each other, sat in awkward silence.

"I'm doing better."

"That's good."

"No, I mean I'm getting better. Really. The meds…I feel like I'll be able to get on top of this."

"Yeah." She held up the list. "All you have to do is start humming the next time the voices tell you to attack someone."

"You're upset?"

"Are you fucking kidding me?"

He shook his head.

"Yes, I'm fucking upset! Our life is shit! We're broke—you've completely trashed everything we've worked for."

"I've—"

"For Christ's sake, Aidan, you showed up drunk on the set of my commercial and picked a fight with the director!"

"That wasn't me!"

"It looked a lot like you!"

"It was the bipolar! We didn't have it under contr—"

"The bipolar? Is that what they're calling it this week?"

"Jesus, Allison! I have a fucking neurochemical disorder."

"Great. That makes it all better."

"Treatment will. Therapy will. Knowing what we're up against and how to fight it will."

"And if it doesn't?"

"It will, Allison. Just give it a chance. Give me a chance."

"Word gets around, Aidan. I haven't had a callback since you trashed that set."

"I will go and apologize to each and every person that was there. I will explain that I was sick, and that I'm incredibly sorry, and that nothing like that will ever happen again."

She shook her head. "You can't know that."

"I do."

"So you're magically better now? Just like that?"

"No. But the meds are helping. Therapy is helping. The ECT takes a hell of a lot out of me, but it's helping too—"

"You started ECT?"

"I told you that."

She shook her head violently. "ECT?"

"Yes."

"They're electrocuting you?"

"Well—"

"You're letting them run an electric current through your brain?"

"I—"

"I need to leave."

"Allison..." he said.

She took her coat from the hook by the door, wound a scarf around her neck.

"Allison, come on."

She ripped her purse off the ground, yanked the door open.

"This isn't fair."

She slammed the door behind her.

Goddamn right it wasn't.

THE GIGGLE HOUSE

And no walking, either. A cop sees you walking down the street—especially if it's a street wypipo use—and he be like, that negro getting a little big for his Fubu's.

And out comes the steel.

So no walking, brothers and sisters, dear God, no walking.

DETECTIVE TURNER

"Whatchya watching, Uncle Mason?"

Turner closed the tab before his niece could see the woman tattooing 'Fuck the police' on the white boy's scrotum.

His niece grinned. "You were watching porn, weren't you? You are so busted!"

"Shouldn't you be getting ready for school?"

"Shouldn't you be getting ready for work?"

"Done. You wish you looked this good."

"So they're letting you work again?"

"Girl, if you think twelve is too old for me to bend you over my knee, you've got another think coming."

She scurried off.

He shook his head, smiled. Little brat.

He'd been suspended for a week, earlier that month. He kept his pay, thanks to the captain. The captain could have burned him, and might have if the guy he'd jacked up had been more than a patrolman.

Turner had let a few days pass, then gone to the precinct to bury the hatchet, offered to cover the guy's medical expenses out of pocket. Patrolman Kelly had stopped him short, apologized to *him*, said he'd made an assumption, and it had been wrong, and he'd carry the boy's death for the rest of his life.

Turner extended the hand that had formed the fist he'd broken against Kelly's face without thinking, and Kelly took hold of it, and the pain blew out his vision, ripped him back through time: *You redneck motherfucker,* he'd snarled. *You murdered that boy.*

Crack!

Turner apologized again when he was reinstated. It had been an all-staff briefing, and he'd asked Kelly, the Captain, the precinct, and "all those who wear the shield" to forgive him for smearing their name. The precinct respected Detective Turner, even if some thought he acted like he carried more of the weight of the world than he could rightly claim, and they were ready to give him a pass if he did the right thing, but it had to be *the right thing*, because the precinct liked Patrolman Kelly, and being who they were, there was the obvious consideration, so while Turner and Kelly's initial exchange was sincere, it was never going to be sufficient. People needed to see; his apology had to be as public as his crime, as his allegation: "Patrolman Kelly is not a racist."

How many times had they made him say it?

"Patrolman Kelly is not a racist. Patrolman Kelly is not a racist. Patrolman Kelly is not a racist."

Maybe not, but a boy was dead because of Kelly, another Black youth chalked on a sidewalk in South Bronx, and yes, the kid was a banger, and yes, he'd been packing when he got shot, but there had been a doctor right there, and everyone who'd ever served knew about the golden hour—Kelly with his three tours, Turner with his one— knew that if the doctors got to you within the hour, as long as you weren't headshot, you had a near-eighty-percent chance of being okay.

The kid should have been fucking okay.

Except the doctor had been Black, so when Kelly arrived on scene moments after reports of shots fired, he didn't see a doctor trying to stop an arterial bleed, he saw a nigger beating on his victim, and so Kelly had ripped the doctor off and cranked his arm high up his back and rode him to the ground, jammed a knee into the base of his skull, and cuffed him. And because the doctor wouldn't stop screaming and trying to get to the victim, Kelly hadn't let up, only leaned harder, grinding the doctor's face into the concrete and driving a shard of glass through his lower lip.

And Turner would have been fine with it, had Kelly been right, had he been looking at a 10-13 about to turn 187—no way that's excessive force with blood flowing and a burner jammed in the vic's pants. Yes, the legality of the technique was questionable, but executed correctly, it was efficient and safe, and allowed the officer to gain control of the situation before it escalated, and if the perp ended up with a few broken bones or torn muscles, well, sometimes shit happened.

But Kelly wasn't right. He wasn't fucking right.

The man he'd cuffed was a doctor, and he'd been trying to save someone's life, the life of a man who was once his friend, a kid he'd grown up with, a kid who'd had more meals at his house than in his own family's, because his mother had died when he was little, and his father had to work three jobs just to get them by. The doctor was six years older than the kid, had become his big brother, walked him to school, checked his homework, taught him to shave, to shoot hoops. And then the doctor had to watch him die, watch him bleed out from a few feet away, knowing he could've saved him.

Seale could have saved Lamar.

But Kelly saw a nigger instead of a doctor, so the point was moot.

Turner shook his head, rubbed at his temples with both hands, pinched the bridge of his nose so hard the two fingers turned white.

He couldn't get clear on this, couldn't think straight.

Kelly. Three tour Kelly. Wounded in action Kelly. Medal of commendation Kelly. Kelly with pictures taped up in his locker of hunting and fishing and screwing around with the guys from his unit: three Black, two white, one something else.

It didn't help that the doctor wasn't just a doctor, that he was Turner's younger brother, and that part of the reason he'd become a doctor was because their father hadn't had a degree, only a G.E.D., and their mother hadn't even had that, and so even though they worked two and sometimes three jobs each, none of them came with medical, and they were only just able to cover the cost of their mother's diazepam, olanzapine, phenelzine, quetiapine, risperidone, and topiramate out of pocket when it was just the three of them, Turner and his parents, but then the twins came, early and ill, and spent eight weeks in the NICU, and after that they couldn't afford anything, especially not doctor's visits. Turner had joined the Army after high school—one less mouth for his parents to feed—and had been shipped to Baumholder, Germany, where he lived frugally and sent all he could home. The day after his twenty-second birthday, the platoon sergeant called him into his office and regretted to inform him that his parents were dead, killed when the Yugo they were driving swerved into the path of an oncoming bus.

The Army was granting him a compassionate discharge so he could take custody of his seven-year-old brother and sister. The sergeant handed him his file and orders and told him to report to admin.

In forty-eight hours, he went from being a soldier in Germany to an unemployed civilian with seven-year-old twins in the South Bronx.

"Nandi." Turner caught his niece's wrist as she hurried by.

She stopped, waited, ready for school, her hair brushed out, lively; she looked at him, trying to gauge whether or not she was in trouble.

"I love you."

She smiled. "You're okay, I guess."

He laughed. "You better get out of here before I come up out of this chair."

She got.

He watched her go, turn right onto the sidewalk in front of the apartment, and disappear.

Her mother just got promoted at work, was in charge of all the hiring and scheduling for the hospital, now, which meant working nights when they were short-handed.

He was proud of her, proud of her brother.

His brother.

Turner had given up everything for them, never had a girlfriend or traveled or went out. But he got his brother and sister through high school and college, and he saw Seale through medical school, and C.J. through her Masters, and he'd worked his way through night school along the way and earned a B.A. of his own.

As terrible as it was to pick up the phone so long ago and hear that his parents were dead, it was nothing compared to the call he got from the detention center, nothing to hearing that his brother had been arrested on suspicion of murder, nothing to going down to the precinct and seeing Seale in a cell, nothing compared to Turner knowing that he didn't hit Kelly just because Kelly roughed up his brother and killed a kid, or because Kelly didn't have the decency to find Seale some clothes and a few wet naps so he wouldn't have to wear his dead friend's blood while he sat in holding—Turner didn't even do it because Kelly read Black men as *niggers* and *criminals* rather than people—what did it, what pushed him over the edge, was the realization that Kelly, and every other Caucasian motherfucker riding the lynchman's rails, had actually gotten to him, had done him so hard and for so long that he'd started thinking like they did, seeing things the way they saw them. Seale had been arrested for murder, his face was bruised and bleeding from being driven into the asphalt, he was covered in Lamar's blood—Turner hadn't even asked him if he was okay, because it never occurred to him, because, despite everything he knew about Seale, despite the fact that Turner had raised him like a son, he saw Seale sitting in that cell and wondered: had he done it, had Seale done murder?

They'd gotten him.

If the Black father of a Black doctor can't imagine a Black man setting his hands on another man apart from malicious intent, what hope was there?

It wasn't just that the scrubs and the hospital ID and the fact that Seale had been administering lifesaving medical care didn't matter to Kelly, that Seale's credentials didn't matter to Kelly, it was that they hadn't mattered to *him*, to Detective Mason Robeson Turner.

He'd looked at his brother and seen a nigger.

He didn't try to hide his tears or staunch their flow, now. He didn't try to make sense of things, or separate rage from sorrow or the fists crushing his lungs or the razor shredding his insides or the desiccation of his heart, and it all merged into a band of immolating pain wrapped around his skull that consumed everything but the hate he carried in his heart, leaving behind something bestial, something that salivated at the thought of tearing the throat from someone's neck and lapping at the blood that surged forth, something frenzied and malignant with serriform teeth and ragged breath, and damned if it wasn't going to unleash itself upon the world.

Blood for parched lips, to sate an inhuman thirst.

Violence, vengeance.

The carnival of carnage shimmering on the other side of *fuck it.*

He shook himself away from the feeling, opened his laptop, resumed watching the movie.

An alert sounded on his smartphone: they'd discovered the boy's identity. He was J. Christopher Fairchild, the son of billionaire mogul William Fairchild.

Turner didn't care.

The boy was a John Doe when they found him, dangerously

feverish, face mashed, nose and cheek and jaw broken, left eye swollen shut, bruising and breakage of the ribs consistent with being kicked and stomped.

But terrible though his injuries were, he was alive, and thus not Turner's problem. The EMTs had strapped the boy to a gurney and loaded him in an ambo, and that was that. Turner called the hospital the next day, to make sure he hadn't become his problem, and half-listened as the nurse told him more than he needed to know:

The boy would live.

Turner, out.

He checked his phone. Seale would be finishing up a thirty-hour shift around nine, and Turner was going to take him to get some breakfast before he went home and crashed. The hospital had offered Seale time off after the shooting, but he'd said no. He'd wanted to get back to work.

Kelly took one life, and there was no way Seale was going to let him or anyone else take more just because he was a little shaken up.

Turner was proud.

THE GIGGLE HOUSE

And don't ever be just standing around when you're in public. A cop sees you standing around, he knows you're selling drugs or casing a bank or waiting for a white woman to rape, or possibly all three.

And when a cop sees that...Y'all want to say it with me this time? Out comes the steel.

V

"Not going to happen," Sol said, hurrying away.

V pursued. "It's a great story!"

"Forget it," he said without looking back, rounding a corner toward the safety of the men's room.

"Why? Just tell me why."

"I—shit."

Libi Altschul stood in front of the men's bathroom with her arms crossed. "Sol," she said.

"Libi." He inched backward, turned, and found V blocking his way.

He looked from one woman to the other, scanned the room, and spotted the paper's longtime photographer. "Mel! Help me out here!"

"Sorry, Sol," he said without breaking stride. "You're on your own."

Sol clutched his chest.

"Really?" Libi gave him a look. "Faking a heart attack?"

"I have a condition!"

"I'll say."

He blinked wildly.

"Mr. Feiner..." V started.

"Why are you doing this to me?"

"Why can't we do the story?"

"What are you, an amoretz?"

"Mr. Feiner," V said.

"You know why!"

The office was run-down, poorly lit. The ancient heating system had caused the wallpaper to blister in places and had dissolved the adhesive in others so that it sagged like a cancer patient's skin. The filing cabinets and desks and chairs were older than the interns, dented and scored from decades of rough use.

Most of the employees capable of finding other employment already had, including the editor.

"Say it, Sol," Libi demanded. "Say it out loud so that everyone knows what we've become."

He looked from Libi to V, sweating, back to Libi. "Our finances are fercockt! We're barely afloat as it is."

He'd worked there for thirty-three years, been the assistant editor-in-chief for twenty-five. Libi had been at the paper for over a decade.

V was four-months-new and just-out-of-journalism-school-young, hungry.

"But it's got everything, Mr. Feiner; torture, sex appeal, racial tension—it practically sells itself."

"Did you happen to notice, perchance, who was involved?"

"Don't be an ass, Sol," Libi scolded.

"Oy gevalt, Libi—she's supposed to be a fekokteh reporter!"

Sol stalked back to his office and slammed the door.

"What was that about?" V asked.

"William Fairchild. His corporation is the only reason the paper hasn't gone under."

"And Sol thinks Fairchild will drop us if we go to print?"

"Knows."

"Fairchild threatened him?"

"His people."

"They said that?"

"In so many words."

"Damn." V paused, staring off into nowhere, her mind racing. "I have to do this story, Libi."

"It will never happen here."

V grimaced, shook her head. "Have you seen the videos?"

"About two minutes of one, which is two minutes too much if you ask me."

"Where would you start?"

"Start what?"

"The story."

Libi stole a glance at Sol's office. "You're ready to lose your job over this?"

V nodded. "I've got a source."

"How reliable?"

"Everything he's given me so far checks out."

"What's he given you?"

"Names and contact information."

"Of whom?"

"Those involved."

"Go write your resignation."

"What? Why? I—"

"I see you put it on Sol's desk and walk out the door, then I'll help you."

"But—why? I thought we were—"

"We are. I like you. You remind me a little of myself thirty years ago."

"Then what?"

"Fairchild would drop this paper in a second if his people told him we were digging into his son's story, and that would kill Sol, literally kill him. He's given nearly half his life to this paper, and watching it go under on his watch would be more than he could take."

"Okay. I'll do it."

"Meet me at Toad Hall at four-thirty."

V arrived first, chose a table by the window. Libi walked through the door at five o'clock, shivering. She ordered a double bourbon, neat, and V, tonic water with a lemon twist.

"So what do you have?" Libi asked.

"One of the tattoo artists, Fairchild's roommate, the guy that ran the tech, Fairchild's former professor."

"How?"

"Packages. No name or return address."

"How many?"

"Two so far."

Libi frowned.

"What?"

"You don't have enough."

"I know, that's why—"

"Listen to me. Fairchild's roommate and former professor are easily discoverable, as is the tattoo artist whose face is visible in a video that has gone viral. There are people out there who know who he is, and given a little incentive, will tell you where he lives. All you have is the name of a computer guy."

"But the why..."

"There's nothing there. Give it a day or two and this nutjob will post a manifesto decrying capitalism and its fascist minions or what have you—or sixteen different people will post sixteen different screeds, all claiming to have been written by Christopher Fairchild."

"But the violence...chains, kink...people will eat it up. And Fairchild and that gay professor, maybe—what?"

"Don't do that." Libi shook her head. "You sound like *The National Enquirer*."

V's eyes fell to the table.

"Every paper, magazine, and blog that covers this story is going to go that route—straight to the sewer."

"That doesn't mean there isn't something there."

"No, but anything you'll find there will be cheap and tawdry. It won't launch a career, and it certainly won't make your name. You'll be just another peddler of drivel."

The waiter brought another round.

"Why let me resign, then, if you think the story is crap?"

"I didn't. I took the letter off Sol's desk. He never saw it."

"Then why—"

"I wanted to see if you'd write it."

"I did."

"Now tell me why."

"I told you, I—"

"You risked your career so you could muck about in some brat's manure? No. I don't believe that for a minute. Why?"

"I can't tell you."

"Won't?"

"Can't, because I don't know."

"Say you work yourself all the way to Fairchild, what exactly do you think he's going to say?"

"Maybe there's not much he can say. Maybe that's the story."

"What is?"

"That some stories are predators, rather than prey. Maybe my piece isn't just on Fairchild, but on all the people caught in the wake of this thing."

"Want some advice?"

"Sure."

"I don't understand what you're after, but I love your fire. You want to make it as a reporter? Don't marry, don't have kids, work your ass off, and don't accept a 'no' from anyone. One day you'll come upon a story that needs to be told.

"This is not that story. Come to work tomorrow, do your job. Work Fairchild on the side, if you have to, but don't stake your future on it."

"I'll think about it."

Libi put a hand over V's and smiled. "Good," —she stood— "I'll see you tomorrow."

V watched her leave before ordering a drink.

Libi was missing something.

V just had to figure out what.

She raised a hand. One more, and she'd get back to work.

THE GIGGLE HOUSE

So just to recap: under no circumstances should a Black person walk, run, or stand in public.

Niggas gotta levitate.

THE REVEREND JEREMIAH CARTER

The Reverend Jeremiah Carter was nearing the last of his twenty laps. He'd been a pastor for fifty-two years, and in those years, he had painted the yellow rectangle around the perimeter of the church property one hundred and four times, every October and June. In that time he'd lost a sister to drugs, two brothers to bullets, and a son to an overzealous policeman. He'd buried two wives, one grandchild, and more parishioners than he could count, suffered humiliation and indignity at the hands of white men not worthy of mention, been betrayed by his own father, cheated by his best friend, and had to hold and comfort his daughter after her rape.

He'd been angry plenty, knew well the feeling of ground glass lacerating his insides, the white heat of rage gone steel-cold beneath enervated hate. He'd succumbed to anger and had to dig deep into himself to find the strength for contrition and humility and the seeking of forgiveness; he'd vented anger from the pulpit in bellows and sighs until church and tabernacle trembled; he'd triumphed over anger, ignored it, buried it so deeply in his being that he'd gotten cancer and had to allow doctors to pump him full of poison and burn it from his bowels.

But he'd never been angry with God before today.

He'd cultivated his mind and tamed his will and purified his heart so that, at the end of days, he might behold the countenance of the Lord and hear His voice say: Well done, my good and faithful servant.

And now he felt contempt metastasizing in his chest, curses

swelling in his mouth, and only the momentum of a lifetime kept him from spewing them skyward.

The Reverend began a twenty-first lap, and at that moment the sexton left his mop to lilt in its bucket and went to the window, and the neighbors across the street ceased their activities and turned their eyes toward the church.

For fifty-two years the Reverend had preached the importance of prayer, of the absolute and incontrovertible necessity that his parishioners seek the counsel of their Creator, and in those same years he spoke to them also of Paul, and of the race each one of them were called to run, and of the importance of exercise that they might care for and strengthen their bodies, and in so doing prove themselves to be good stewards of God's gifts, fleet of foot and long in endurance. And because faith without works is dead, he had, for the entirety of those fifty-two years, walked twenty times around the quarter-mile perimeter of the church property every day, starting at two o'clock, regardless of the weather, and in this and the general conduct of his life his parishioners saw that he was faithful and fit, and knew him to be a man who placed no burden upon another that he did not also bear up under himself, and they came, with varying levels of awareness, to live in accordance with his rhythms and example, and to depend upon the constancy of his presence.

Few could have said why they stopped what they were doing that day, but stop and watch they did, and minute by minute an hour passed, and then another, and yet another, and the Reverend was still walking, and the number of spectators had grown to more than thirty, and the number of times he had compassed the church had surpassed fifty, and still he walked.

Because no one could have stopped to watch the Reverend from the near sidewalk without interrupting his progress, the sexton was the closest to him, and because it had become apparent that the Reverend was in the middle of a great struggle, the next closest people were across the street, held there by the intensity of his battle; one of the deacons would later say that he was wrestling an angel in the manner of Jacob, and though the deacon's remarks were as true as any offered on the matter, it was known that he had been on the other side of the city at the time, tending to things unbefitting a man of God, and so people closed their ears to him, and his words fell barren from his lips.

The Reverend's mouth bent and flexed as he walked, but no sound escaped them, at least none that anyone could hear.

He was angry, though, about that there was no mistake; his complexion was ordinarily that of umber, and yet now there was red burning through, the red of dead fathers and incarcerated sons, the red of the lochia of mothers and daughters raped and forced to bear the issue of their violation into a heartless world, of mothers and daughters given no choice but to love and raise those children.

And why was he mad? Why now if not at so many times in the past, if not after having been accused of theft when he was innocent, accused in public as he stood with the white of his clerical collar blazing in the afternoon sun?

Why not after seeing his father, a man as strong as Samson, as gentle as Ruth, and more generous than Solomon, a man who, having never been to school, had taught himself to read and write, and having learned one language, had not been content to stop until he'd learned four more—why not after the Reverend had been forced to watch his father endure humiliation at the hands of an insecure, illiterate fool intent on groping and degrading his wife, the Reverend's mother?

Why now if not at innumerable moments when the white world and the Black world and every world seemed to revel in violence and the denigration of everything that he loved, every worthy, just, and gentle mote in the whole of creation?

One amidst the spectators claimed to be able to read lips, and according to his account, the Reverend, between the ninety-fourth and the ninety-sixth laps, demanded that God explain to him how, after all he had allowed to befall his people, after all the pain and tribulation and torment he had allowed them to endure, all the slings and arrows and lashes and wrongs—all the seeds of rage he'd seen plowed into the soil of their hearts as he stood by—how could God permit the Great Deceiver to tempt them so deviously, to set their damnation before them disguised as satisfaction—as justice, as righteous retribution?

The lip-reader was almost as old as the Reverend and greatly respected in the community. He'd been a lawyer before he retired, and had gained a well-earned reputation for representing the least of these, whether or not they could pay him.

He, too, had buried a wife in his forties, but unlike the Reverend, his faith failed him, and so he faded through the decades, a lonely man, known to turn to drink early in the day.

It is said that the Reverend's anger gave out after his ninety-eighth lap, and that he had begun to appear unsteady on his feet as early as the ninety-sixth. Several people remember Mrs. Fisk saying that someone should go to him, and that in the event he could not be convinced to cease his exertions, that the saints should offer their arm and walk beside him.

Ms. Brown is supposed to have said that she'd been worried about the Reverend since two months prior when he'd done eight funerals in three and a half weeks, all for parishioners who were too old to be considered children, and too young to have become men, and while church records confirm that the funerals took place, there's no way of knowing if the Reverend ever gave her cause for worry, or if she was merely trying to look out for a man too busy looking after others to spare a thought for himself.

The Reverend had always kept his own council, and the tendency only became more pronounced after his second wife died and the last of the men he'd grown up with passed away.

What is known, absolutely, is that the Reverend Jeremiah Douglas Carter collapsed after completing his hundredth lap around the perimeter of the church, and that he died on snow-covered ground in the city he loved and in which he'd lived his whole life, having pastored his congregation for more than half a century.

Barack Obama was the President.

The Republicans controlled both the House and the Senate.

The country had just watched Black men torture a white boy for three days.

We pray for Reverend Carter, that he may rest in peace and God's everlasting love for all eternity.

THE GIGGLE HOUSE

We'll get back to the po-po—for the melanin-deficient in the audience, that's another name for the police—but first we need to cover some tips for surviving the next greatest threat to African-Americans: namely, wypipo.

STEVE

Steve looked at the men waiting outside his office. "This couldn't wait? I had Mahler's Ninth on the Ultima and a bottle of scotch I've been saving for twenty years."

"Had to be now."

Steve sighed, flicking through his keys, found the one he needed, opened the door, and waved the men in.

"We've been infiltrated," one of them said as soon as the door clicked shut. "There's a race traitor in our midst."

Steve took off his glasses and rubbed his eyes.

"Did you hear me? I said we've got a nigger-lover in our midst!"

"Dicky—"

"It's Garth!" Dicky thrust his hand at the third man.

"Race-traitor?" Garth growled, jumping up from his chair. "You're a fucking liar."

"You betrayed us!" Dicky shoved him hard in the chest. "You betrayed your own brothers—your own race—just so you could fuck some monkey."

Garth swung at him. "Fuck you."

"Sit down, both of you."

"But—"

"And shut up. Jesus Christ, look at yourself. Did you think we didn't know Garth was engaged to a Black woman?"

"I—wait—You knew?"

"Of course we knew."

"But..."

"Some girl shook her tits at him twenty years ago, and he thought he was in love. Do you really want to have to answer for every piece you've stuck your dick in your entire life?"

"But—"

"We're moving on, Dicky, you're going to have to accept that."

"Moving on how?"

"Same goal, new message. Greater clarity and precision."

"But—"

"No more nigger, no more kike or fag. From now on we leave that to the idiots wearing pillowcases."

"But we're in danger. The niggers—"

"Where is our event taking place tomorrow?"

"In the Marriott."

"Correct. In the Marriott."

"So what?"

"So everything."

Dicky shrugged, palms up.

"Have we done events in a Marriott before?"

"Once or twice. Not really, no."

"No, we haven't. We've met in rec centers, in people's basements, in the back room at rotary clubs, but never at the Marriott."

"So what?"

Steve squinted at him. "All the work we've been doing online, building a respectable community—we're stepping out into the light now. No more hiding, no more slinking about or apologizing for who we are and what we believe."

"Right, I get it. Raise 'em high and proud. Sieg Heil! Heil Hitler!"

Steve closed his eyes, opened them after a ten count.

"If I ever hear you say those words again, Dicky, I'm going to shove my boot so far up your ass you'll taste polish."

"But—"

"We can't step into the light with 'nigger.' We can't go mainstream with Nazi salutes."

"So, what, they're not a threat, suddenly?"

"Who?"

"Niggers—"

Steve silenced him with a hand.

"We're not after Joe Misanthrope, anymore; we're hunting bigger game now. The skinheads and KKK have their role to play, but the cause—we need more than broken down, blue-collar nobodies to achieve our objectives."

"Which are?"

"The same as they've always been: an America for Ameri-cans, an identitarian, ideologically conservative society that rejects global multiculturalism."

"But we can't say nigger or ki—"

"Absolutely not. Ever. Leave that to the trolls."

"Why?"

"Because now we're going after people that wear suits to work—nice suits. Respectable, upstanding citizens who coach little league and serve on the town council. People who vote with their money."

"Since when are we concerned with the high rollers? I thought we were out for the people."

Garth shot his friend a look.

"Sometime in the next few years, the great unwashed will realize that we and the people that bankroll us have been making promises that we not only couldn't keep, but which we never had any intention of keeping. They'll realize we screwed them."

"We did?"

"Yes, Dicky, we did. Coal is not coming back. The middle class will continue to shrink, and the threat posed by radical Islam will grow unabated so long as we continue to bomb the Middle East. People are going to figure this out, eventually, and when that happens, we're going to need to have established a new base, a constituency both willing and able to keep us moving forward."

"Including Jews and niggers?"

"And fags. We've already got some working for us."

"We do?"

"You might consider following some of our online platforms and the work we're doing."

"I'll leave that to you. I've got work to do, getting the word out. There's an army of niggers and Jews and other racial trash gunning for America, and most folk don't even know it. That's why I'm here."

"Be that as it may, we're not going to use those words anymore."

"What words are we going to use?"

"We're not going to talk about race, or racial threats, or racial violence. We're going to talk about the tribe."

"The tribe?"

"Before race, there was the tribe, a group of people that looked alike and lived and acted together for a common purpose. We'll talk about strength, tradition, and community. We'll talk about the long-lost days of power when men were men and protected their families by the might of their hands."

"But the niggers and Jews..."

"Will identify themselves."

"I don't understand."

Steve stared at Dicky in silence.

"How will they 'identify themselves'?"

"By doing what they do."

"Which is?"

"A Jew is as a Jew does, same for a Black man. Those who make it clear that they are not part of the tribe, that, on the contrary, they wish to do it injury, will be excised."

"Excised."

"Yes. Naturally, and without unnecessary racial terminology that obfuscates the fact that the individual has proven himself to be a threat to society."

"No," Dicky said, shaking his head. "No, Sir. This is not right. We got a race war coming: niggers are breeding like rabbits—we're facing a goddamn nigger apocalypse, and there ain't no way I'm going to stop telling people about it—we need to prepare!"

Garth fidgeted in his chair.

"Blacks make up less than fourteen percent of the population, Dicky, and they control less than three percent of the country's wealth; the only way America will ever see a racial apocalypse is if the whole of white America hops in its Range Rover, heads to the ghetto, and proceeds to beat the residents to death with a nine-iron."

"So what, then? It's all a lie?"

"A lie?"

"The whole racial thing."

Steve threw his hands up. "Can you help me, Garth? I'm not getting through."

"I think what he's saying is—"

"I don't need no help from a monkey-fucking race-traitor!"

"Fuck y—"

"Enough! Both of you! Dicky, take a good look at Garth, because

87

this is the last warning you'll get: clean contemporary haircut, button-down shirt, cardigan, khaki pants, adult shoes; no tobacco stains on his teeth, speaks English—this is what you're going to have to become if you want to stay with us."

"And if I won't?"

"I can connect you with one of the screamer groups: KKK, neo-Nazis, paleoconservatives, skinheads, take your pick. But I don't think you want to do that."

"I don't?"

"No, you don't."

"Why?"

"Because right now, the greatest threat facing America isn't Blacks or Jews or gay people, but our own lack of self-regard. We've lost faith in ourselves."

"I don't understand."

"Have you seen the Fairchild video?"

"The one with the niggers beating on the kid?"

"Try to get yourself out of the habit of using that word."

"Sorry. The African-Americans beating on the kid."

"Precisely. Fairchild put himself in that position. No one ordered him to do it, no one forced him. He chose to do it because he believed that it was what he deserved, what all white people deserve. He held himself, you and me, and our whole tribe in such low regard that he considered his own torture an act of justice."

"What we need to do is string up the niggers that beat him."

"No! What we need to do is combat the culture that has us attacking ourselves from within. You say it's the Blacks that are the problem, the Jews, the feminists, homosexuals, the LGBTQ lobbyists, and pinko-commie bleeding heart liberal cucks. Fine. But we are better, smarter, wiser, wealthier, and more numerous than they are, so they aren't the real problem. We are, and that's why we don't need to name any of them."

"We don't?"

"No. We need to help people realize that the son of a man who built a billion-dollar empire with nothing but his bare hands and the sweat of his brow is a god, that a boy earning top marks at a prestigious university should be proud of himself, not apologetic.

"We need to remind them that tradition, community, and a legacy of accomplishment bestow an identity that deserves to be celebrated.

"We need to tell them we have a responsibility to ourselves and to our tribe to be the best we can be. That's going to be our primary job: to create an identity they can step into."

"And then what?"

"Give them something to do—tell them they need to learn survival skills, go to the gym, make a ton of money."

"Why?"

"To keep them busy while culture shifts."

"Shifts?"

"There are deep wells of wealth and power waiting to be tapped, people of great consequence who are tired of apologizing and tripping over their words. People who long for the good old days, Judeo-Christian America, the land of the free, white, and brave. All they need is the thinnest veneer to protect themselves from accusations of racism."

"But the nig—"

"Get out of my office, Dicky."

"But—"

"Now."

"That's not—"

"Go, Dicky. You're done."

"I tried," Steve said to Garth when Dicky'd gone.

"Some people are just dumb motherfuckers."

"Are you tracking, Garth? Is this making sense?"

"Yes, Sir."

"Good. We've got work to do."

THE GIGGLE HOUSE

The first thing to know is wypipo are some wiley bastards. They know how to butter us up real good, right?

"My, Jamal, you do run so quickly! And those muscles! So strong! So...ripply! I dare say, your people are exceptionally talented at athletic endeavors!"

"Oh, just look at those dance moves, Laquanda! However do you rotate your hips in such a fashion? We whites could simply never be as smooth on the dance floor!"

And we eat that shit up. We're over here all high-fiving each other, like, "Yeeeeeah dawg! Fuck wypipo! We da shit!"

DR. SCOTT

Knock, knock.

Go away, he thinks.

Knock, knock.

Go away, please.

"Dr. Scott?"

He opens the door.

She is beautiful, which sets him on edge—Senegalese braids, tawny skin, business casual.

Attractive women don't just show up on your doorstep.

Or at your office, as the case may be.

And how did she know he'd be here on a Sunday morning?

"Dr. Scott, hello. I'm Vivian Carver-Brown; it's a pleasure to meet you."

"Likewise," he says, shaking her hand, polite, but not warm.

He's waiting; she's smiling.

Neither of them speaks.

He clears his throat.

"Do you have a minute?" she asks. "I was hoping I might ask you a few questions."

"Regarding?"

"A former student of yours. Christopher Fairchild."

He frowns; she presses the advantage, pushes past him and sits in the chair opposite his desk.

Scott stands motionless for a moment, sighs, allows the door to close, and moves toward his desk.

"You knew Mr. Fairchild?" Carver asks.

Scott nods.

"Well?"

"What do you mean?"

"Were you close?"

"He was one of many students..."

"Of whom you were particularly fond."

"Why are you here, Ms. Carver?"

"I told you, I have a few ques—"

"To what end, Ms. Carver? What are you after?"

"I was hoping you could clarify the nature of your relationship with Mr. Fair—with Christopher."

"Why?"

"Are you aware of what happened to him?"

"I assume you're referring to his performance art piece?"

"You mean the video?"

"Yes."

"And you—"

"Have no desire to be quoted on the matter."

"Why?"

Scott purses his lips, but remains silent.

"Why are you so reluctant to talk about Christopher?"

"Why haven't you told me why you're here?"

"I told you. I'm here to talk about Christopher Fairchild."

"And I already asked you why you want to talk about Mr. Fairchild and got no answer. So, since you're either unable or unwilling to tell me where you're going with this, I'm going to ask you to leave."

He gestures toward the door.

"Dr. Scott, I—"

"Let me get you started. You're articulate and have had a sufficient amount of education to be able to use 'whom' correctly without much effort, which means you're either an English major, or you have a graduate degree, because we haven't taught grammar in this country since the '6os."

She starts to speak.

"Please," Scott says, lifting his hand, "Let me finish."

She crosses her arms.

"Thank you." He offers a thin smile. "You're too old and too polished to be an undergraduate student, but you're too young to have completed a doctoral program, which puts you at a Masters, a professional degree, or something in the humanities, because you'd be doing something more lucrative than stalking college professors, otherwise. How am I doing?"

"Were you and Christopher close, Dr. Scott?"

"Right, I'll wrap things up, then. So you're a reporter, you got wind of the Fairchild story through a friend of a friend, and you saw an opportunity to make a name for yourself, only whichever publication you were working for at the time wouldn't touch it, either because William Fairchild owned it directly, or one of his company's subsidiaries owned it—or maybe there was no connection between Fairchild and your company whatsoever, and it was just that your publication didn't want to incur the unholy wrath of Daddy Fairchild and lawyers by making his son's humiliation national news.

"At any rate, you were given an ultimatum, and being the idealistic, type A, go-getter you are—no tea, no shade—you quit your job to chase the Fairchild story through as many seedy, sensationalist, and atavistic cesspools as possible, starting with the professor who had the audacity to introduce the boy to the idea that the end of slavery didn't mean the end of racism, and that white America continues to enjoy privileges procured on the backs, blood, and suffering of African-American men and women, among others."

She folds her hands in her lap and meets his eye.

"So let's be real, shall we? Put all our cards on the table?"

He flattens his voice, wringing all the emotion from his words so as not to appear threatening.

She nods.

"You're looking to advance your career by doing me very publically, so to speak, but don't come for me, Ms. Carver, because as we say in Chelsea, I'm not featuring that, so I'll serve you some realness: it's none of your business."

"You misunderstand me, Dr. Scott, I'm not asking if you slept with him."

Scott looks at her, blinking, opens his mouth to speak, closes it again.

"Even if you did, it's not a crime, not even a problem, really, so long as he wasn't still your student. The age of consent in New York is seventeen."

Scott clenches his teeth. Unclenches.

"Look, I know you and Christopher spent time together outside of class. I'm not looking to burn you or to print some lurid tale. All I'm asking after is the nature of your conversations. What did you talk about?"

Scott stares hard, off-balance, skeptical, trying to peel back the layers of her face and lay bare her intentions.

He fails, leans back into his chair.

"He was part of an informal reading group I led. We met every other week at a bar not far from here. Chris tended to linger. He was new to CRT—critical race theory—and he had a lot of questions."

"Such as?"

Scott's eyes laze over the room, moldings and bookshelves, diplomas on the wall, a painting. "I think I've said all I'm going to say, Ms. Carver, so with all due respect, I'd like you to leave."

"Why are you so reluctant to talk about Christopher? I'm not accusing you of anything, the—"

"I've done nothing to be accused of."

"Exactly. All I want is to understand why Christopher did what he did. You said you'd discussed the performance piece with him?"

Scott steeples his fingers.

"Can you elaborate? When did that discussion take place? In what terms?"

Scott looks out through the window, cracks his knuckles, and follows the progress of a particularly gaudy delivery truck until it passes from view. "Purely theoretical ones. The idea was to try to account for the full range of the effects of racism, to go deeper than slavery and Jim Crow and lynching—not to dismiss them, but to trace their effects."

"So the war on drugs and police brutality..."

"Deeper."

"I don't follow."

Scott screws up his face. "Really?"

She shakes her head. "Tell me."

Scott lets a bark of laughter escape his lips. "We'd been discussing the concept of reparations," he says. "The question of the true cost of slavery."

"The true cost?"

"Beyond what is calculable. Not just the lost wages, lost

investment opportunities, the physical injuries, the men and women murdered, the unconscionably disproportionate incarceration rates, predatory lending practices—"

"Et cetera, et cetera," she interrupts. "I'm familiar with the litany."

"You dispute it?"

"No, but I think it's time we stop whining and start doing what we can to elevate ourselves. No one's going to help us, so we've got to do it on our own—stop slinging rock, put down the guns, and pick up a book. Get educated, take back our communities, start our own businesses, buy Black."

"All that would help, but take back from whom?"

"Pardon?"

"You said take back our communities. I'm wondering who you think has them."

Ms. Carver is silent.

"Right." Scott glances at his watch. "I really need to be going, Ms. Carver, so if there's nothing else..."

"Just finish telling me about the thought experiment. Please. Then I'll leave."

Scott speaks for ten minutes while she takes notes, and when he's done, he stands, takes his coat from its hook, and puts it on, while she caps her pen and tucks it away.

He lets her leave first, locks the door, and pulls it shut behind him, testing the knob before following her down the hall to the street.

Carver turns left at the sidewalk and begins trying to hail a cab. Best of luck with that, Scott thinks, and turns right.

He hasn't seen the video. He started it once, saw Chris being led down a snow-crusted street, naked and shackled, and turned it off.

He can't remember everything that was said, or how far they'd gone, whether or not they'd discussed guilt or atonement. Probably.

He and Chris spent more time together than most students and professors do, but they only ever talked about course materials, CRT, liberation theology, African-American literary criticism, and the like.

Snippets of conversation drift through his mind, the voices indistinct, but the words pristine.

The CRT group was meeting, a half-dozen people including himself.

Imagine, a voice says, *that you were taught the concept of* comparative value even before you acquired language, were shown images that you would later link to the words 'good' or 'bad,' 'better' or 'worse,' 'best' or 'worst.'

It is cold out.

Scott quickens his pace.

Imagine that it dawned on you, one day, without reason or warning, that there was no place for you within 'good' or 'better' or 'best,' no possibility of connection between those admirable, desirable states and your own being.

What would that mean?

Imagine that you not only realized you were excluded from 'good' and 'better' and 'best,' but that the very content of 'good' and 'better' and 'best' were constituted as your antithesis, as 'not you.'

Imagine that you realized it was too late to fight it, that your understanding of yourself and truth and value and Heaven and Hell and God formed around the notion that the only meaningful contribution you could ever make to the world was to die.

If you want to understand racism, imagine that 'not me' was the only answer to the following questions:

If you could be anything you wanted to be when you grow up, what would it be?

If you could have any quality, what would it be?

What is the most beautiful thing you can think of?

What's the most valuable thing a person can be?

Six blocks south, Scott turns into a bar, sits down at the counter, and orders a beer and a bourbon.

Got it? Now take a moment to realize that 'not me' was the only answer your mother could give to those questions, the only answer your father could give, and your husband or wife, your daughters and sons, the only answer their children will be able to give...

Scott shakes his head.

Now imagine you're gay on top of that, Scott says to his beer. And you live in Arkansas. And your Daddy's a minister.

"Excuse me?"

Scott looks up, surprised by the bartender's voice.

"You say something, man?" the bartender asks.

"Did I?" Scott says.

The bartender laughs. "You would know better than me, bro!"

He had.

But he wasn't sure what.

THE GIGGLE HOUSE

So now they've got us all congratulating ourselves 'cuz we have crazy ups and can bust a move. Then they pull out the big guns, and I do mean BIG guns, if you feel me.

This is when wypipo start telling us how hung we are. White honeys start talking like, "OMG, Madison, you know Jamal, right? OMG, I heard his...'thing' is, like, massive!"

"OMG, Stephanie! I, like, wonder if I could, like, even fit it!"

"OMG, Madison, have you, like, never been with a Black guy before?"

"No...wait, OMG, Stephanie! Have you? Like, OMG, you have to tell me everything, like, right now! Is it, like, as good as they say?"

"OMG, Madison, you have to try it! You'll, like, never want to be with a white guy again! They all just seem, like, so small now!"

"OMG, Stephanie! You mean it's, like, true?"

"OMG, so true!"

I mean, they ain't wrong, but...

FR. DIEGO GRACIA

It isn't that Diego Gracia doesn't believe in God—how could he not? He'd stolen from Nazario Ortega and lived.

Ortega had sent Gracia's friends to his apartment, men he'd grown up with, whom Gracia had himself initiated into the cartel. He'd been expecting them, knew he couldn't run fast enough or far enough to escape *El Más Loco*, so he'd attached a trip wire to a sawed-off shotgun in the front room, duct-taped a grenade to his bedroom door, a string running from the door handle to the pin. He'd had two FN-57s and an AR-type 223, and planned to go out his bedroom window and start shooting. Instead, he set the guns on his bed, disarmed the traps he'd set, and walked out the front door with his hands above his head.

He knew what would happen to him, that it would be slow, excruciating, that Ortega's men would place an IV in his neck and torture him until his body gave out. He didn't do it for Alejandro, his secret son, *El Bastardo*. He'd felt nothing for the boy, then, nothing for anyone or anything. He'd spent his days sitting in his apartment or at the compound, motionless, not thinking or talking or reading, not even listening to music or watching television. He smoked or drank or did lines if someone put something in front of him, but he never sought anything out.

They'd called Gracia *El hombre que no quiere nada*.

The man who wants nothing.

It was why Ortega trusted him, why he'd been in a position to steal from Ortega in the first place.

They took Gracia to Ortega's house, a massive Spanish-style mansion in the center of a gated compound, led him through the house to a courtyard.

Ortega sat beneath a large umbrella drinking juice from a tall glass. There was a pair of shears on the table in front of him along with a large knife and a box with a towel draped over it.

How long have you worked for me? he asked Gracia.

Since I was eleven, Señor.

And how old are you now?

Thirty-nine, Señor.

Almost thirty years, then.

Yes, Señor.

And in all this time, have I ever mistreated you?

No, Señor.

Have I ever denied you anything?

I've never asked for anything, Señor.

And why is that?

I was always content.

What changed?

Nothing, Señor.

We are talking now, Diego. I'm giving you a chance, but if you insist on lying to me...he gestured to the table.

I'm not lying, Señor.

You stole from me.

Yes, Señor.

Why? Dime, or you'll end up like your partner.

My partner? Gracia shook his head. I didn't have a partner.

Me voy a la mierda con este machete, Diego, al igual que con tu pareja—Ortega ripped the towel from the box—y luego voy a cortarte la cabeza.

A boy's head lay on its side, eyes frozen wide, mouth open in a shriek that would endure long after the earth swallowed him.

His cowlick still hovered atop his head.

Gracia had fallen to his knees, certain he was about to die, that someone had plunged a knife through his back and into his chest, but when he'd looked down, there hadn't been any blood.

Gracia looked both ways, then crossed the street, doing up the top button of his shirt and inserting the white plastic into his collar.

Good evening, Father, said the young man walking the other way. Gracia waved in response.

The woman on the young man's arm had turned fifteen two years earlier. Gracia had danced at her quinceañera.

She'd had an abortion last year, told him so in confession.

Her parents didn't know.

He'd given her seven Our Fathers and seven Hail Mary's, but all he'd wanted was to hold her and tell her that God loved her.

Gracia had been hard. He'd grown up tough in a time before gangster was cool, before the world decided that dealing drugs and shooting people and getting shot were glamorous. He believed in God not because he was alive, but because of what he'd been allowed to become and the manner in which he'd become it, and because of the way in which even the worst, most humiliating, and painful part of what had happened to him had been used for good.

Dime, Diego. Dime todo, y te mato rápidamente.

Diego told him.

The man Ortega had sent him to kidnap had been having a party; Gracia and his men had killed a mother and father and a sister and two uncles because they'd stolen from their boss.

They hadn't seen the boy hiding under the table, hadn't known he was watching as they tortured his father. Gracia discovered the boy as his men found the drugs and some cash under a floorboard in the child's bedroom.

He'd given the cash to the boy.

You expect me to believe that, Diego?

Gracia shrugged.

Why?

I don't know, Señor.

What was the boy to you?

Nothing. I don't even know his name.

¡Mentiroso!

It's the truth, Señor.

Gracia could give so many reasons now: guilt, shame, remorse, but none of them were true then.

If Nazario Ortega had been a monster, Diego Gracia had been...nothing. An emptiness.

Ortega cut Gracia's testicles from his body with the garden shears and ordered his men to dump him outside the hospital afterwards. He was sutured, given antibiotics and something for pain, and discharged. Ortega's men watched him limp a few blocks before pulling up and yanking him into the open door of a van. They put a dark hood over his head, bound his hands, and drove for a very long time. Then they stopped, shoved him from the vehicle without a word, and drove off.

I'm Father Doloroso, a voice said.

Diego Gracia.

How're you feeling?

I'd be better if you'd take this hood off.

That I can do. As for your balls...

Chinga tu madre, Father.

With what?

Pinche culero. Are all priests such grandes cabrones?

Claro que no. I am the greatest of the assholes. You are very lucky.

No mention was ever made of Ortega, nor was Gracia ever forbidden to leave, but he had nowhere else to go. He was given a room in the back of the parsonage and three meals a day, which he took with Father Doloroso, who liked to go for a walk afterward. There were no orders to follow, and no objectives to achieve, and Gracia began to grow restless, and because of this, he started accompanying the priest, who tried to engage him in conversation. At first, Gracia had nothing to say, but then, for reasons that were unclear to him, he began borrowing the father's books. Shortly after, he tried his hand at helping out around the grounds, which were plagued by the signs of poverty and indifference: a leaky roof, broken toilets, missing knobs and hinges and dials, a faulty pilot light.

Then, one night, his son came to him. Gracia couldn't understand why. He had never met his parents and had no idea what parents were meant to say to their children, and so he and Alejandro stared at each other. Then he came back, again, and again, and again. The dreams were vivid, terrifying, Alejandro's eyes penetrating his own and boring down into his emptiness.

At first, he came once or twice a month, but then it was every week, every other night, and Gracia fled from sleep, reading deep into the night and fixing things that needed fixing, and after enough pages had been turned and nails pounded and screwdrivers cranked and wrenches torqued and shocks suffered, Gracia learned enough carpentry and plumbing and circuitry to keep the parish in repair, and read enough theology that he could talk with Father Doloroso about the ultimate, the things that stirred the old man's heart.

You should go to seminary, the priest said eventually, and Gracia asked him why, and Doloroso asked if he really wanted an answer, and a day later Gracia decided that he did.

You think I'm talking about matemáticas, tus deudas, the priest said, but the reason has nothing to do with your former life. Lo hecho, hecho está y está en manos de Dios. The reason you should become a priest is because you have the heart for it. You have a desire to give gifts, Diego; all you do all day is work, and yet you are happy. But you could do more, you could become the conduit through which Dios otorga los dones finales.

What about faith? I'm not sure I believe—

The priest waved him away. La fe viene y va. I take communion twenty times a week: sometimes it's his body and blood, sometimes it's a cracker and cheap wine. Tener fe es tener una relación con Dios. The point of faith is to struggle; he who believes something once and for all time can't grow, because he isn't interested in learning anything new.

I'll think about it, Gracia had said.

The priest shrugged. Hardest part's already been taken care of for you.

What do you mean?

Un hombre sin huevos no tiene que preocuparse por despertarse a tiempo para decir unas cuantas avemarías antes de la misa, porque cada vez que ve a sor Carmelita, quiere...

Gracia frowned.

Cálmate, Diego, the priest smiled, laying a hand on his shoulder,

¡No huevos, no problemas!

Eight years after he castrated Gracia, Nazario Ortega suffered a massive stroke, and two years later, almost to the day, Diego Gracia was ordained Father Diego Gracia, O.F.M. And though he had no desire to go, the order sent him to New York, saying only that the parish there had need of his particular gifts and graces. The night before he was to leave, he and Father Doloroso drank from a bottle of mezcal that seemed to have existed from the beginning of time, and afterward, for the first time, he wept bitterly. He collapsed into sleep and dreamt he could fly, and that his tears were rain, and his son did not come to him. He knew no more about America than he had the night before, and nothing of South Bronx, only that he wanted to care about his son, to stay and learn what that might mean, and maybe, after he'd done penance, to see him. He wanted to beg the diocese and Fr. Doloroso to let him stay.

But he didn't. And so he'd flown from Benito Juarez to La Guardia to begin a new life, only to discover on the way to the rectory, block by block, tag by tag, and boarded-up storefront after boarded-up storefront—seeing gang signs being stacked and thrown, drugs changing hands, pockets and waistbands bulging—that it wouldn't be so different from the one he'd left behind.

Gifts and graces, my ass.

The turn of a century, more than a decade into the new millennium, and now Fr. Gracia was in his seventies, on his way to visit one of his parishioners at Lincoln, and enough had changed in him and in the world that the tears forming in the corners of his eyes weren't only due to the cold or the wind or the fact that he'd become old when he wasn't looking, but because the priest had thought the man in the hospital was one of his success stories.

Yes, the man still went by Lobo, but he had two brilliant little girls under the age of five and had opened up a tattoo shop that was thriving, and he'd told the priest that he was going to change because he wanted to dance with his daughters at their weddings, and to see the children they would have, and the priest had believed him. Lobo said that he was done with all of it, that the Brims had granted him special dispensation and were going to let him buy his way out, and the priest knew that wasn't really how it worked, but chose to believe him nonetheless, because he wanted it to be true.

He allowed himself to think of Alejandro from time to time, after mass. Maybe Javy was a stand-in, and maybe that was why Gracia had promised that he'd let Javy ink him if he stayed out of legal trouble for a year, and why he'd been so happy when Javy had, why he'd relished watching Javy's jaw drop when he showed up at the shop on the appointed day, at the appointed hour, with a design for a full sleeve and asked him to cover up the ink he already wore.

The police had found Javy bleeding out on a sidewalk at three-thirty in the morning, miles from his family's apartment.

Things like this made him feel old: his utter surprise at this turn of events.

Gracia walked into the hospital, grateful to be out of the wind, rubbed his eyes dry, then moved toward the hospitality desk.

Father, the woman greeted him.

Angela. How are you?

A day late, and a dollar short, I'm afraid.

Better late than never, though.

If you say so, Father. What can I do for you?

I'm here for Javier Cruz.

The woman clacked away at her computer. He's still in the ICU.

He nodded his thanks.

You know where the elevators are?

Not if they've moved since yesterday.

Anyone ever tell you you've got a lot of smartass in you for a holy man?

Every day.

He grinned. She waved him away.

He found the elevators without issue, but was still having a hard time curbing his emotions when the elevator spit him out onto the fourth floor. He couldn't swallow the lump in his throat or keep his eyes from tearing up, so he ducked into the bathroom.

The most important thing was that Javy was alright, would be alright; Gracia didn't pray all that often, preferred doing something to talking to the ceiling, but he was praying now, his lips moving soundlessly, forming the words over and over.

Let him be okay, God, just let him be okay.

Gracia knew what Javy had been doing that night because he'd just seen the movie; so many of his parishioners had been buzzing about it yesterday that even Fr. Julian had heard.

Javy had been tattooing that boy.

Goddammit, Javy.

They'd gone at the boy for over twelve hours, stuffed pills in his mouth to keep him still.

The video shocked him—not the torture, but the fact that it'd happened in his community, and that he hadn't heard about it until the movie surfaced.

He knew some of his people sold drugs, were in gangs, but this?

He was forgetting what it had been like.

And Javy?

Memories Gracia thought he had buried came slinking up out of their graves, smells, sounds, pleas. They were pushing their way up through his throat. Gracia bit his cheek, dug his fingernails into his palms until they raked blood.

Javy.

Alejandro.

Javy.

He thought he'd seen Alejandro once.

There'd been a woman behind him, Alejandro's mother, hollow-eyed, dead: choked out and shot in the head.

Another thing he did.

Gracia pushed the images away.

He had no idea what his son would look like now, or if he'd managed to escape the guns and drugs and violence.

Probably not.

Pull it together, he commanded himself.

Your son is lost, but you can help Javy.

He turned the knob on the tap and ran some cold water, splashed it on his face, dried himself with a paper towel.

Now go.

Go.

THE GIGGLE HOUSE

I know you caucasian ladies in the audience are trying to figure out if I'm just playing with you, wondering how big we talkin', so I'm just going to settle this for you.

We ain't talking elephant, we're talking mammoth.

That's right. Mammoth. Fucking. Tusk.

KOLYA

He was making grilled cheese with an iron when he heard the knock at the door. It was Chris's thing: slice of bread, two slices of cheese, slice of tomato; iron on both sides.

They didn't have irons where Kolya grew up, or tomatoes. In Russia, yes, but not at the *sirotstvo*, the orphanage.

"Pechkin?" the voice on the other side of the door said. "Kolya Pechkin?"

Kolya's eyes ricocheted around the apartment. Run, he thought. Hide, at least. If they know your name, they're there for a reason.

"Mr. Pechkin, please. I received an envelope from a courier. No sender, no return address or explanation. Just your name and address, and a website."

Goddammit, Chris.

Kolya waited.

"I just want to know why I'm here."

He shut his eyes as tightly as he could and grit his teeth.

"Why are you here?"

"I'm hoping you can help me figure it out."

Fuck, he thought, undoing the chain. Fucking Chris. He slid the bolt and opened the door.

The woman on the other side threw him. "Vivian Carver-Brown," she said, extending a hand. "I go by V."

He didn't take it. "Who are you?"

"How do you know Christopher Fairchild?"

He started to close the door.

"I'm a reporter."

"For?"

"Freelance."

"What do you want?"

"I just—"

"What do you want with Chris?"

"I want to tell his story."

Kolya sighed and opened the door enough to allow her in.

"Tea?"

V nodded.

Faucet, hotpot, two tea bags in two fourth-hand coffee mugs.

"I hope you like it strong."

V nodded. "So where do you want to start?"

"You're the one with the questions."

"How do you know Christopher?"

"He's my roommate."

"Your roommate?"

"Yes."

"Nothing more?"

"That's his girlfriend," Kolya nodded toward a picture in a cheap plastic frame. "Or she was. I haven't seen her in a while."

"May I?" V gestured toward the picture.

Kolya shrugged.

"Do you remember her name?"

He stared at her.

"What?"

"Of course I know her name."

"And?"

"And I'm still not sure what you want, or why I should answer any more of your questions."

"He must have sent me here for a reason, right?"

"I don't know. You said you didn't even know who the package was from."

"I can show you the envelope and card," she said, reaching into her bag.

It was still half-concealed when he waved her off. "Put it back."

"You don't want to—"

"No. That's his handwriting."

"If he sent me here, then he must have had a reason."

"Chris is full of reasons."

"What do you mean?"

"I mean he doesn't do anything by accident. We'll study for hours in silence because he won't say anything that he hasn't considered from a dozen different angles. And when he decides it's okay to say something, he repeats it over and over. 'Want to get pizza tonight, Chris?' 'Sounds good.' 'What about sushi?' 'Sounds good.' 'What about pounding nails through our feet and chewing broken glass?' 'Sounds good.'"

"Did he tell you his reasons for making the video?"

Kolya frowned. "I told him not to do this."

"To do what?"

"To drag me into this…stupidity. I told him from the beginning I wanted nothing to do with it, that I wouldn't help in any way."

"Yet here we are."

Kolya didn't respond.

"How'd you meet?"

"At a bar. I was looking for a place to stay and made plans to meet someone, but the guy never showed. I called him a couple times to see if he planning on showing up, and Chris overheard. He told me he had an empty room in his apartment. I moved in that night."

"Just like that?"

"I wasn't happy about it, but I didn't have many options. If there'd been anywhere else I could stay I would have, but I didn't know anyone or have any money, so I drank the beer Chris bought, and followed him through Washington Square to this place."

Kolya barked a wry laugh.

"Into an apartment building that looked like it had been airlifted from the old Soviet bloc. I slept with a switchblade."

"So you didn't know who he was?"

"You mean that he was William Fairchild's son?"

V nodded.

"No."

V was silent.

"You don't believe me, do you?"

"I—"

"There were certainly clues, in retrospect, but I'd never heard of Kopi Luwak or Black Ivory, then. The only coffee I'd ever had was instant.

"And, yes, Chris helped me find a job at two of the toniest bars in the City, and gave me his 'old' laptop to use for school, but I was fresh off the boat and everything was coming at me so fast that I didn't have time to think.

"Plus, look at this place. There's nothing on the walls, we don't own a TV, and the furniture was all salvaged from sidewalks and alleys."

"Do you and Chris party together?"

Kolya shook his head. "We're here to study. We don't party, we don't do drugs, and we don't drink."

V looked down at her notepad. "You said you and Chris met in a bar, and drank beer together."

Kolya waved the comment away with a frown. "We rarely drink. Sobriety is a strategy, not a dogma. Both of us want to do well in our programs."

"What program are you in?"

"International business. I receive a full scholarship."

"And Chris?"

"African-American Studies and Religious Studies. Double major. Or maybe philosophy. He switched recently."

Kolya looked across the room and out into the city. V would write something about their place being small and dingy, out of character for a billionaire's kid. And it was. The walls hadn't seen paint in thirty years, and could easily have been the walls of the orphanage he'd grown up in, he and his sister shivering beside the same miserly radiators as these that did no more than keep the pipes from freezing. The windows were no less cracked and scum-smeared than those through which he imagined his sister's and his own escape.

Here, there was a valence across the window, though. That was different. There were no valences in Russia. At least not in the parts he'd known.

He turned back to V.

"Can I see his room?" she asked.

Kolya frowned.

"Please."

"Why?"

"Do you want me to tell his story or not?"

He pushed himself off the couch. "Not really."

V entered the room while Kolya leaned up against the door jamb and watched her open Chris's minuscule closet, a half-width, white door that ran on plastic rollers on a plastic track. She took inventory: six hangers held three shirts and three pairs of pants; two belts hung from nails, one brown and one black. There were three pairs of shoes lined up neatly beneath the hangers: sneakers, black dress shoes with tassels, and brown leather docksiders. There was a black tie, a red tie, and a navy-blue tie with gray pinstripes, all hanging on a makeshift tie rack.

"I will never understand why he made it," he said.

"But you said he had reasons—"

"Yes, many of them."

"But you're not going to tell me what they are?"

"No."

She closed the closet, turned to the bookshelf. He watched her eyes pass over the books: Baldwin, Bakara, Brooks, Brown, Chestnut, Cohn...

"Can I ask why?"

Douglass, Du Bois, Dunbar, Dyson, Ellison, Equiano, E. W. Iola, Hansberry, Frances, Leroy Harper, Hayden.

"Because they are absurd and grandiose and incoherent, and because if people heard them they would never stop mocking him."

Hughes, Hurston, Harriet Jacobs, James Weldon Johnson...

"So you're protecting him? By refusing to do the very thing he's asked you to do?"

"People that are incapable of protecting themselves need protection most of all."

King, Larsen, Lorde, Paule Marshall, Morrison, Albert Murray, Petry, Ishmael Reed, Shange, Toomer, Walker, Washington, West, Wheatley, Wright, X...

V sunk down onto Fairchild's bed.

"Do you know why I came to America, V?"

She didn't answer.

"My parents died when I was nearly fifteen. My sister was eleven. We didn't have any other family so they send us to a *sirotstvo*—an orphanage, which kicked me out when I turned eighteen. They wouldn't let my sister go, though, and no one would help me, so I came to America to make enough money to buy her way out and bring her here."

"I quit my job for this story, Kolya. It wasn't a high-paying job, but it paid the rent. I raised myself, took care of my grandfather, and got through high school with a four-point-oh to get that job. I danced and waited tables to put myself through college and graduate school, to get that job."

"I don't have to worry about money anymore," Kolya said. "Or my sister."

"I quit that job because I know there's more to this story than carnage and smut, more to it than a billionaire's son with daddy issues, and that story isn't going to get written unless I do it."

"Chris would appreciate the sentiment."

"But you're still not going to help me?"

"No."

"Why?"

"Chris found out about Faina—my sister—and called his father, made sure everything was taken care of. She lives in California with the Fairchilds."

"You think you're protecting him, but you're not. You're gagging him. He had something he wanted to say, and he said it in a way he knew would force people to listen."

"He said something that no one will hear."

"A self-fulfilling prophecy."

Kolya shrugged. "Aren't they all?"

V sighed, pushed herself onto her feet, and left the room.

"Are you familiar with the term wigger?" V asked.

Kolya nodded.

"Was Chris—"

"You're asking me if Chris wished he was Black."

"Did he?"

Kolya shook his head. "No. Some people said so, but no."

"So what did he want, Kolya? Help me out."

Kolya looked away. "He called it performance art."

"Performance art."

Kolya nodded.

"So he was trying to say something. Jesus, I'm a reporter, let me tell his story. You've seen the video, right? If you don't help me do this, he will have suffered for nothing."

Kolya scraped a sleeve over his eyes. "He said lots of things, and very little of them made sense, especially at the end."

"He'd stopped eating, right? The police report said he was starving."

"Yes."

"How long?"

"A month. Maybe longer."

"What about sleep?"

"Hardly ever."

"Why?"

"Why do you think?"

"You tell me."

Kolya stood, motioned toward the door.

"You're kicking me out?"

"I have somewhere I have to be."

"Can we talk again? I have questions—"

"You know, you aren't all that different from Chris."

"How's that?"

"You both think that everything can be said, and that something can be heard just because it can be said."

"There's no way of knowing until we try."

Kolya opened the door. "I think we both know that's not true."

V stepped into the hall. "So what's your solution? Magic? Prayer?"

Kolya smiled. "Would that gods and angels had ears to hear."

THE GIGGLE HOUSE

And while we feeling it, rocking a Mandingo strut and swinging a crack dick—being all we're told to be—wypipo watching, one hundred percent convinced that we just can't wait to get our dicks in their antidepressant guzzling, anorexic, assless wives and daughters.

This is how we get Lebron James as the Great Black threat.

Know-nothing bobble head be like, shut up and dribble.

Bitch, the number of dollars that Nigga's donated to charity is higher than your husband's sperm count.

THE TEACHERS

"What's up?" Marcus pulled a chair out from the table and sat.

"S'up?"

"You talk to Jeff today?"

Jamal shook his head, chewing, swallowed. "I try to avoid it as a rule."

"Talking to Jeff?"

Jamal nodded.

"He's thinking of resigning," Marcus said, unrolling the top of a brown paper bag, reaching in, and retrieving an apple and a sandwich.

"That would make avoiding him exponentially easier."

"What've you got against him?"

Jamal rolled his eyes. "How much time do you have?"

"Seriously? Have you talked with him? He's a nice guy."

"He's creepy."

"Creepy?"

"Yeah. He creeps me out."

"Why?"

Jamal shrugged, took a pull of his Diet Coke. The teacher's lounge was empty except for the two of them.

"Don't like the guy."

"Yeah, I got that."

"What can I say? He just rubs me the wrong way."

"When did he even get the chance to do that? He's only been here a few months."

"Yeah, why is that?"

"Why is what?"

"Why's he here?"

"You're on that again?"

"Like a fat kid on a cupcake."

"You know, when people do this shit to us we call it racism."

"Actually, racism requires—"

"That the person engaging in discriminatory behavior belong to a group with the power to force oppressive effects on the group in question...blah, blah, blah."

"You've read your Dyson."

"Stokely Carmichael. Don't try to out-Black me, bitch, I'll break you."

"Says the man who just called me a racist."

"Says the man who thinks you're being an idiot."

Jamal waved him off. "Jeff graduated from Yale. He's just another white guy who feels vaguely bad that his great-grandparents bought and sold our great-grandparents, so he's doing a couple years with the niggers in South Bronx before going on to Harvard or Stanford or some equally lily-white bastion of privilege, from whence he'll launch himself into fame, fortune, or, if the gods deem him white enough, both."

Marcus laughed. "Lighten up, brother," he said, chucking Jamal's shoulder. "It's February! This is our month!"

"Yeah, we know how that conversation went down. Well, Nigel, darn it, it can't be helped—we have to give the negroes a month. Oh, I dare say you're right, George. Oh! Oh! I've just had a capital idea! Let's give them February. Oh, yes! The shortest month of the year! Nigel, you old rapscallion, you, you're absolutely wicked!"

"Nigel?" Marcus asked, laughing. "And what the hell was that accent? Forrest Gump meets Monty Python?"

Jamal shrugged.

"Seriously, though, I get it. Shit is fucked up. America is broke, no doubt. But Jeff is a decent guy."

"Maybe." Jamal worked his twist absently. "It just pisses me off that people don't give us the same props he gets, you know? I mean, we're putting our lives on hold the same as him, but people look at us and just assume we belong here, that either we couldn't do any better, or we somehow owe it to our Black brethren."

"I hear you."

"Someone should ask Jeff why he isn't with his people in West Virginia, you know, spreading the word to the crackers: *Sorry, Bradley, but the Civil War's over. You lost, and Black folk are human now.* He could even try teaching them to read, while he's at it, maybe even convince them to stop fucking their sisters."

"He'd probably agree with you."

They heard footsteps and fell silent just as Jeff entered the breakroom.

"Fellas."

"Jeff."

"Whatchya up to?"

Jamal lifted his sandwich.

Jeff sat. "Everything okay? It sounded like things were getting pretty intense in here from the hall."

"Dumbass white folk who think they can make up for three hundred years of institutionalized racism by talking nice and making inconsequential symbolic gestures."

"Right." Jeff cringed. "I can see how that could eat at you."

"Don't mind him," Marcus said. "The Fairchild thing's got him all pissy."

"Yeah, yeah, Fairchild, that's it," Jamal said. "What kind of idiot lets people tattoo his junk?"

All three men winced.

"Did you see the latest?" Marcus said. "Apparently he wrote some kind of 'manifesto.' Showed up online last night."

"And?"

"The fucking moron says he was—hold on, let me get this right." Marcus reached for his phone and pulled up the page. "Here it is. He was 'offering himself as a sacrifice of atonement, allowing himself to become a living text on which the silenced could inscribe their words.'"

"So, he's more or less retarded."

Jeff's eyes were glued to the tabletop. "I know the guy."

"Of course you do," Jamal said.

"The whole thing is bullshit, if you ask me. Chris has always had daddy issues. This is just a crazy way for him to get some attention."

"Pretty extreme."

"Of course, that's the most charitable reading," Jeff said, wringing his hands. "There's a chance Chris actually meant everything he said, and he's just the most recent megalomaniacal idiot to think the Black savages need a white savior."

"Make you wonder how much of a difference there is between the poverty tourist who spends a year or two teaching nigglets in an inner-city school before heading off to bigger and better, and your boy letting pissed-off niggers tattoo his dick."

Marcus glared at Jamal. "Jesus, you're an asshole."

"No," Jeff held up a hand, "I get it."

"And that's why I don't like the bitch," Jamal pointed at Jeff, "because he actually thinks he does."

"Experientially, I obviously don't. Point taken. But conceptually, for whatever little that's worth, I think I do."

"Right. My bad for arguing with a white man. Sorry, Massa, I won't let my nigger-self get uppity with you ever again."

"Jamal!" Marcus shook his head. "Forget him, Jeff."

"No, it's okay. I appreciate it, but I've got this." Jeff turned to face Jamal. "It's like white people have had you bent over for centuries, and for centuries we and our families and our friends have been taking turns jackhammering you in the ass without lube, and Chris's bullshit gesture—hell, me being here now—it's like we're taking a break and shaking a few aspirin out of a pill bottle to give you before we have our next go, and expecting you to be grateful."

Jamal winced. "Well, that was vivid."

"And you're absolutely right, Jamal, it wasn't that hard for me to put things on hold for a couple years, because I am more or less guaranteed to move on to 'bigger and better things,' and ever after, I will be able to point to my time in the Bronx if anyone ever accuses me of being racist, all while reaping the benefits of a system designed to ensure my success at your expense."

"Shit."

"I get that in your mind Chris and I and white America are essentially sodomizing Black America while congratulating ourselves for our magnanimous generosity in tossing you an over-the-counter analgesic every so often to ease the pain we're causing, and that white America has no plans to stop anytime soon."

Jamal waved him away. "You're fucking nuts, dude—you know that, right?"

"I don't dispute any of it, but let me ask you this, Jamal, what am

118

I supposed to do?"

"Whatever the hell you want to. I don't care."

"Ah, but you do. You care a whole lot, that's why you've been on me since I first arrived. It's why I've overheard a half-dozen conversations about how much you hate me."

"I don't know what the fuck are you talking about."

"Look, things are fucked up. I and 'my people' owe a debt that can't be calculated, let alone repaid. My family has a disgusting amount of money, and though we never bought or sold slaves, the business we did was possible because of an infrastructure built and maintained on the strength of their labor. I can't undo any of that, and even if I were to give up my inheritance and all my privileges, we live in a system that's designed to ensure that they come back to someone who looks just like me. So now what?"

"Fuck you is what." Jamal stood and shoved his chair under the table.

Jeff backed away from the table with his hands up. "The guy who had my position last year is doing 10-20 at Rikers because the administration found child pornography saved on his school computer."

"So?"

"I don't know what the solution is to systemic inequality. I don't. But I can't not be white, and I can't change the past. What I can do is teach my kids for as long as I'm here. It doesn't make things right, but—"

"At least you aren't a pedophile."

"There you go. I have to run to class now. Sorry to ruin your lunch."

"Later." Marcus nodded.

"Later."

"Well, shit." Marcus looked at Jamal. "You happy now?"

"Shut up and eat your lunch." Jamal sat back down.

"Don't mind if I do." Marcus bit into his apple, spat the flesh into his bag. "Man, I just bit into a damn worm!"

"Told you, you shouldn't buy shit from those discount fruit vendors."

Marcus spat again, dug worm from between his teeth. "Your compassion is touching."

"Whatever, man. All I'm saying is if you weren't so cheap—"

"You'd have to find someone else to hit up for money."

"Whatever! I owe you, what, like a buck?"

"Try two-fifty."

"Bullshit!"

"The two hundred's legit. The fifty is for the juice."

"Right."

"Tell you what."

"What?"

"You stop riding Jeff, I'll forget it."

"The juice? I ain't worried about that, because there is no way in hell I'm paying you no juice."

"The whole thing."

"Say what, now?"

"The whole thing."

"Just like that?"

"Just like that."

"The whole damn thing?"

"The whole damn thing."

"Why?"

"What do you think is going to happen if Jeff quits?"

"I don't know. They get a sub until they get a replacement?"

"You have got to stop sleeping through faculty meetings."

"What the hell are you talking about? I don't sleep..."

Marcus made a face as the bell sounded.

"Damn," Marcus said. "Gotta get to class."

"Go. I'm not keeping you."

"You don't have class?"

"I have class. But I'm going to finish my Coke, first. Students aren't going anywhere. They can wait."

"Whatever. Listen, even if they could find one, there's no money for subs and replacements. Jeff quits, his kids get divided between you, me, and Joy."

Jamal's mouth fell open. "Naw man! I already got thirty-five! How can they send me another dozen of these animals?"

"I'm right there with you, man, but that's how this is going to go down if Jeff leaves, so quit riding him, okay? Maybe even talk to the guy."

"And that's that? I owe you nothing?"

"It would be the best two hundred dollars I ever spent."

"No doubt."

THE GIGGLE HOUSE

You wanna know the best thing to do around wypipo? Play down your cool. Keep that shit hidden.

Mention your small, ideally impotent, penis as frequently as you can while flailing around the dance floor off the beat.

And if you can spill your drink, too, well, fuck it, homie, you golden. You basically white.

Just make sure it doesn't get on some white girl's shoes. That shit is crazy-expensive.

DR. DARIUS BELL, M.D.

"How can you just sit there, William?"

Fairchild and his wife sat awkwardly across from Dr. Darius Bell, M.D.

"What would you have me do, Genevieve?" Fairchild spoke to his wife without looking away from the doctor.

"Something! Anything! Jesus! This is Christopher we're talking about! Our son!"

Dr. Bell took care to maintain a neutral expression. He took in the degrees and certifications he'd had framed and matted and hung on the wall, the photograph his wife had taken on the day he'd been ordained a deacon, the photos of his family sitting on his desk, turned so only he could see them.

The Fairchilds had appeared without an appointment, and since there was no question of turning them away, he'd told his secretary to bring them to his office and stolen a moment in the men's room to ready himself. The doctor didn't anticipate the interview going well.

He walked into the room intent on saying as little as possible.

"I'm aware," Fairchild told his wife.

"Then do something!"

"Genevieve, the man's one of the top doctors in his field, he—"

"For Christ's sake! He's a state employee! How good can he be?"

"Medical school in Chapel Hill, residency at Hopkins... his credentials are impeccable."

"Our son let himself be stripped naked, William, stripped naked and marched through the streets of New York in the middle of winter. He allowed himself to be chained in a cage, and never tried to free himself, even after people forced drugs down his throat, tattooed his genitalia, and beat him with shovels. What part of that sounds sane? Which of those decisions makes you think Christopher is capable of acting in his own best interest?"

Tears blazed in her eyes, hurling fluorescent light at her husband like daggers.

Fairchild closed his eyes a moment. "Genevieve..."

"Jesus Christ, William! Can't you see? He's one of them!"

That was when Fairchild broke away from the doctor to look at his wife. "Them?"

"Did you even read the report?"

"Yes, I read—"

"The subject is lucid and articulate..."

"Genevieve."

"He demonstrates an acute awareness of his surroundings, readily identified his present location, and supplied the correct day, month, and year when asked."

"Genevieve, please."

"The day, month, and year!"

"Mrs. Fairchild," Bell interjected. *God, grant me the patience.*

"No! My son's been disfigured, Dr. Bell!"

"I understand th—"

"Do you have a son, Dr. Bell?"

"Genevieve—"

"Shut up, William!"

Genevieve turned to the doctor. "Do you have a son?"

"I don't see—"

"Do you have a son?"

The doctor glanced at Mr. Fairchild.

"Don't look at him!" Mrs. Fairchild demanded. "Look at me! I asked the goddamn question!"

The doctor stared at her. *God, grant me the wisdom.*

He saw a mother protecting her cub.

Understandable, even if the cub's wounds were self-inflicted.

"Well?"

"A son and a daughter."

"Then let me ask you this: if your son had allowed himself to be exposed, mutilated, sodomized, defecated upon, and battered to the point of deformity, and subsequently refused to press charges against the people that had brutalized him, would you deem him competent to decide whether or not it was in his best interest to have the 'Eat shit and die you white mother-fucking faggot' tattoo removed from his face?"

Bell blinked, crossed and uncrossed his legs, set his hands in his lap.

"He didn't declare Christopher competent," Fairchild said without inflection. "Competence is a legal term. The doctor declared him capable. From a medical perspective, the relevant issue is whether or not Christopher possesses the ability to understand the nature and effects of his actions, which, having talked with Christopher, we both know he does."

"You agree with Dr. Bell?"

"Agreement isn't the issue. He gave the only answer possible to the question put to him in his position as a psychiatrist. What we're asking him isn't within his power to grant."

Bell watched Genevieve Fairchild collapse upon her husband's words, her eyes fluttering, her body tottering to one side of her chair, then the other, then lilting forward until her husband grabbed her arm. And though he had not felt hate in a long time, he knew that it was hate that ripped through him as he watched Fairchild quash his wife's resistance with a sentence, and only part of him pleaded for forgiveness.

Bell's great-grandparents had been slaves on a Georgia plantation, but they'd been both fortunate and skillful in their post-emancipation endeavors, and so two generations later, Bell's father had gone to law school, become a judge, and then a successful politician. Bell's mother had been a physician.

Bell had grown up in an affluent enclave of Baltimore County, cosseted within the Black elite. He'd boarded at Trinity School in New York before moving on to college and medical school and his residency.

He was used to being in the presence of whites, and used to those whites knowing that the combination of his parents' money and influence, and his own achievement, made him their equal, if not their superior. He knew of racism's existence, encountered it every day of his life in a thousand small ways, but such was his privilege that it was never more than an irritant, never, to his knowledge, kept him from his goals, even if, on occasion, he was forced to work harder than a white man would have had to in order to achieve the same success.

He'd been detained by the police only once while touring the Capitol on break from medical school. He'd used his phone call to call his father, and less than an hour later, he was back in his car on his way home, knowing that tomorrow there'd be an official letter of apology in the mail signed by the chief of police.

Bell knew his experience was atypical, knew of and sympathized with the travails of those of his kind who were neither so fortunate nor so well-protected as he had been, but atypical though his experience was, it had formed him, led him to certain conclusions about the world and his standing in it.

If God is for us, who can stand against us?

But he saw now that his conclusions were naïve, self-aggrandizing, and misguided. Fairchild's God had made him stronger, dominant. Even in the department of the hospital that Bell oversaw as the Chief of Psychiatry, Fairchild's word was decisive. Not just in terms of ending his wife's belligerence—that was only the final instance. Fairchild had walked into Bell's hospital, into Bell's department, and in an instant, overwritten every rule and protocol Bell had established in twenty years' time.

He'd done it without yelling or threats, without raising his voice, merely by his presence. He'd been neither condescending nor antagonistic—had been nothing but courteous, even acknowledging Bell's superlative credentials. And now Bell knew all his achievements and degrees, all his certifications, plaudits, and laurels amounted to little more than baubles which he had allowed to distract him from the fact that no amount of distinction, excellence, or expertise would gain him equality. As far as America was concerned, he was a guest in a white world, and anything he ever had or achieved belonged to its citizens. He could get away with success as long as he was careful to make them feel a part of it, to make them feel like his achievement was their achievement, and to reassure them time and again that he hadn't forgotten that he needed their permission, that the only reason he was allowed wealth and education and whatever else came his way was because they had signed off on it.

For the briefest of moments, he thought that maybe it had nothing to do with race, and everything to do with the fact that he had chosen his career poorly, and Fairchild, optimally, with the fact that, increasingly, doctors were regarded in the same way as hairdressers and auto mechanics, as workers in a service industry of which the rich availed themselves when the desire arose. One needn't look too hard to find evidence of the precedence given mammon over men in the calculus used to dictate policy be it corporate or governmental, domestic or international, economic, legal, or medical.

He glanced across his desk at the Fairchilds; at Mrs. Fairchild who was covering her face with one hand, and Mr. Fairchild who had taken her other hand in both of his.

He's one of them!

Had she really said that, or had he imagined it? And if she'd said it, did she mean what he thought she meant?

So this was how the other half lived, and he was among their number: the African-Americans, Blacks, Negroes, Niggers—the people to whom he had always belonged, and to whom he had always been regarded as belonging, even if he rarely felt the kinship.

Here he was, out-maneuvered, trapped, frustrated, and wondering if the color of his skin had colored their reaction, but also simultaneously wondering if he had finally succumbed to the pathological paranoia of one who'd been too long under the microscope.

Mrs. Fairchild left the room, and Bell realized after the fact that Mr. Fairchild had spoken, only catching the word 'question.'

He and Fairchild stared at each other, and Bell understood that Fairchild was asking permission for something, so he nodded.

"Christopher explained his reasons to you, right? Explained why he did what he did?"

"Yes."

Fairchild nodded. "I know..." his voice trailed off. "I know this is...irregular... And, I promise not to repeat your answer to anyone, not even to my wife."

Fairchild was squinting as he talked, looking just to the right of the doctor's head, staring hard at the space as if he expected the words he was looking for to materialize from the air in just that spot.

"I'm not asking you to speak for anyone other than yourself..."

"I'm not sure what you're asking, Mr. Fairchild."

"I'm not asking as William Fairchild, and I'm not asking you as a doctor..."

The beginning of tears flickered in his eyes, then pulled back.

"I'm asking as a father...trying to understand..."

And in a moment, Bell knew where he was going.

Don't say it! He wanted to scream.

"Is there any truth..." Fairchild said.

Bell's mouth filled with bile.

Just stop!

"Was Christopher...at all right..."

Stop!

"Was it...?"

Bell screamed for the vomit to remain in his throat.

"I mean, is it..." Fairchild stopped himself. He squeezed his eyes shut, took off his glasses, ran a hand over his face, put the glasses back on, and looked directly at Bell. "I'm sorry," he said. "I know...I'm sorry."

"You've been through quite an ordeal, Mr. Fairchild. You and your family."

Fairchild nodded.

"Is there anything I can do? A prescription, maybe? Something to help you or your wife sleep?"

Fairchild shook his head. "Thank you. That's a very kind offer. Especially considering how brazenly we've imposed on your time."

"Completely understandable."

Fairchild nodded, kept nodding, looking like a doll on the dashboard of a car.

"I have no idea what to do next," he admitted.

Bear with each other and forgive one another if any of you has a grievance against someone. Forgive as the Lord forgave you.

"I can give you a few names," Bell said, "colleagues of mine who might be able to be of help."

"I'd be grateful."

Bell wrote the references on the back of a business card and handed it to Fairchild, who put it in his wallet without looking at it.

"Thank you," he said.

"My pleasure."

"I'll go find my wife now."

Bell nodded. "Call anytime."

"Thank you."

Fairchild turned to go, then paused for a moment at the door, and Bell thought he was going to turn back and finish the question he'd started to ask earlier.

Bell wondered if it was pride that kept the question back, that overwhelmed Fairchild's desperation to hear that his son had been right and true, and that his actions were more than just symptoms of affluenza and a hyper-inflated sense of his own worth.

But that thought faded quickly.

Dr. Bell thought of his son and his daughter, and he thought of his wife.

He thought of all the things he'd done right, of the sixty years of Friday and Saturday nights and Sunday mornings spent in church, of the thou-shalt's and the thou-shalt-not's, of the thus-sayeth-the-Lord's, and the justice that would rain down like water, of the oaths he'd kept and the rules he'd refused to break, and of all that he'd forgone lest he lead himself into temptation.

And he thought of the Fairchilds, of William and Genevieve, but mostly of Christopher.

Of the contrast between his ice-blue eyes and the tattoos covering his face.

The boy had looked demonic.

THE GIGGLE HOUSE

What's most messed up about the whole Black-white clusterfuck is that, on some level, white people know that what they're doing is wrong, and they're due a two-hundred-year ass-whooping.

So, if any of you wypipo out there ever want to do the right thing, give me a call. I've got a wife and three kids, and my momma's still got her switch hanging in the closet, just in case I slip up.

And she's only two blocks from the hospital.

BRIDGET

Bridget unlocked the door to her apartment. It was a hundred years old and wooden, and swelled in the winter because the heating system was even older than the door, and her landlord was a cheap asshole who would sooner cut meat from his own flesh than spend money on his tenants. Opening the door required Bridget to throw all six-feet-two-inches and twenty or thirty more pounds than she cared to admit possessing against the door, which she hated doing, especially now, because she was still recovering—hadn't even had her stitches out, yet—and it hurt like a bitch. But it wasn't just because of the pain, or even primarily, but because she had been given a different name at birth, and it had taken her thirty years to accept that it was the wrong name, and another year and a half to work up the courage to the tell the people who had named her and to begin referring to herself as *she*, and then two more years after that to grow out her hair and start wearing makeup and dresses and shaving her legs, and the brutal inelegance of leveraging her size and strength in order to force her will upon an inanimate object made her feel like she was back on the other side of things again, too large and too strong and too awkward, bumbling and trying to cram herself into a space she wouldn't fit in no matter how violently she cursed and thrashed.

Her mother had called again, not on the cell, which Bridget carried and occasionally even answered, but on the ridiculous landline that her mother had insisted she have installed when she moved in. The preternaturally bright '1' blinking madly on her correspondingly absurd answering machine turned all 480 square feet of her apartment into a demonic disco replete with hell-haze strobe lights.

Bridget threw herself back against the door, yelping in pain, and managed to get it closed, forcing it into its misshapen frame with tears in her eyes. She drew the chain and locked all three deadbolts.

Her mother left the same twenty-minute message every time she called, an absurd routine for which Bridget was immensely grateful, especially today, given the day she'd had, since one of the very few positive continuities between her former and current lives was the fact that the sound of her mother's voice still soothed her.

She set a kettle on the small stove to boil water for the ramen that, along with a pear, would be her dinner, and pressed the 'play' button on her answering machine.

Her laptop sat on a battered plywood stand that was both her desk and dinner table; she cut the volume off so it wouldn't mitigate the salve of her mother's voice, and started up the video that she kept open in her web browser. She'd seen the truncated version first, which reduced the three days to five hours; then she'd gone and found the other three versions: the seventy-two hours from the still camera, the seventy-two hours from the camera that swiveled and zoomed, and the seventy-two hours that had been produced by cutting back and forth between the two, though she hadn't had time to view them in their entirety yet.

He'd been suffering for some time when she was attacked. So much of the video was horrific and unwatchable, but she'd had twelve hours from the second day—from the seventy-two-hour still version— playing on loop for a couple of days now, the segment that began with the artists' appearance. She couldn't say why, really, though there were particular moments she liked: the artists finishing their respective parts—the corpses and tree—in perfect synchrony; the way they didn't look at each other or speak, but stood up at the same time and tucked their irons in their back pockets and lit cigarettes to allow another woman using the tattoo machine the masked priests had provided to finish her contribution, the 'i,' 's,' and 'e' from the last *I rise* of a poem Bridget had thought she recognized, but ultimately had to look up.

Bridget—who eked out a precarious subsistence by working part-time at the NYU and Columbia libraries and writing on political aesthetics for various underground publications—was particularly sensitive to synchrony, so watching the convergence of a man whose corpses radiated elements of Woon Kim and Regino Gonzalez, and a woman who managed to evoke the styles of Jun Cha, Bugs, and Julie Becker in sixteen square inches of landscape was arresting, the gradual recognition of their collective vision not merely conceptual, but somatic, transmuting itself into a palpable knot where Bridget's womb should have been.

But there was only accident, chance—not even indifference. *Art* saved her; it spoke to her of the beauty of truth, and the truths of anger, rage, and pain. It filled the hollow of her absent womb.

She decided she wanted tea as well as noodles, pushed herself away from her desk reluctantly.

She was sufficiently self-aware to recognize that *art*, for her, typically designated only art-objects produced in a particular style post-1980 in accordance with a fairly specific set of aesthetico-political criteria, and part of what she liked about the video was how different it was from those artifacts or art-objects she usually considered art, and how present and yet, simultaneously, strangely absent, were the aesthetico-political elements that she normally demanded of an "object" before she would confer on it the status of *art*. The first time she saw the video, she wondered why the artist abandoned the tree mid-trunk, with no sight of roots or suggestion of ground, but that answer came quickly, or rather, began quickly. A woman finished her Angelou inscription, and the two artists tossed their cigarettes aside and fired up their machines while a clutch of homeless men fought over the remnant of the man's cigarette while the woman's lay burning on the asphalt, untouched.

The artists returned to their work, their canvas hanging insensate from bloodstained handcuffs.

The answer began with the outline of a cheekbone and the slope of a hat, elaborated itself as the artists blocked out the figures, one after another, partial figures, obscured behind others that were themselves partial, arms disappearing into chests and backs and legs until there were so many people beneath the tree that there was nowhere to walk, bodies pressed so tightly it wasn't possible to say where one ended and another began. And slowly, Bridget started to feel she got it. Having blocked out the figures, the artists began to articulate their features, and while the corpses and the tree were heavily stylized, the people were rendered with such meticulous reality that it appeared as though the artists had grafted their flesh into the boy's: the man pointing ominously at Shipp's and Smith's corpses had a Hitler-mustache, a pointed nose, and a receding widow's peak; the teenage girl holding her boyfriend's hand had buck teeth and slouched; a young man in a shirt and tie was grinning as if he'd just been flatulent, though the expression on the face of the comely woman in front of him seemed to suggest that he'd just groped her. Several of the figures were looking away, though mostly out of boredom; only two men, neither of them more than a few steps into adulthood, seemed genuinely unsettled.

The beauty of truth, Bridget marveled, chewing on a lock of her hair and watching the artists' sequence for the fifth time, *death opening into life, deceit into revelation.*

Bridget picked up her phone, but didn't know who to call, who might have seen the movie and gotten what she had from it and wouldn't be totally freaked out that she'd watched it multiple times.

She found the artists' inversion of the dynamic flow of the event stunning. Their instantiation of the painting within the grotesque figures of Thomas Shipp's and Abram Smith's corpses, the mytho-poetic tree, and subsequent articulation of the ordinary, recognizable elements of mainstream Americana in terms of the spatial and thematic dominance of perversity and death effected a trenchant and poetic unveiling of the pernicious foundations of the American consumerist cosmology.

She twirled her fork in a steaming bowl and wound a tangle of noodles around its metal tines.

The merging of styles was aesthetically and ideologically remarkable, hyperrealism conjoining with the mythic and forming a harmonic, yet disjunctive frame for the photographic realism that underscored the jarring contrast between appearance and reality, fact and fantasy, juxtaposing the assembled collective of next-door neighbors and PTA moms, town councilmen, varsity athletes, and Boy Scouts with the carnage wrought by the collective, thereby doubling the American Pastoral as the American Psycho-pathological, revealing the extent of the imbrication of patriotism, the American dream, and mom and dad and Jesus and apple pie in the fantasy of White righteousness and the necessity of pornographic acts of sexual violence and domination in the face of a looming racial apocalypse.

Absolutely, Bridget nodded, yes, that's it. They want you to believe that hate and violence are anomalies, but the reality is that our hetero-normative, phallocentric, racist, capitalist society is predicated on annihilation and enslavement, on the subjugation of the many in order to sate the voracious appetites of the rapacious few.

Lynching wasn't an anomaly within American society, but foundational to it.

Her mind raced as the film played, speeding for the duration of her mother's message, hurrying through her Sriracha-saturated ramen dinner, and flying as she washed her dishes and placed them in the drying rack.

Tears glistened in her eyes for Fairchild, tears that carried her to other names, to the names of women she'd only recently come to know: Rita Hester of Allston, Massachusetts; Gwen Araujo of Newark, California; Nireah Johnson of Indianapolis, Indiana; Shelby Tracy Tom of Vancouver, Canada; Angie Zapata of Greeley, Colorado; Paige Clay of Chicago, Illinois; Deja Johnson of Miami, Florida; Kendall Hampton, Agnes, Dwayne Jones, Ashley Sinclair, Kelly Young, Betty Skinner, Brittany-Nicole Kidd-Stergis, Mayang Prasetyo, Mia Henderson, Jennifer Laude, Ashley Sherman, Gizzy Fowler, Papi Edwards, Lamia Beard, Ty Underwood, Penny Proud...

And there were so many more...she couldn't remember them now, but one of the first things she'd done after she came out, after she decided that this would be her life now—honesty and pride and self-acceptance from here on out—was to go to Wikipedia and look up her genealogy; she'd been stunned by the legacy that was her inheritance, and set out to memorize the names of the martyrs.

Her people represented every color of the rainbow, Black and White and Red and Yellow and Brown, and that was part of how she knew that what she was doing was right, because she never felt *White* or *Male*, never felt *Straight*, even as William O'Hara growing up in his parents' Republican Catholic household, even when he was living with a woman and thinking of adopting her children.

On her computer screen, the artists had spread some kind of ointment over the tattoo and were wrapping the boy's torso in saran wrap.

She'd read somewhere that the insulation provided by the saran wrap had probably saved his life.

Unintended good.

She smiled to herself.

It happens.

Just like shit.

She was about to pause the video, but decided to watch her favorite part again, just short of the fortieth hour. A massive Black drag queen in a Marilyn Monroe wig, full makeup, a Black sequined unitard, and a girdle with attached angel wings draped a blanket over the boy.

You go, girl! Bridget gushed, before remembering almost immediately that no one said that anymore and blushing scarlet.

These were her people now.

She'd chosen well.

THE GIGGLE HOUSE

I don't know how it was for you all growing up, but my Momma used to make me get the switch off the hook and pull my own pants down, while she stretched and did some light calisthenics. Then she'd beat my ass bloody, and if I didn't sit up straight at dinner, I got it again.

The biggest reason your average Black man is always going to be tougher than your average white man—aside from the genetic mettle imparted by four hundred years of racial violence—Black mommas.

NTOZAKE

"Ntozake."

The girl turned toward the voice. "Nikki! Hey!"

They embraced.

"How are you?"

"Good." Ntozake smiled, pointing to one of the children playing on the playground. "That's my niece, Keisha. She's six tomorrow."

"She's so tall!"

Ntozake nodded. "Tallest girl in her class, and she's still growing like a weed."

The women sat squinting into sunlight that leapt off the snow hot and sharp and aggressive. Keisha's hoodie blazed blue, and the playground equipment was a searing red, and beneath their hand-shade and through the flicker of sunspots and shadow and brilliant white nothing, the women could see that Keisha's height and the length of her limbs made it difficult for her to dart and dodge between and behind obstacles and opponents as her friends did. Instead, she ran toward and then past them, rounded a jungle gym, and burst into a straightaway along the edge of the playground, breaking away from the boy pursuing her; the women watched blue torn from red and white.

"She's fast," Nikki said.

"You should see her going after the ice cream truck."

They smiled and were silent. Ntozake continued watching her niece, while Nikki's eyes fell to her jeans.

137

"So how are you, really?" Nikki asked, glancing sideways.

"Good. I really am."

"I heard you and Chris broke up."

Ntozake nodded. "A month ago. Six weeks."

"You broke up with him?"

"I guess. It was more a mutual thing, though."

"That doesn't sound like Chris."

It was a crisp Saturday afternoon; though the temperature had climbed into the thirties, Ntozake wouldn't have been outside if it weren't for her niece. Keisha had been practically vibrating with energy, so Ntozake had agreed to take her to Washington Market Park.

"Oh, he didn't want to break up, but he said it was obvious I wasn't happy, and he wanted me to be happy more than he wanted to stay together."

"That was sweet of him."

"He's a sweet guy."

"So what happened?"

Ntozake shrugged, shook her head. "Nothing, really. He didn't do anything wrong; we didn't fight. It was just...something was always off. He was a little too thoughtful and attentive, a little too careful choosing his words. If we started to argue, he'd back down right away. He gave me too many gifts for no reason, tried too hard to make my parents like him."

"Nice, generous, and understanding? What a nightmare."

Ntozake laughed. "I know, right?"

"Well at least now I know to cross sweet and thoughtful billionaires off the list of people to set you up with."

Ntozake laughed again, turning away from her niece to look at her girlfriend. "Seriously, though. Chris was a nice guy, but we didn't have all that much in common, weren't into the same things, didn't hang with any of the same people...I never really knew if we were together because he was into me, or if there was something else going on. My parents weren't all that crazy about him either."

"Yeah."

"It's not like Daddy's going to like anyone I bring home, no matter what—the guy could be Black Jesus and Daddy'd be like, 'Stay away from my little girl!'"

Nikki chuckled. "Your father is definitely a little extra."

"But Mom didn't like Chris, either—well, didn't like him is the wrong way to say it—it was more that there was something about him that sketched her out. I thought she was just being paranoid, at first, but the longer we were together...and now..."

"You saw the video?"

Ntozake shook her head. "I heard about it." Her teeth started to chatter. She peered through the steady stream of people passing by the concrete half-wall they were leaning against and spotted a nearby vendor. "Coffee?"

Nikki nodded. "Have you heard anything from him since?"

"He sent me an email telling me he'd be okay."

"That's hard to believe."

Ntozake shrugged.

"Did he say if he was coming back to school or not?"

"Didn't mention it."

Nikki nodded. "Well, I'm just glad you're okay."

"I am."

"Good."

The women ordered their coffees and walked back to their perch.

"I just can't get over the fact that I know him, you know?" Nikki said after a while. "I mean, we've eaten meals and studied and gone to movies and hung out together, and he always seemed like this nice, normal, good-looking, shy guy."

"You know, if he does come back, and you want to take a shot at him, don't hold back on my account."

"You're joking with me? You think this is funny? Chris is our friend, and now you can go online and watch—how does that not bother you?"

Ntozake's smile faded. "I told you I hadn't seen the video."

Nikki's face fell. "Sorry."

"No," Ntozake shook her head. "You're good. You're right. The whole thing is horrible."

"I just don't understand why he...I mean how he—what led him to..."

"Me either. But you know what—and I know this is going to sound awful and inhumane, but it's true: people do awful things to themselves and others every day, and we only have so much energy and so much time. We can't care about everyone, so we choose a few, and do the best we can."

"I guess."

"I like Chris. I think he's a good person, and I hope he ends up happy, I really do."

"But he's not one of your people."

"No. He isn't, and I don't think he ever really was. I think a part of me knew that all along, and that was what he picked up on, how he knew I was unhappy."

"That's tough."

"That's life."

The women drank their coffee in silence, sharing the brownie they'd bought and watching Keisha play. She was running and laughing, moving in and out of different groups of kids, multiple games of tag. Her smile was wide and easy, and her teeth matched the white beads swaying and clicking in her hair as she ran. Keisha's playmates shrieked with laughter every time they were caught or the person who was "it" got near, but no one ever caught Keisha, and eventually they stopped trying and she phased seamlessly into a game of double dutch, and then into a group of kids dancing to a radio. Keisha was like the wind, and that was what Ntozake wanted to be, how she wanted to be. She wanted to flow, to live her life and do her thing and express herself. She didn't want to have to try so hard all the time.

"I should be going," Nikki said after a while. "It was good to see you. I'm really glad you're okay."

"Me too." Ntozake smiled. "It was good to see you, too. We should grab coffee sometime."

"Definitely."

Nikki left, and Ntozake watched her niece a while longer while she finished her coffee.

She was cold again, but she didn't want Keisha to have to stop playing.

Maybe Chris would come back whole.

Or maybe not. Either way, the world would continue as before.

Watching her niece play reminded her of how much joy there was in the world, how much laughter and how much light.

One day, she was going to find hers.

THE GIGGLE HOUSE

I'm a big man. No, wypipo, I'm not talking about my dick—not everything is about my dick. Seek help.

But I'm six-foot-four, I weigh three bills, and I grew up street, so I can handle myself. Anyway, I used to chill with this white guy, Walter. He was a cool dude, chill, and always ready with a blunt, but he wouldn't stop using the word 'nigger'—not nigga, which is borderline acceptable for white people to say if they have the written and notarized permission of no fewer than three Black people, but the whole violence, and I finally told him, dude, I like you, but you're on notice. I'm going to lay you out every time you use that word going forward. Yeah, he nods, that's fair.

Now Walter was five-eight or five-nine, and maybe a hundred and forty pounds, and I wasn't pulling any punches, so when I hit him, it was nap time.

I knocked Walter out two or three times a day until I went away to college.

Wypipo crazy.

ELROY

Elroy didn't mind his name—it sounded like someone you wouldn't notice nohow, someone you'd walk right past if you was anybody, and that was exactly the way he liked it.

People didn't see you, you couldn't get in no trouble.

People didn't see you, they'd say things in front of you they wouldn't never say otherwise.

Elroy had been born in the Mississippi Delta, just outside Vicksburg. Daddy was a laborer, but didn't care much for it, and was gone as often as not, up in Memphis, searching for more civilized work. His Momma never said nothing or complained that Elroy heard, but then one day he woke up and she was gone, hadn't left no breakfast for him, and no food in the pantry, neither, and when lunch and dinner passed without any sign of her, he figured that maybe she hadn't been none too happy with his Daddy running off for weeks at a time.

It was ten more days before Daddy come back. He hadn't seemed overly surprised when Elroy told him he hadn't seen Momma for over a week, only looked around some and asked him what he'd done for food.

142

Elroy's Daddy took him to Memphis where he worked as a bellhop in the Peabody, and elsewhere cleaning offices after hours, and at first, he seemed to enjoy his son's company, telling him stories and showing him around town and watching the boy's eyes pop, but that weren't never going to last, and though Daddy never said nothing or treated him bad, Elroy could see he was restless. Most nights he made like he was asleep so his father could sneak out and go wherever it was he needed to go.

Then, when he was ten, his Daddy got in a car with some men after they trapped him in an alley. Elroy had been on his own ever since, more than sixty years now. He'd been hiding behind a dumpster and Daddy had dropped his wallet and kicked it back toward him before getting into the car. That was when Elroy knew his Daddy weren't never coming back, because there weren't no way he'd have given up his wallet if he thought there was a chance he'd live to spend the money in it.

Elroy counted backwards from a hundred before he moved, staring at the speckled leather wallet the whole time. It was beat-up and misshapen and bulging, the seams loose from being overstuffed, and he was surprised because his Momma was always saying they didn't have no money. He got down to zero and stood up some and crept around the dumpster and got the wallet. It was surprisingly light for how fat it was, he couldn't even get his hand all the way around it. He started to open it, but thought better and stopped, not wanting to invite the wrong kind of attention. Better he go back to the hotel and do it in private. But then he got to wondering if the people that took his Daddy might be waiting for him back at the hotel and ducked back behind the dumpster to see what he'd been given.

Labels.

Beer labels and mayonnaise labels, labels from canned sardines and potted meat, Coke labels and liquor labels and cigarette labels, a label from a can of shoe polish and several from congolene bottles that still reeked of lye. Elroy took them from the wallet one by one; the smaller were folded up to look like charga-plates and the bigger ones made into the shape of bills, and he undid the folds, and saw that they were bright red and shining gold and spectacular orange and brilliant blue. So many colors, and not one of them green. He held them up and let the wind take them.

He was about to drop the wallet in the trash when he noticed a tiny label stuck in its folds with a scrawl running across the back: *Elroy, PO Box #X. Key taped to toilet cover. Sorry.*

With his father gone, Elroy didn't have no relations, so he moved around. He didn't reckon himself overly smart, but he had the eyes and ears his Momma gave him, and he figured he'd be okay so long as he paid attention to what they was telling him, and he didn't waste no lessons and have to learn them over again.

He knew that things like food and rent cost money, and that the $142.59 his Daddy left behind would run out sooner or later. He spent a week trying to find work, but no one wanted to hire a ten-year-old, and though he only bought the cheapest food he could find, and didn't let himself eat but once a day, sooner came on the first of the second month after his Daddy died, when he couldn't make the rent.

Not knowing what else to do, he started walking toward Vicksburg.

It was two hundred and fifty miles from Memphis to Vicksburg, and he walked every step of it save for the few he was spared by a negro driving an old farm truck. It took him months to make the distance, but he weren't in no hurry. Vicksburg was a place, not a destination—weren't no one there he knew enough to impose upon. There was something to the road he liked, anyway—it kept you moving so you didn't have no time to overthink things or feel sorry for yourself. He hired himself out when he could, earned enough to eat and slept in the labor camp when there was one, or in a barn or an abandoned shack or under the stars if there weren't, and if he couldn't find no work, country folk was mostly nice and would feed you a meal or two if you looked hungry.

You had to mind you didn't look too hungry, though, or they'd start asking questions like where's your parents and where you stay at, which was a problem when there weren't no answers to give them.

The problem with the delta was that it was full of country folk and small towns where everybody knew everybody, so folk knew you didn't belong from the moment they first seen you, and if they saw you again after that, they was on you—usually out of goodness and not wanting a boy to be lost or hungry, but on you nonetheless. And when they found out you didn't have no people, well, then they got meddlesome, and you'd find yourself in some stranger's house or at some church, and people would be asking you things that weren't none of their business and getting mad cause you didn't talk or act the right way, and if you was there long enough, they'd make you go to church and school, which Elroy didn't have no use for.

And God forbid the people was white, because then it didn't make no never mind that the South lost the War—they'd be working you like you was their nigger and they was on a deadline, or they'd be setting the police on you.

Time he was fourteen, Elroy done snuck out of three white folks' places and a few colored houses, too, and made it south all the way to Florida, only to decide it was too damn hot, and worked his way back north, train-hopping along the Atlantic Coastline railroad and walking when there weren't no trains.

By fifteen he was bussing tables in Philly, and after that he was in Jersey, and finally, New York City.

He'd wanted to drive a cab from the moment he first seen one, scrimped and hustled and saved with the idea of buying one, shining shoes, selling apples at the park for a nickel, running messages, and doing deliveries or sweeping and mopping shops after close of business.

He'd learned to pick a pocket somewhere along the way, so he could do that if he had to, if it got to be a few days since he ate something, but he rarely did. New York kept him fed and clothed, if not well-fed, or in anything you might call style.

He'd always had rules, even as a kid. He never stole within a mile of where he was sleeping, never stole from someone who looked like they couldn't afford it, never stole in the same place two times in a row, and never flashed any of the cash he pulled, not even the time he'd lucked into a wallet with almost $200 in it. No benders at the bar or fancy threads for him. He did like music, though, that deep, soul-churning sound he got a taste for growing up, and which by the fifties was all over New York, even at the swankiest, high-falutinest clubs where the guests and wait staff were white, and the performers and kitchen hands Black.

He introduced himself to the bellhops and elevator men, got to know them and did them little favors if and when he could, brought them coffee or covered for them if they needed an alibi for the cops or their wives, and eventually one of them knew someone who could get him a job emptying the trash at one of the clubs the big names played.

He was twenty in 1961, working nights at the club, teaching himself to play guitar, and trying to get so he could really play the harmonica he'd carried since he was a boy. By 1963 he finally had enough scratch for a secondhand cab that leaked oil, but which he learned to fix and drove during the day.

Elroy bought his first limo just as he was set to turn thirty. He'd survived unlicensed for the better part of a decade, picking up fares no white cabbie would in parts of town that few drivers ventured into. He had a shotgun under his seat and a revolver in his jacket pocket, and he'd only had to use the revolver once for word to get around.

He hadn't planned to buy a limousine when he woke up that day. He'd showered and dressed and skipped breakfast as was his way, stopped for coffee at a diner, and overheard a conversation between a limo driver with a gambling problem and a coke habit, and another man. Coke habit was asking the other man for money: I don't get my hands on $6,500 by tomorrow, he said, I'm a dead man.

The friend couldn't help him. Tapped out, he said. Might not make the rent.

Elroy left, waited by the man's Cadillac.

Your nigger-ass better not be leaning against my car, the man said when he saw Elroy.

Elroy squinted at him, looked from the man to the car three and a half feet to the left and back at man.

I was wondering if you'd be interested in selling me your limousine.

How much you offering?

$6,520.

The man scowled. You heard me inside.

Yes, Sir, I surely did. Couldn't help it.

The man pointed. That's a 1970 Cadillac Fleetwood Seventy-Five Limousine.

Yes, Sir, it surely is.

I paid over $11,000 for it less than a year ago.

Elroy shrugged.

You trying to cheat me, nigger?

No, Sir. I made you an offer. Yes or no is up to you, I ain't no way forcing you to do anything, one way or another.

You goddamn nigger trash—you're taking advantage of me!

Yes, Sir, I am. I was standing in line when you was talking to your friend, and I heard what you was saying through no fault of my own, and I thought, Elroy, you didn't have no plans to buy a limousine when you woke up this morning, and you don't have no $11,000, but you do have $6,520 tucked away, and that man need $6,500 mighty bad—maybe you can make a deal.

Go to hell!

Sir, I can see I done offended you, and that weren't never my intention. I apologize. I'll be on my way.

Elroy had gone about thirty feet when the man called after him. Wait! he said. How soon can you have the money?

Elroy pointed. My bank's ten blocks from here.

The man looked in the direction he was pointing, then down at the ground. Fuck. Fine. Deal.

You'll sell me the limo?

I don't have a choice.

Elroy nodded, started down the street. I'll meet you there.

I can give you a ride.

Thank you kindly, but I'll walk. It'll just be a minute more. I got long legs.

Suit yourself.

Elroy withdrew the money, took possession of the title and keys.

Good luck to you, Sir, Elroy said, offering his hand.

The man ignored it. One question, he said.

Elroy dropped his hand.

Why the extra $20?

Elroy shrugged, made to go, but the man grabbed his arm.

Elroy frowned, met the man's eye. You got yourself in a tight spot, and I reckon getting out of it just cost you about all you had, and if I were you, I'd be wanting a drink about now.

The man nodded.

Elroy turned to go.

What's a nigger going to do with a Cadillac limousine?

Elroy didn't answer.

He spent some time thinking about it that night, though, and over the next couple days. He thought about taking the limo to a dealer and getting his money back plus whatever he could get on top, and he might have if he hadn't—for no real reason—thought about a TV show he'd seen once or twice whose name he'd long since forgotten or never knew. The star played a millionaire police chief who got around in a Rolls Royce. Elroy remembered him handling business and investments and talking about the details of murder investigations as if his driver didn't exist, and that made him think that he'd come to own the Cadillac the same way, by being invisible and paying attention to what folk said when they thought weren't nobody listening, and so he kept the limousine and got an official license, registered with the New York State Limousine Commission, and did what he could to ensure that he drove as many businessmen and bankers and stockbrokers as he could.

And he saved near everything he earned, found the cheapest place he could in a livable part of Queens, and banked eighty percent of what he brought in.

He had some luck, picked up a few stock tips that his caution and limited funds had prevented from leading to a real windfall, but which he'd turned into the beginnings of his retirement fund. He chuckled, thinking about it now, remembering how for a time he'd been convinced that some CEO or banker or politician was going to let something slip that would make him the Black Rockefeller.

And now he was seventy-three, had never been married, never had kids.

But he was okay with it. He had a good life, a busy life, the life he wanted, though he'd probably back off the eighty-hour weeks sooner rather than later.

He still drove, and his friends thought he was crazy, but the truth was he liked to drive.

Elroy would admit after a few whiskey sodas that not having any kids bothered him sometimes, but he didn't drink much, and drank alone when he did, in a booth reserved for him at the jazz club he frequented.

Almost no one knew the club belonged to William Fairchild. Elroy only knew because he'd driven him in his limo once, Fairchild and another man. They was doing business with the partition down so Fairchild could tell him which streets to take as they went, which had made Elroy's butt itch a bit at first because he prided himself on knowing the city better than anyone, but after Fairchild told him to make three or four turns that Elroy would've made on his own, he had to grant Fairchild his due respect. The men were negotiating a deal for Fairchild to buy a jazz and blues club, one which Elroy knew to be a hot mess and poorly run. They'd dropped the other man off and were heading to the airport when Elroy had taken his shot, said excuse me, Mr. Fairchild, Sir, and, I didn't mean to eavesdrop, but I couldn't help but hear what you were discussing, and I know it ain't none of my concern, nohow, but I don't think you want to do this deal, Sir.

He'd met Fairchild's eye in the rearview mirror, but couldn't say whether the man was irritated, interested, or indifferent.

If you's looking for a partner, Sir, I know for a fact that the proprietor's in a bad way owing to heroin and booze, and that the manager and the bartender help themselves to the till. If you're after the building, the pipes need to be replaced, and the foundation's a damn mess.

Elroy'd glanced in the mirror again and saw that Fairchild was losing interest.

Last thing I'll say, Mr. Fairchild, Sir, is that even if all you want is a club, you still don't want this place, no how: they ain't bothered to put no anechoic panels up so the alcons is damn near fifteen, the sound system is for the birds, and the stage is so small it can't hold a drum rig, let alone a full band.

And that was when Fairchild got interested, not just in what Elroy had to say about the club, and what he knew about the New York scene and which joints one might go to if he found himself hankering for some Delta Blues, but about Elroy himself. So Elroy told him about meeting Robert Johnson and Chester Burnett, Huddie Leadbetter, Billie Holiday, and Albert King, about seeing them play, seeing Blind Willie McTell, Johnny Lee Hooker, Lonnie Johnson, Muddy Waters, and others. He told him about the half dozen jam sessions in which he'd blown his harmonica alongside famous musicians, and then Fairchild told him he was looking for a place to hide when he was in New York, and all the better if it were a place where he could go and listen to the music he'd loved since he was seventeen and stationed at Greenville Air Force Base, since before he made his money, back when he went by Billy.

Elroy offered to show Fairchild around sometime, to take him to some of the venues where the Blues still happened. He'd scribbled his number on a scrap of paper he tore from an envelope and given it to the billionaire, and didn't think no how, no way he'd ever hear from him again, but a couple weeks later the phone rang, and a week after that Elroy met Fairchild at the airport and took him around, introduced him to some of the musicians he knew, people without national names, but the real deal, people whose lives were all about sound and the alchemy that made it possible to express the whole of the world's truth and sorrow in a twelve-bar progression, and Fairchild had bought everyone's drinks to keep the energy going as they'd talked the Blues, laughter and smoke curling in and out and above them as they argued amongst themselves about whether Chicago Blues was better than Country Blues, and if it could hold a candle to Delta Blues, and could Electric Blues ever be as raw and pure as all the others.

Elroy helped Fairchild pick the spot for his club, helped him select the staff, suggested certain musicians. Fairchild reached out whenever he was going to be in New York, and Elroy made himself available when he could, but he never called first, never asked for nothing, because he knew Fairchild expected it, was waiting on him to ask for money or a job or a stake in the club, but there weren't no way in hell that was going to happen, and after a while, after ten or fifteen years of riding in the back of Elroy's limo, Fairchild seemed to get that, and relax. He'd offered to stake Elroy about the time Elroy was fixing to start his company, and Elroy'd said no, thank you, and he'd offered again in October of the company's third year, when Elroy was all but bust, and it was looking like the company was going under, and Elroy had said no again, and thank you, but that he'd been on his own since he was a boy, and that was how he liked it.

That was the last time Fairchild offered him money, and though Elroy didn't know nothing about friendship, and hadn't never had no friend his whole life, he reckoned that was when he and William Fairchild became friends, after twenty years of knowing each other.

Elroy peeled the label from his beer bottle absently, a crest with an unlikely green hop crowned by the brewery's name, slowly curling over and into itself as he worked at it. Fairchild had turned him onto it, had the full selection of beers made by the Lazy Magnolia brewing company shipped up from Mississippi. Fairchild always started the night drinking the $1,000-a-shot scotch he imported from Scotland, but switched to bourbon and Lazy Magnolia after the first or second round, for which Elroy was grateful as Fairchild always ordered drinks for both of them, and the bartender wouldn't take his money. It wasn't that Elroy wasn't okay with the free drinks. He'd shown who he was, and if after twenty-odd years Fairchild chose to pick up his bar tabs, it could only be that he was showing his regard for Elroy, his respect.

It was just that he couldn't no how, no way understand shelling out $1,000 for an ounce of anything.

Elroy looked at his watch; he'd pick Fairchild up at the courthouse in an hour.

He'd never imagined he would meet a billionaire, and having met one, the thought that they might become friends had never occurred to him.

This morning, he'd learned that it was possible to feel bad for a billionaire, too, and to know there weren't no way and no how he'd trade places with him, given the chance.

One of Elroy's drivers showed him the article about Christopher just before he left to meet Fairchild, and Fairchild told him that his son wouldn't allow the tattoos to be removed unless all charges against the men who'd assaulted him were dropped, and a statement he'd written was read at a press conference.

Fairchild wasn't but three or four years older than Elroy, but he'd looked for all the world like time itself was hanging on him.

If that was what kids did to you, Elroy was okay with not having any.

Besides, if Fairchild, with all his money, who'd actually been a presence in his son's life, had been unable to keep the child from woe, what chance would Elroy have had?

About as much as his Daddy, probably.

THE GIGGLE HOUSE

Walter wasn't smart, he wasn't dumb either, and I think about him a lot, because he knew I was going to knock him out if he said nigger, and he never meant anything by it, so why?

I think maybe it's related to the white-run corporations and studio owners and producers that throw mix gangsters, guns, bitches, and bling together, and call it "Black culture," and the fact that we— Black and white— just internalize the fuck out of it.

You speak the words we're given, even if we don't know what they mean.

Y'all looking at me like I'm crazy—that get a little abstract?

The dude in front of me decked out like he an OG, his name's Percy. He's a fucking accountant.

JEREMY

The man grabbed his friend's shoulder. "Yo, check it out—yo! Barkeep! Turn it up!"

Too early to get riled, man, Jeremy thought, grinding his teeth as he cranked the volume on the TV, trying not to glare at the jackhole all decked out in his gangsta costume: jersey, sideways hat over some kind of bandana, or do-rag, or whatever they called it. Pants hanging below his ass.

In a shocking turn of events, two men were gunned down today in the shadow of the courthouse, only minutes after their unexpected release from the Criminal Court of the City of New York. Stacey Harris and Terrance Green were set free when reclusive Billionaire William Fairchild made a rare appearance to announce that his family would not be pressing charges against them. The two men were caught on tape brutally beating Fairchild's son and heir, John Christopher Fairchild, with shovels, in a video that has gone viral after surfacing online earlier this month. William Fairchild read a statement written by John Christopher, and left the premises immediately thereafter, without comment. Those in attendance were left baffled by the young Fairchild's statement, which included apologies to Harris and Green

for, quote, "the immense suffering and irreparable damage that had been inflicted upon them."

The elder Fairchild appeared frail as he read the address, leading to speculation that he might step down from his position as CEO of Prosperitatis Absque Limitatione Eligi.

—WE INTERRUPT THIS BROADCAST FOR A BREAKING NEWS SPECIAL REPORT—

We have unconfirmed reports coming in that a standoff between a man and the St. George police has ended without casualties. While we have yet to ascertain the alleged gunman's identity, eyewitnesses describe him as a thin, clean-shaven Caucasian male, approximately six feet tall, with a military haircut.

We can also now confirm that police have recovered an HK417 A2 twenty-inch sniper rifle from the crime scene, leading to speculation that they may have apprehended the courthouse gunman. While ballistics have yet to be run, authorities believe that the rounds that killed Stacey Harris and Terrance Green will match the rifle.

Jeremy didn't have a problem with Black people, just assholes who took up a spot at his bar and didn't tip or care enough to thank him when he handed them a drink.

He knew Black people didn't have an exclusive on that crap—Canadians didn't tip either, Asians were hit or miss, and then there were the tourists from Europe who liked to pretend they didn't know you had to tip in America.

Assholes.

The Jesus crowd didn't tip either. Men usually tipped more than women, especially if they were with a woman they were trying to bang—but give him a table of homos any day. That was where the money was.

Jeremy hadn't even bothered applying at the bars and clubs in Chelsea, though. He knew what he was, nothing special and not much to look at, and he was okay with it.

His hairline had started receding in his early twenties, and three years later his waistline was making tracks in the opposite direction, but he hated running, and gyms in New York were hella expensive, so he just did his best not to eat that fifth slice of pizza or order that third pitcher.

He was forty-two and single, had an associate's degree in business management, and worked all the time, saving as much as he could, because he thought that maybe he might open a bar of his own someday. Upstate where things weren't so damn expensive. And as little as it was, it was more than his people ever achieved, a bunch of white trash ex-con, drug addicts, and alcoholics living in sixty-year-old single-wides in trailer parks that charged $250 a month for a lot, barely able to make rent after they got done buying booze, cigarettes, and chaw.

"Yo, Barkeep! We could use another set up down here, you know, if it's not too much trouble—and don't be so white with your pour this time!"

"Clinton say, don't be so white with yo' pour!" the man beside him echoed, bumping fists with his friend. "Nigga got jokes!"

"Hey! Watch your mouth, man! There are people in here."

The friend made a face. "What I say?"

"Come on, man, don't give me a hard time, alright? Just keep it clean."

The friend looked from Jeremy to Clinton and back, shook his head.

"The n-word, man, you can't talk like that in here."

"Dawg," Clinton said, "you realize he Black, right?"

"Doesn't matter. House rules. Come on, Clinton, this isn't news; you're here like every other day."

"You'd think I could get a decent pour, then."

"You start tipping, and we can talk."

"You tell your people to pay me more than dick-fifty an hour, and I'll think about tipping."

"My people?"

"Yeah, the ones with all the money," Clinton said, waving his hand dismissively. "Everyone know all you white folk got money."

"Man, I grew up in a trailer. My 'people' don't have a pot to piss in."

"Yo," the friend interjected, "what the fuck you want to piss in a pot for?"

"Come on, man, don't make me cut you guys off."

"Speaking of that," Clinton said, "have you cut us off, or might you feel like doing your damn job sometime in the near future, and pouring our motherfucking drinks?"

"Last warning, Clinton."

"I still want to know why you pissing in a pot," the friend said.

Jeremy drew the men's beer, poured them each a shot, and pushed the drinks across the bar. "It's a figure of speech," he said. "Just means we were poor."

"Shit, man," the friend said, taking the drinks, "everyone poor where I come from."

"You want to figure something," Clinton said, pointing to the television, "figure me how the great white psycho there steps out in front of the cops with two handguns and a big ass rifle, and he alive, but my boy Kimani get lit up for no damn reason."

Jeremy shrugged. "Don't know what to tell you, man."

"Oh, wait, I just figured it for you. Your boy white. Kimani Black. That clear enough for you?"

The friend nodded. "Pretty messed up."

Both men looked at Jeremy.

"What do you want me to say? I didn't do it."

"Naw, dawg, you didn't have to—your brothers did it for you."

"You know, man," Jeremy said, grabbing a rag and scrubbing at an invisible spot on the bar, "you're being a real dick tonight. Someone steal your lunch money or something?"

"Yeah, and a shot on the house would make me feel a hell of a lot better."

"You want a shot?" Jeremy grabbed a rocks glass and poured a double. "Fine. Here's two! Feel better now?"

"Actually, yeah, dawg. But I think my boy Da'quan feeling a little left out."

Jeremy poured another double, pushed the glass toward the friend. "Here you go, Da'quan."

"Thanks, man. Name's Mike, though."

"Screw you, Clinton."

"It'd take a lot more than one of your weak-ass doubles for that to happen."

"I think it's about time you went home."

"You cutting me off?"

"Yeah, man. You don't have to go home, but you gotta get the fuck up out of here."

"I thought there wasn't no profanity allowed."

"Pay your tab, Clinton. Go home."

"Whatever." Clinton turned to his friend. "You got this one?"

Mike handed Jeremy four twenties. "That cover it?"

"More than," Jeremy said. "I'll get your change."

"Keep it."

"You sure? You know you've got like fifteen coming back, right?"

Mike waved him off.

"Thanks, man," Jeremy said. "Thanks a lot."

Mike nodded. "Be easy."

"You, too, man."

Jeremy watched Mike walk through the door, a little wobbly but otherwise fine. He and Clinton lit up and started on down the way.

Jeremy put the change in his tip jar.

Another day, another dollar.

And after rent and groceries and bills, not much more than that.

THE GIGGLE HOUSE

You want more proof? Show of hands, how many of your pants are below your asshole?

Wypipo say, we criminals, give us movies and television shows and music hyping Black criminality, and specify pants-below-ass as an essential part of African-American haute couture.

Now, I ask you, what kind of criminal can we be if we can't slip the 5-o, and how're you supposed to run with your pants around your knees?

Wypipo be diabolical.

ORLANDO

"Fuck you, man! Why you always sweating me? You a faggot or something?"

They were in his office, just the two of them on a Sunday afternoon, Orlando and the kid.

"You're the one who offered to fuck me."

It was the wrong thing to say. He knew it even before the words came off his tongue.

He was pissed.

Orlando had been a punk when he was coming up, hadn't been able to see the things he saw now. He'd been Dante, jambing himself up for no fucking reason.

He could help if the boy'd listen.

He'd survived Mott Haven, the drugs, gangs, streets, the crappy schools and beat-your-ass-for-fun cops. He'd survived the foster home shuffle, the deadbeats, crack-fiends, and perverts.

He'd gone to college, then law school, and made himself a few million a day trading while he was at it.

Now he wanted to give something back, not out of gratitude—no one other than a handful of teachers and church ladies ever did anything for him—but because he could see all that the neighborhood could do and be if it weren't so busy strangling itself, mired in a system that was only too happy to give it a hand.

"You know what?" Dante said. "Fuck this. I'm out."

Orlando knew better than to expect gratitude, but this went

beyond.

"Dante," he said, "sit down. Now."

Dante didn't sit, but he took his hand off the doorknob. "Naw, man, I'm done. I don't need this shit!"

"Explain that to me, Dante."

"I don't gotta explain shit to you, nigger!"

Orlando glared. He hated that word. It was one of the few ground rules he laid out when he started mentoring someone.

Nigger means trash, he'd say. *You calling me trash?*

Orlando was a large man.

Nigger means not human, undeserving of life. You calling me inhuman? You saying I don't deserve to live?

I didn't mean nothing, they'd stammer.

He'd cut them off.

No, you don't. Not a goddamn thing. And you never will in this world unless you make something of yourself, unless you do something they have to respect.

Even if Orlando couldn't really walk, now, and it hurt to stand, he could still throw a punch if he needed to.

He hated that he had to retain that threat to get through to these kids, but that was how it was, what the system did.

If you think you're trash, he'd say, *if you think you and the people you roll with don't deserve to live, you keep on calling each other niggers. But you will not disrespect me in that way. Am I clear?*

"You don't have to explain it to me, or you can't?" he asked Dante. "Because where I'm standing you need it bad."

"Man, you ain't nothing but a broke down old nigger ain't never mattered to no one," Dante sneered.

"Is that right?"

"That's right."

"What kind of car you drive, Dante?"

"What?"

"You got a nice whip? You ride spinners? You hitting them corners in your low-low?"

"Fuck you, man!"

Orlando grimaced. Check yourself, O, he thought. Keep it tight, or you'll lose the kid.

"You absolutely need this, Dante, whether you know it or not."

"Or what? You going to violate me?"

"Me? No, that's on you. You know the terms of your parole. I won't be making any phone calls to rat you out, but I'm not breaking any laws either. Your PO calls and asks me how our sessions are going, I'm going to let him know."

"Man, this is bullshit!"

"You know what's bullshit? Gang banging, selling drugs, packing heat...the whole act you go through to convince yourself you're hard. You tell yourself you're King Fucking Kong all strapped out with chrome, but what you don't realize is that it's just another way for them to get what they want, which is Black bodies."

"Who the fuck is *them*?"

"They'd prefer you alive and in a jumpsuit so they can use you to keep their multi-billion-dollar-a-year prison industrial complex humming, but they aren't going to shed any tears if you end chalked. There are plenty of other bodies."

"We all gotta die someday—I going out on my feet, busting."

"That's exactly what you don't seem to get, Dante, you're not on your feet. You're on your damn knees. You say you're all 'no homo,' but every time you strap up and go do more of that thug life bullshit, you're getting down on your knees in front of the man and asking for a taste."

"Hell, no!"

"Hell, yes. That's exactly what you're doing. I'm trying to help you out, to show you there's another way to do things, but you're not making it easy."

"Don't talk to me about easy, bitch! You know what it costs me to get here? How long I gotta wait just to get on the motherfucking, piss-smelling bus?"

"I told you I'd pick you up."

"Oh, great! Just what I fucking need, be seen with you. That'd do me real good."

"What the hell are you talking about?"

"I take major shade because of you!"

"How you figure?"

"How I figure? Man, everyone knows what you did."

"What I did?"

Orlando looked out the window for a moment. The skeleton of a tree quivered in the winter wind.

"Okay, Dante. Fine. I'll bite. Tell me what I did."

The boy started in.

Orlando had heard various stories over the years.

September, 1994. Thirteen-year-old Nicholas Heyward Jr. was playing cops and robbers in the stairwell of his family's apartment building in Brooklyn until a policeman shot him. The District Attorney refused to press charges against the officer, and the borough exploded in violence. The police retaliated. Orlando held one of his neighbors while the cops beat him.

February, 1999. The NYPD had just fired forty-one at Amadou Diallo, nineteen of which hit him. Orlando was demonstrating with a bunch of people from his block; the police came. Everyone else held their ground except Orlando, but the police chased him down and beat him, broke his arms and legs and a hip and three vertebrae.

March, 2000. The NYPD had just killed Patrick Moses Dorismond...

May, 2003...the NYPD...Ousmane Zongo...Orlando sided with the cops against his own people...

January 2004...the NYPD...Tim Stansbury...Orlando ran. The police cornered him in an alley. He pissed himself.

The version Dante repeated had Orlando helping two NYPD officers run down Tamon Robinson in their police cruiser in April of 2012.

"And you believe that story? After all the time we've spent together, you believe I punched a Black woman in the face for swearing at a cop?"

Dante shrugged. "Everyone be saying it."

"Everyone?"

"They saying you's a punk-assed bitch."

"How old are you, Dante?"

"Sixteen."

"And it's 2014, right? Which means you were born in 1998?"

"You a smart nigger."

Orlando slammed his fist on his desk so hard the wood cracked.

"You use that filthy word in my presence again," he said, his voice low and flat even as his eyes snarled, "and you will not be able to walk yourself out of this room. Do you understand me?"

"Whatever, man."

"Now, were any of the people in your crew alive in 1992?"

Dante stared blankly.

"Any of them twenty-two or older?"

"D-bol twenty-seven, and Mario twenty-eight."

"No one else?"

Dante shook his head.

"Have you ever heard of Rodney King?"

"He in a Tupac song, ain't he?"

"But you don't know who he is?"

"Another deadass nigg—" Dante froze.

Orlando stared.

"Man—who the fuck cares?"

"Rodney King was a drug addict who ran from the LAPD. But they caught him, like they always do, because street thugs haven't figured out that you can't outrun a police cruiser with your belt around your knees and your ass hanging out of your pants. They broke his skull, and kept on beating him."

"So what?"

Orlando stared at the kid. "I was in LA on business a couple days after. Lots of people protesting, rioting. I came around the corner and saw three cops sticking people with nightsticks, trying to start something, so I got between the officers and the men to try to calm things down. One of the cops reached around me and cracked one of the men in the face, so his friend swung at the officer, and hit me instead, knocked me to the ground. His friends stopped going at the cops, and stomped me."

"Bullshit."

Orlando shrugged. "You can believe what you want. The whole thing was caught on video, though. And the city of Los Angeles was sufficiently embarrassed to see four of their finest watching a group of men beat another man without intervening that they cut me a fairly substantial check."

"How much they give you?"

"You're angry, Dante, and you have every right to be. But your anger has got you doing stupid shit and fighting the wrong people. Your beef isn't with me, and it isn't with the Crips—it's not even with white people. For Christ sake, stop being pissed off for a second, and look around."

Dante started shaking his head.

"No, of course you can't! You can't turn off the rage, and you can't think because the people that run this world don't want you to. It's like Malcolm said, 'They put your mind right in a bag, and take it wherever they want.' They keep you mad and stupid so you can't help yourself or anyone else, and they make money off you any way they can for as long as they can, and then they kill you, or they push you aside, and leave you to die on your own in the shit-world that they built for you."

"Man, seriously. How much they give you?"

Orlando just stared at the boy.

"How much?"

"That's all you've got for me? I said all that, and all you want to know is how much money they paid me for wrecking my leg?"

Dante shrugged.

"Goddammit, boy, I'm telling you, you can win—you can beat them at their own game. You ever hear anyone say that before?"

"What the fuck you talking about? Who the fuck is they?"

"Malcolm X said—"

"Man, fuck Malcolm X. Who the fuck is Malcolm X?"

"Someone who said, 'When a person places the proper value on freedom, there is nothing under the sun that he will not do to acquire that freedom.'"

"Man, I'm free as a motherfucker. Now you going to tell me how much they gave you or not?"

Orlando stared at the boy, clenching his jaw. He closed his eyes and counted to ten.

"What weird-ass thing is you doing now?"

Orlando opened his eyes and regarded the boy a while before speaking. "Not nearly enough," he said finally.

"Fine, man. Whatever. Be like that."

"Well, I guess it's late enough that we can call time. Would you like me to take you back? We can grab a bite on the way if you want."

"Nah, man. I'm good. I'll just hop a bus."

Orlando nodded.

"Later."

And then Dante was gone.

Orlando didn't know what was left of the boy; if there was enough humanity left to save.

He looked down at his desk calendar, at an appointment he'd canceled. A high-profile case. He barely knew the men when he agreed to represent them; he did it as a favor to a judge, and because the only alternative was a public defender suffocating under an impossible caseload.

The men had been caught on camera beating a billionaire white boy with shovels, so the best Orlando could have done was to negotiate a plea bargain, but it hadn't come to that.

All charges were dropped, out of nowhere.

His clients were in holding, had said their goodbyes to their families, and then, suddenly, they were free to go. No explanation given.

Freedom lasted for fifteen minutes.

They dropped like rocks outside the courthouse, blood and brain oozing from the holes in their skulls.

Dead.

But then, they'd always been dead, hadn't they.

Always already dead from the day they were born.

And Dante, too.

Orlando wound a scarf around his neck, took his coat and hat from the chair in the corner.

At least he had Knicks tickets for tomorrow, box seats. He'd planned to take Dante.

Maybe he'd call Dave, he thought, locking his office.

Or maybe he'd just scalp the extra ticket and buy a nice bottle of scotch.

THE GIGGLE HOUSE

Alright, we Black.

Cálmate hermano—for the next twenty minutes, you a nigga.

We want to survive.

How can we save ourselves?

We are going to follow the master. All of us are going to become Jaleel. Fucking. White.

Seriously. Jaleel White.

My boy Jaleel is the alpha and omega of Surviving Black.

His voice.

His style.

Even his motherfucking name.

RYU

What is good? Garlic. A leg of lamb on a spit. Wine with a view of boats rocking in a cove.

Ryu tilted his head and exhaled a stream of smoke into the night. He was sitting on a milk crate in the alley behind Alain's restaurant wearing only his uniform, sans apron and toque; he'd be cold soon, but for the moment the change in temperature was a grace, a reprieve from the kitchen's flames.

Garlic. A leg of lamb on a spit. Wine with a view of boats rocking in a cove.

The man who wrote the words was dead by the time Ryu heard them, as was the fifteen-year-old boy who discovered the poet all those years ago in a paper sack of books given up for rubbish.

The boy, Angus Patrick Duff, ceased to exist in 1983 with the flourish of a fountain pen he had purchased for the occasion. His parents were dead and he had no other family, no prospects to speak of, and so he ceased to be, and Alain-Laurent Alkan rose in his place.

He remade himself as a Parisian, spoke French even in the privacy of his own home.

Our home, Alain insisted.

The chef garde manger appeared in the doorway. "Tu es besoin."

Ryu nodded. "Je serai bientôt en. Une minute."

He stood, took a long drag, savoring it deep in his lungs, exhaled slowly, and flipped the cigarette into a bucket, but didn't return to the kitchen. A few minutes later, Alain stepped into the alley.

"Est ce que tu vas bien?" Alain asked.

Ryu nodded.

Alain frowned, searching Ryu's face.

"Je vais bien, Alain, vraiment." He pushed the tears from his eyes with the blades of his hands.

"Is it your friend?"

Ryu nodded.

"Do you want to talk about it?"

Ryu shook his head.

"Alors bouge toi le derrière!"

"Tout de suite, Chef."

The chef de tournant muttered under his breath as Ryu and Alain returned to the kitchen together.

Ryu took his apron off its peg and put it on. He knew how it looked, that he'd be jealous were their situations reversed.

Beyond jealous.

People called Ryu a gold digger, Alain's calendar boy, and so on. Alain was a somebody, though, a world-class chef, and so people were forced to temper their scorn, to sling it from behind fake smiles and between gritted teeth.

Ryu learned not to listen.

He hurt more for Alain than for any indignity he was made to suffer. Alain had the thinnest of skins, the most tender of hearts, and such words bit him like a scourge.

Ryu's rapid ascent of the kitchen hierarchy only made things worse, the criticism of their relationship more strident.

Alain had found Ryu picking through the dumpster behind his restaurant years before. It was two-thirty in the morning. Ryu was a week from his fifteenth birthday and had been on his own for months, had become adept at dodging DCFS, rapists, and pimps, those hungry for blood. He was emaciated, his clothing threadbare, and he would have been filthy but for the kindness of a local priest who allowed him to shower at the parsonage. Alain piled the evening's leftovers on a plate and gave it to him, filled four large takeaway containers. Ryu ate deliberately, which surprised Alain, intrigued him. He told the boy that he could come back as often as he wanted, and that he would make sure he was fed, and so Ryu did.

After six months, Alain offered him a place to stay, and Ryu accepted, and that was the first time Ryu spoke to him.

"I thought you were mute," Alain said.

Ryu shook his head.

He moved in shortly thereafter, and when he asked about a job, Alain hired him. At first, Ryu washed dishes, then he made porter, and later, after only eighteen months, he was named steward.

Alain taught him the dynamics of a professional kitchen and, when Ryu expressed an interest, the fundamental elements of cookery: flavor profiles and the proper way to use a knife; how to make roux and stock and consommé, the mother sauces. At first, everyone loved him because he came to work with Alain, which is to say, very early, and left with him, which is to say, very late, and each day the chefs and line cooks arrived for their shifts and found their scutwork was already done, the mirepoix and mise-en-place prepared, their stations set up. And though people took notice when Alain promoted him to steward after less than two years, no one grumbled. Stewards were glorified lackeys. No threat at all.

Ryu asked questions of everyone, from the commis to the sous chef, and he took great care to do so in a way that flattered them, and so they shared their secrets and took the time to give precise, thorough answers, and even demonstrated the techniques in question whenever possible, and only Alain and the sous chef realized what was happening.

"Filet up!" Ryu called out, making one last pass with a cloth to ensure the plating wasn't marred by an errant peppercorn before surrendering it. It had been three years since Ryu had been promoted to steward, and a little over one since he was elevated to commis.

Modi, he thought. *Merde. Not even a week removed from the sous chef's warning.*

It was the last entrée of the night, the final of four going to a table of VIPs too famous to turn away despite the fact that the kitchen had been closed for an hour and a half, and the staff was deep into its preparations for the following day. Alain and the sous chef had retired to his office to plan the spring menu; the dishwasher was neck-deep in the pots and pans and plates, and the leftover produce and herbs and spices had been sealed beneath plastic wrap and returned to the refrigerator.

The maître d' sat the party, whereafter the loudest of their number proceeded to summon the sommelier across the restaurant with a flick of his hand and dispatch him to the wine cellar in search of a vintage that didn't exist, while the rest of the men peppered the waiter with off-menu orders. The maître d', having recognized one of the group as a prestigious food critic, hurried for the kitchen, burst through the door, and caught the garde manger in transit, knocking him into the chef de tournant and sending both men careening into a kneeling prep cook. The garde manger landed hard on his face, knocking two teeth from his mouth, while the chef de tournant lurched into the friturier, who braced himself against a burner that had yet to cool, filling the kitchen with the sound of sizzling flesh and a vapor of burnt hair and char while the unmaimed prep cook stood blinking, and the oysters Rockefeller, the petite filet with gorgonzola and porcini mushroom sauce, the seared duck foie gras slices over Black truffle couscous, and the five-spice grilled Cornish hen with Mongolian barbecue sauce remained unrealized.

Without meaning to, Ryu began calling out orders, directed the rotisseur to fire up a filet and repurpose his pan peppercorn sauce on the fly to approximate the gorgonzola and porcini sauce, told the poissonier to throw the oysters Rockefeller together, the saucier to concoct the Mongolian barbecue using the plum sauce he'd been serving over lamb, and adding cayenne, garlic, and ginger, while the boucher found the pheasant that would have to stand in for Cornish hen, which Ryu pan-seared and passed to the grillardin before starting on the foie gras, au torchon, molding a lobe in a towel and searing it over a fire of sarments before slow-cooking it in a bain-marie and plating it atop a Black truffle couscous.

The food was out and tabled before anyone realized what had happened. Five minutes passed, ten, fifteen; the maître d' stood helplessly and the sommelier peered at the table from behind an art deco screen, while the waiter watched behind the door to the kitchen.

Apprised of the situation, Alain and the sous chef joined the kitchen, and when the inevitable call came, it was Alain who went out to face the table.

He was inscrutable as he walked back to the kitchen.

"That was Auguste Gusteau," he said upon returning.

"From Elle à Table?"

Alain nodded.

"He ordered the foie gras."

"I'm going to kill that—" the potager muttered, but Alain looked up, eyes bright, cutting him off.

"He loved it! He called it a revelation!"

The kitchen erupted, thrilled to a man, even those who resented Ryu's presumption, elated for the restaurant's good fortune and the gravitas its standing would lend to their resume when they moved on. Soon they were passing bottles of champagne back and forth, popping off volleys of toasts and corks.

Knowing Alain couldn't, the sous chef went looking for Ryu, and found him in the alley, smoking.

Alain waited for some time before going out to Ryu, needing his kitchen to see him touting their victory, to know that, above all, he was their executive chef, that even if he was Ryu's lover outside the restaurant, inside, he looked after his kitchen, after everyone that was a part of it. After Ryu, yes, but no more than any other member.

Finally, he was able to break free.

"René said you were out here."

He spoke from the doorjamb so as not to intrude, halfway in and halfway out, so he could stay or go as Ryu wanted.

"Aren't you even going to ask about the food?"

"What food?"

"Now you're just trying to piss me off."

"You're talking about that last party? I assume their food was fine or you or they would have reamed me out by now."

"Were you aware that one of the men in the party was Auguste Gusteau?"

"Karl said something like that."

"But you took it upon yourself to cook his meal anyway? Rather than getting me or René?"

"I didn't take it upon myself, I just did it—I didn't even think. We were there, and the orders were there, and no one was moving, so I did."

"Don't you want to know what they said? They called me out to the table."

"Oh?"

"They said the food was marvelous, a revelation! Your cooking!"

Ryu smiled. "I had a good teacher."

"Have a good teacher."

"Yes, yes. There is no end to the wisdom you can bestow upon me."

"Doesn't that make you happy—alive?"

"I generally feel alive."

"But—"

"It's what I expected, Alain, that's all. It makes me very happy—for you, for me, for the restaurant—but I never imagined it any other way."

"That's—"

"What? You're an amazing chef, an artist, and a brilliant teacher. And we have put in so many hours, so much blood—did you really think it would it be any different?"

"You don't seem happy."

"I don't mean to be unhappy."

"Good. Because I cannot have an unhappy chef de partie in my kitchen. Your sorrow would ruin the food."

"Chef de partie? But I'm only twenty," Ryu protested.

"I don't give a damn how old you are."

"I've never been to culinary school."

"Neither have I."

"But—"

"Assez! Cette conversation est terminée! La nourriture décide: tu es mieux que tout le monde dans cette cuisine, de sorte que tu es le nouveau chef de partie, si tu veux que le travail ou pas!"

La nourriture décide.

The food decides.

Alain stepped into mystique and danger and art and sex as others did into fresh clothes—that was another difference between him and Ryu: Alain had killed Angus Duff in order to clear space for Alain-Laurent Alkan and the attention, fame, and fortune that were always going to be his, but Ryuken Nakahara was born into mystique, into exoticism: the narrow eyes, soaring cheekbones, and the thick hair that came by way of his Japanese father; the bottomless complexion—honey and copper—and height bequeathed to him by a mother who was half-Haitian and half-Dominican and had burned brilliant and wild and hotter than the sun unto the very moment she was snuffed out.

Only the gods knew where he got his eyes, which phased between waterfall gray and sapphire blue according to his mood.

He couldn't remember a time when people hadn't stared at him, even before he turned sixteen and his muscles began to swell and his jawline thrust itself into a composite of angular lines, and the eyes that set upon him became pregnant with hunger and began to cut like teeth.

Had Alain groomed him as people said when he wasn't around? They called him a Derek and a chickenhawk and a manther, and sometimes he wondered if it were true.

Groomed him.

As if he were a poodle.

Not much got to him, but that did. Screw them. How many of them could have survived as he had?

And it was never like that. Ryu knew that, despite his doubts.

Alain had never tried to be his father or his lover, or to coerce him in any way.

Ryu had made the decision.

He'd been nineteen; Alain, forty-five.

It was the year the restaurant was awarded its third star, but three or four months afterward.

Alain had been distracted for weeks, poring over the menus by Adria, Redzepi, Achatz, Ducasse, Blumenthal, Atala, Dominque Crenn, Marcus Samuelson, and others, flailing for inspiration, groping for the new, silent except for when they went on their walks, schizophrenic perambulations that unfurled over miles according to an indiscernible logic, vacillating in pace between a manic near-run and an excruciating shuffle, words and gestures coming in torrents or not at all.

"La nourriture est l'existence, Ryu, existence. Sight and smell and touch and taste—it consumes them all, tout! Every last one of them."

Ryu listened without comment.

"It is so much more...to experience food is not merely a matter of the tongue detecting ingredients—it isn't reducible even to the web of relations between the ingredients, or the play of taste, temperature, and texture. It involves all these things, yes, but most of all it is the imagery and horizons that arise within the one who eats—always new, toujours brillant, toujours unique! Ce qui ne peut être dit émerge—éclate—the unprecedented, and suddenly something new exists, and new possibilities..."

Alain trailed off, looked at Ryu, blushed, and broke eye contact.

"I'm babbling," he said.

Ryu smiled. "I like it."

"Really?"

He nodded. "It's the best you."

"Mais de quoi parles-tu, pour l'amour du ciel?"

"It's the part of you that I love the most."

Alain stopped walking. "Tu aimes? Moi?"

Ryu met his eye, threaded his fingers through Alain's, nodded. "Oui."

They walked on in silence until they reached the East River.

"You were saying?"

Alain frowned, scrutinizing his face. "I can't tell if you're teasing."

Ryu shook his head. "I'm not."

Alain hesitated, turned away, and looked out over the river.

"I'm not teasing you."

"It's just that it's so much like us, tant que le monde. We die and become ash, and one day our sun will exhaust itself and the planet will turn to ice and everything and everyone else will die, too." He shrugged. "Même le plat le plus exquis se tourne vers la merde."

"That's beautiful."

"But it does, right? No matter what we eat, it turns to shit."

"Poetry."

"But that's how it is: always the same. Only the way we view it changes, the things we look at and for and do and eat, how we relate to them, consider them, prepare them, and consume them—maybe it's only those changes that matter. Life will destroy us, one day, but in the meantime—in the everyday—it can transform us."

"Indeed."

"Our lives...ludicrously inconsequential. We are born and live and die a short time later, and we lose everything we worked so hard to attain. Tous. Our part in the world is nothing if not for cookery—for food, drink, cuisine. Mais la nourriture existe—we have only to eat, to cook, to serve—pour engager le monde dans lequel nous, nous trouvons—to become beautiful, to partake of immortality."

"No one but ourselves can deny us this, if only we are willing to reach up."

"I'm going to kiss you now."

"Baiser? Moi? Qui?"

Ryu kissed him, and it was a good kiss, long and hard and gentle.

Words came hard for Ryu, and sometimes not at all, but easily for Alain, and sometimes Ryu thought it was because his cradle had been so crowded: Japanese and English from his father, Spanish from both parents, French and Haitian Creole from his mother.

He thought that it might be easier if he only had one or two of them to sift through.

But what did it matter?

He was what he was, had what he had.

Ryu recalled another one of Alain's Milosz poems went something like, *You see how hard I try to reach words, to say what matters most, and how I always fail.*

That was how it was for Ryu. It wasn't just poetry that eluded him—he had so much he wanted to say that it felt like there was something swelling in his chest, pressing hard into his heart and lungs so that it hurt to exist.

And it seemed like so little to ask—he wasn't trying to be poetic or profound, only to say the things he knew Alain wanted him to say, to share conversations and thoughts and feelings, and express what cooking meant to him, and explain why—Alain had never asked the question, but it was never more than a soft moment or bottle of wine from his eyes—to explain why Ryu was with him, an old man, as Alain described himself, with thinning hair and dark bags under his eyes accentuated by his pasty-white complexion.

Part of why he liked spending time with Chris was that Chris didn't seem to want anything from him but his company, companionable silence.

He never once made Ryu feel as though all that he was interested in was Ryu's body, or having a Black friend, an exotic prop that might increase his own social currency.

Alain had never done any of those things either, but somehow other people's shit injected itself into their life together.

It wasn't a comparison so much as a point of fact; Ryu relaxed around Chris, at ease in a way he hadn't been since his father died and his mother took her life.

Nonetheless, he loved Alain.

That's why he struggled to understand why Chris had become a thing between them, even as he knew that it was because Alain sensed the ease he and Chris enjoyed, and felt hurt and insecure and guilty, and Ryu, because he couldn't find the words he needed, said nothing.

Ryu was planning a surprise party for Alain's fiftieth in April, and since a man of Alain's standing had certain obligations, there would be people in attendance who would spit at him with their eyes, people who would condemn and denigrate and sneer at them even on the night of their joy, and Ryu would have no choice but to deal with it.

He could handle it. It would be easier if Chris were there, but he could handle it.

An image of Chris being lashed with a lamp cord burst into his mind, a cloud of blood and jagged flesh.

He braced himself against the wall until it passed.

How was he supposed to explain to Alain that he was terrified, terrified that he needed Chris in his life, and terrified that, having watched his movie, he might not be able to even look at Chris ever again?

He concentrated on his breathing until the pain passed: in, 2, 3, 4; out, 2, 3, 4.

Alain would be home soon.

Ryu decided he would test the waters one more time before he sent the invitations.

"You still think I slept with him, don't you?" Ryu asked.

"No."

Ryu looked up. "Really?"

"Forgive an old man his petty jealousy?"

Ryu made himself smile. "You are pretty old."

Alain barked a laugh. "Little snot."

"So, you're really over it?"

"Over what?"

"Your obsession with Chris."

"I wasn't obsessed."

Ryu raised an eyebrow.

"Fine. I was obsessed. Are you happy now?"

"He's just a friend. Nothing more. But I need you to be okay with our friendship."

"I thought he'd gone back to California?"

"So, you're not okay with it?"

"I'm fine with it."

"Good. Now come here and let me give you something else to be fine with."

A pipe had burst at the restaurant the night before, forcing its temporary closure. The temperature had fallen below zero and remained there for more than a week, and pipes in older buildings were bursting all across the city.

Ryu and Alain would have all day together, lounge in terrycloth robes, read, and sip espresso. Alain would put on his reading glasses to do the crossword in the *Times*, and Ryu would make fun of him, and then they'd bake madeleines and brioche, and the arctic weather beyond their walls would give them an excuse to drink mulled wine from morning till evening.

They'd eat fresh bread and cheese for lunch and dinner, apple slices and grapes and jamón serrano. They'd listen to Alain's old records, Billie Holiday and Ella Fitzgerald, Bessie Smith and Sippie Wallace.

And then they'd step into the shower together, and Ryu would feel Alain's stubble against his neck and cheek as Alain bit him, and Alain would inhale deeply as his nose pressed into the nape of Ryu's neck, and muscles would tense and hearts pound as they became tumescent, and their difference receded into the external world.

THE GIGGLE HOUSE

You want to know how to become Mr. White?

Let's start with his voice. Mr. White is one observant motherfucker—he noticed wypipo don't talk so much as squeak in belligerently alpine octaves. So while the unenlightened niggas all 'bout that bass, we going to take a page outta our boy Jaleel's playbook and make some modifications to our, um, sound system. See, when wypipo see Jaleel's Black-ass skin and start to get all twitchy, all he has to do is open his mouth, and the wypipo hear that reassuring, glass-shattering squeal and think, "Oh, thank goodness! I thought he was Black there for a second!"

OFFICER REILLY

Conversation died whenever Reilly entered a room. His colleagues developed a keen interest in their paper-work, in their fingernails.

At home, he sat on his couch, his self-regard insufficient even to power him to self-medicate with booze or pills or mindless television.

Reilly had been sent to grief counseling with the police psychiatrist after his son overdosed, was pulled off the street and deprived of his weapon at the psychiatrist's behest after his wife took her own life less than three months after their son's death.

He spoke no more than a few hundred words in the entirety of the following year, lost nearly thirty pounds, forgot to eat, mostly, and almost never slept.

Eventually, the psychiatrist recommended he remain a desk officer indefinitely. Reilly didn't protest, bore no resentment. He took up his post and did his job, and at home, and in bathrooms stalls, and alone in the break room his tears became seasons: a winter of ice-sharp pain yielded to spring and gales of rage, a deluge and churning whitecap river of grief that overflowed its banks and drowned and destroyed all but everything, only to see what did survive burn beneath summer's heat as his heart withered in his chest and everything lush and soft desiccated in a sun-scorched silence.

A woman came to the station to press charges against her rapist, and Reilly processed her paperwork and directed her to the psychiatrist that had benched him, failing to register the victim's humanity and trauma as he writhed beneath iron and stone and self-recrimination: shit father, worse husband.

His son dead, a junkie, overdosed. His wife, a suicide.

The woman returned, and Reilly's wife and son were still dead. Then she came again, and again.

And now she was back once more, twice raped, thrice battered. Bridget O'Hara, legal name, William O'Hara.

She was walking gingerly, leaning on a cane, guarding her stomach with her arm.

A charge of emotion detonated in his chest, staggering him; he'd already seen her once this month. This time a beating, from the looks of things.

Last time she'd been knifed.

He passed her the forms she needed and asked if she wanted a chair, and she shook her head and handed him a copy of her discharge papers from the hospital and a sheet of paper with her statement, signed 'William Arthur O'Hara,' because the police reports she tried to file under the name Bridget O'Hara were rejected.

Another wave of emotion: a lance of pain that buckled his legs and thrust him forward against the countertop.

There was no reason he should be as familiar with Ms. O'Hara as he was. The precinct had implemented a new policy concerning victims' statements; as part of a statewide effort to encourage law enforcement officers to be more conscientious in their handling of victims, the precinct now sent two uniforms to the victims' places of residence to take their statements in the privacy and safety of their homes. Victims of violent crimes had priority, so the precinct would have sent someone to Bridget's place if she had been agreeable, thus sparing her the travel to and from the station and precluding the contact that resulted in their familiarity with one another.

But she wasn't agreeable, so here she stood.

Reilly didn't mind speaking with her, or taking statements, or writing up reports. Most within the precinct considered desk duty a dumping ground for incompetent police and therefore hated and avoided it, but he was indifferent. He noted that he was exempt from the stigma imparted by being placed on modified duty, and he understood that the exemption meant no one considered him real police anymore, because when real police got put on modified duty they took shit from everyone until they got their piece back.

Hey, Tommy No-Gun, the other cops would say. Hey, limp dick.

But no one knew how to be around Reilly, or what, if anything, to say to him; he didn't deserve punishment, because he hadn't done anything wrong, hadn't screwed up, and collegial ragging was out of the question as what had happened, happened outside the context of the police, and was irreversible.

Dead was dead.

And Reilly was hollow, or rather he aspired to hollow, hoped for it, but was instead choked with pain. It registered in some shuttered-up recess of his mind that Bridget might be struggling similarly, but also that she was merely another luckless mope in the inexorable parade of the brutalized, another pilgrim in the land of pain. The report he filed would go unread, as so many others had, would be followed by another, and then another, and another until finally, the fact of Bridget O'Hara's existence—William Arthur O'Hara's—ceased to matter.

Reilly's relation to his colleagues was equally diaphanous: if the execution of his duties or his colleagues' execution of theirs required that they interact, all involved took pains to conclude their business as quickly as possible and with the greatest economy of words; they made sure there was a partition between them, a cubicle or coffee pot or water-cooler, a refrigerator door, and if no such object could be had, they stood perpendicular to each other with their hands deep in their pockets or wrapped around their chest like a shield, assiduously avoiding eye-contact as they shifted uncomfortably from foot to foot.

And it was fine. None of it bothered him. His coworkers avoided him, and he kept to himself, and after work, he went home and sat on the couch and forgot to eat or picked at a TV dinner, never feeling sorry for himself or lamenting the cruelties of fate or hoping that any particular fact or circumstance would change. He was a world unto himself, hermetic: he had no friends and no family and missed no one and longed for nothing.

And now this—this hobbled, ungainly woman.

Suddenly this.

A feeling, or perhaps feelings: sorrow with a tincture of compassion and another of loss. That, and the broken creature standing in front of him with his heart in her fist. She, a victim made to sign the receipt for her victimhood in a name no longer—if ever it was—hers, forced to do so by the poverty that prevented her from taking a day off work to go to the courthouse and wait in the necessary lines and pay the necessary fees in order to legally change her name to *her name*. And forced, also, by people like him and their need for the power of absolute specification and an impregnable fortress of certitude from which to rule the world.

Reilly had felt the familiar contortions of revulsion when he first met Bridget, felt them deep in his flesh and muscle, in his organs and the marrow of his bones. He saw the earliest bristles of her five o'clock shadow and recoiled at their incongruity with the makeup she wore, and the dress and heels and pearls.

And now?

"Are you alright?" Bridget asked.

He couldn't speak, so he just nodded.

She forced a tight smile.

She had his son's face, somehow, sleek and fine and with none of the aggressive lines and angles of Reilly's. He hadn't understood his son any more than he understood this woman or why her presence sent spasms of pain ripping through his body.

His son had been goth for a while, eyeliner and makeup and spiked collars, had gone vegetarian, and then vegan. He'd done steampunk and Larping, and announced he was bisexual, and Reilly had tried to remain calm through it all. He'd sighed in relief when his son joined a band.

Music. Music was a step toward normal.

He'd bought his son a guitar and an amp, and off he'd gone, and eventually Reilly was invited to the band's first gig, and that was where he learned of the existence of a type of music called death metal, and a year later, having been invited to his son's second band's first show, that there was such a thing as noise music, and he hadn't known what to say to his son afterward, only that he felt entirely cut off from him, as if they didn't have a language in common.

And in the end, it was the music that killed him, the very thing Reilly had thought a lifeline.

He did everything he could for Bridget, which wasn't much. He tried to connect, empathize, said I'm really sorry this happened to you, and she said me, too without looking at him, and left. He headed for the subway after work, as he always did, though for the first time in a long while, he stopped and bought a coffee and an éclair from a vendor, and the day's paper from a newsstand. He walked down the stairs and through a turnstile just in time to catch his train.

The warning chimed and the doors closed, and Reilly fell into a reverie as the train picked up speed. Ten minutes later the PA system announced his stop, and he shook himself awake, stood up, and left. A cleaving wind cut across his face as he emerged from the subway station and into the open air; winter had the city by the throat, and his fingers curled hard around his coffee cup. He opened the tab, took a sip, and scalded himself.

He wondered if his son had really looked anything like Bridget, but was still undecided when he reached his brownstone, unlocked the door, and stepped into the relative warmth of his house. The heat was set at fifty-eight degrees, and he couldn't remember if he'd put it there, or if his wife had done it before she died.

Reilly hung up his coat, walked past the couch into the kitchen, took his éclair out of its paper bag and a plate from the cabinet, and set the one atop the other on the kitchen table, and his coffee beside them, and spread the paper out in front of him. He had read *The Times* back when he got a daily paper, but all the newsstand had left at the end of the day was *The Post*, which was fine.

The pictures of the Fairchild boy were on page three, stills from the movie blown up large enough to see the viscera in all their horrid detail. In one of them, you could see his hair in snarls, matted with clots of blood. His head was bent forward like an altar boy or a saint at prayer, but a smile played on his lips, fit for Lugh, the trickster god so often the hero of his grandfather's bedtime stories.

Reilly held the newspaper straight out, turned it left and right, looked and looked: his son...Bridget...Fairchild... the quarter-life he was living...

Reilly stared harder and harder and harder still, straining to pierce the darkness. The picture began to swim, and this time it was not vertigo, nothing like the surges of emotion that staggered him at the precinct, but tears that were not yet ready to fall, and as the tears bled one into the next, so too did all the things he saw or thought he saw in the Fairchild boy, and in Bridget, and in his son. And they didn't just mix, but churned, and rut, and everything was destroyed.

Every certainty.

Every detail.

Everything that was once tied to a person or memory or emotion was severed and swallowed by the vast expanse of the unknown.

It was all irretrievably lost.

And Reilly wept.

THE GIGGLE HOUSE

Now, gentlemen, you're not going to like this, but the way to turn your bass into a treble like Mr. White is to take your balls in your hand, lift, squeeze, and twist.

I recommend doing it in the car just before you get out, or hurrying into a bathroom as soon as you find yourself engulfed by white people, because each lift, squeeze, and twist only gives you about twenty minutes of bass-less existence.

You'll need to experiment some in order to find the altitude, pressure, and severity of rotation that works for you, and if you do it too hard or too many times it's likely to make you sterile, but, shit, if sterile is the cost of living, that's a price you best be willing to pay. You can always adopt.

Plenty of nigga children to go around.

MARY

A pelican's a funny-looking animal if ever there was one. Mary Williams liked to watch them dive for fish; she'd sit on her back porch in a sunhat with a glass of sweet tea, reading or staring out at the water, watching greater yellowlegs and black skimmers and seagulls. She never thought she'd leave New York, not once in the fifty-five years she'd called it home. She'd arrived at seventeen, a refugee from the Mississippi Delta, over the moon for the man she loved. They'd started with nothing but each other. Ronald took what work he could find, and she cleaned whatever people would pay her to clean; they'd lived on the cheap and gone out dancing every night.

She might have been a fool in love like her Momma and Daddy said, but even so, she'd been a fool in love with the same man for more than fifty years and hadn't stopped loving him even after his heart attack, although his death made it harder.

Ronald was a carpenter, so they'd never had much, and being a negro didn't help any, but they got by. There was never any question of them starving, which was more than some could say, and though he'd been self-employed and didn't leave her a pension, she had social security, and they had been sensible their whole lives long, and set aside a quarter of their income for savings, which Ronald invested.

Mary shifted in her chair, looked at her watch; the women's choir had rehearsal at six, but it was only three-thirty.

She could have stayed in New York if she'd wanted. Her budget wouldn't have had much fat to it, but she would have been happy. She loved Hamilton Heights, and her friends, and the little townhome she lived in, and her daily walks.

They'd been lucky, started on a rent-to-own agreement against their better judgment, shaking hands with an old white woman who promised them she'd see the deal all the way through, and kept her word. All bets are off if I die, though, she'd warned, no telling what my son will do.

It was her next-door neighbors that put Mary on to the idea. They were moving to Florida; some real estate developer had offered to make them millionaires if they'd sell.

Millionaires?

They'd given her the man's card before they said their goodbyes. It took her a few days, but she called, dropped the phone when the man made his offer, the plastic cover shattering and the batteries bouncing end over end across the kitchen floor.

$1.2 million.

Where did you even start?

But there it was.

And now here she was, Cape Coral, and though the sun was always shining, and she had the oceanfront cottage she'd allowed herself to fantasize about off and on for as long as she could remember, she knew she couldn't have left New York any other time than when she did, in February, with the city buried beneath eighteen inches of snow. Any other time and Ronald's gardens would be in bloom. Spring: an eruption of soft pastels gilded in lush green, the air pungent and heady; summer: bold colors shimmering in the heat, giant sunflowers stretching skyward. Autumn was her favorite. Asters and Toad lilies and Russian sage; Colchicum, Helenium, and Sedum.

Ronald built the gardens after Ronald Jr. died, in the weeks and months when they couldn't even look at each other and Ronald was so ashamed of himself that Mary hid the gun they kept and the kitchen knives and extension cords, and turned the house and garage inside out looking for any rope he might have tucked away somewhere.

Ronald had only ever done what he thought was right. He'd been over to see the Reverend at least a dozen times before he'd made Ronnie move out, had prayed and prayed and prayed.

That was the difference between men and women, Mary knew, or one of them, anyway. A man would do the right thing even if it was wrong, would do it just because it was the right thing, even if it felt wrong in every fiber of his body. A woman knew, though. Knew that not every right thing had to be done, that not every right thing was right—that there were things more important than rules, more important than the law, even God's law.

Of course, Reverend Carter couldn't say that, being both a man and a man of God. Rachel would have set him right straightaway—Lord Almighty, she was a remarkable woman—but she'd been gone twenty years by then.

Reverend never did stop missing that woman.

No one did.

Ronald had tears in his eyes as he turned Ronnie out, and that was what made it all so hard. Mary couldn't be mad at her husband—how could she when he never yelled or screamed or said anything to make Ronnie feel bad other than quoting the scripture: *Thou shalt not lie with mankind, as with womankind: it is abomination.*

How could she when he'd given Ronnie his own suitcase, the only thing that his father had ever given to him other than carpentry know-how?

Ronald had held the door for Ronnie as he carried the suitcase out of the house and given him money when he thought his wife wasn't looking. He gave up his two packs a day and sold his truck, and all of it went to Ronnie.

Their daughter, Leah, had stopped talking to them after Ronald made Ronnie leave, and didn't start again until Ronnie told her he saw his parents every week at church, and that they always took him out for a meal afterward.

Mary and Leah and Ronnie had even been able to laugh about it, after a time. They joked that they'd spent more time together since Ronald "booted him out," and Ronnie would laugh, open-mouthed, his brilliant white teeth gleaming as if they were their own source of light.

But they never joked in front of Ronald, at least not about that. He didn't laugh much anymore, only gave his son every spare cent he came across, and hugs that squeezed the air from their lungs.

It broke her heart. It broke all their hearts watching Ronald crush his son in his arms, Mary and Leah shifting their weight from leg to leg and averting their eyes as tears fell from Ronald's eyes and the hug went on and on because he didn't want Ronnie to see that he was crying.

Mary didn't understand her son's lifestyle, but Leah told her it wasn't a choice, and that she didn't need to understand anything in order to love Ronnie—and how, she asked, was being gay any harder to understand than kicking your son out of your home when it was clear you had no desire to have him gone?

Mary couldn't argue with that. Ronald barely ate anymore, had lost almost forty pounds.

And then Ronnie was dead.

They knew now it was AIDS that took him, but not then.

Then was the early eighties, when plagues and pestilence were safely contained within scripture and other books to which few people really paid any mind.

Ronnie's death...they couldn't believe it, and then...

The sorrow...

Wrapping itself around them so tightly...

Cold and wet and aching...

So many what-ifs...

Would he have died if...

Mary had gone to see Reverend Carter, fired to a white-hot rage, tore into and slapped him so hard his face rose in a blazing wheal and her hand throbbed. She said things no man deserved to hear, even if they were true, and was so incensed by the shame on the Reverend's face she hit him a second time and a third until his face was that of a brawler.

That was the last time she ever laid eyes on the Reverend, the last time she ever set foot in his church.

Her son was gone, and now her church, too, another trowel of gut scraped out and thrown away, her heart growing more and more tired, day by day, brittle.

But she couldn't make herself go back.

She couldn't.

Mary looked out over the gulf, watched a man tear across the water and two or three dolphins keep pace. She was wearing the pearl earrings Ronald gave her on their twenty-fifth anniversary, and the matching necklace, touched them gently. They'd had dinner at a fancy French bistro, and he'd given them to her while they waited for their dessert. Afterward, they'd gone in a horse-drawn carriage, and she couldn't stop touching them, couldn't believe they were there. They went home and he kissed her, slowly unzipped her dress. They were only in the kitchen, but she let him, taking tiny steps backward toward their bedroom and tugging at his belt as he removed her undergarments. She was going to take her pearls off, too, but then they were in the bedroom and he was inside her and...

Mary felt herself flush and a bead of perspiration blossom at the nape of her neck, which fell over her shoulder and down along her spine, landing in the swell at the small of her back.

She shivered.

The man on the jet ski was alone now.

Alone.

She'd only just heard that Reverend Carter had died, and she'd been relieved to find she felt only sorrow, sorrow that he no longer existed, and at the bitter loss suffered by all those who loved and relied upon him.

He'd been a good man, just like her husband. Better than most. A man who only ever meant well, even if he'd done harm on occasion.

Men and their folly, she thought. Their pride.

Leah had stopped speaking to her father again after her brother's death, and twenty years passed between them in silence.

Ronald died in early spring, a week before he and Mary were to plant their dahlias. And though her son and husband were dead, and her daughter had refused to attend her father's funeral, there was a smile beneath Mary's tears as her husband was lowered into the ground.

Like a seed, she thought.

Like a seed.

Their gardens were the greatest of the many miracles of her life. She'd been angry as she watched Ronald build them; how frivolous, she thought, terraces and the loud, garish flowers. How could he do that? How could he betray their son again?

The only flowers he should have been planting were black ones with black stems and black leaves.

But then...he hammered the nails as if they had made Ronnie leave, as if they had failed to convince his daughter to forgive him, as if they were AIDS itself, and death, and human frailty, and he was taking vengeance on them all. And when the last plank was in place, and he'd poured the soil, he wasn't angry anymore, not even at himself. They'd planted the seeds together. He'd bought two watering cans, and they'd carried them up the terrace steps, day after day, and poured them out on the garden, the bulbs and seedlings and flowers, and since they'd wept so much after Ronnie's death that they'd run dry of tears, this was the first time they'd been able to cry together in a long while. And they poured can after can of tears into the ground and brought agony to good in the bloom and blossom of the tulips and roses and lilies and chrysanthemums and pansies and crocuses that became the body of their son. And as their son grew before them, they said the things they should have said when he was alive, separately at first, and then together. And Mary saw Ronald turning and fertilizing the soil, and knew that it was his way of teaching and giving Ronnie everything he had meant to teach and give him in life. And when Ronald deadheaded the heavyweight wisteria hanging from the archway, he always lifted a handful of blossoms to his nose to inhale their sweetness and to speak to them, and Mary knew he was giving them messages that he hoped the bees and butterflies that lit upon them would carry to his children. And seeing this, Mary's happiness was restored because all she had ever really wanted from the time she brought her children into the world was for her and Ronald to love them, and to be loved by them.

The developer was going to raze the gardens along with the house.

But it was okay, because the gardens had done more for her than she could have asked or imagined. And though as she lay down for her last night's sleep in the townhome, a part of her hoped she would slip away in her sleep and be spared boarding the plane that would carry her away from the city in which she'd lived and loved and wept and dreamed for over half a century, while the larger part of her wanted to live and get on that plane because her daughter lived in Florida, and Mary knew that life had not been kind to Leah. She knew that the man Leah had married had gambled and cheated and spent every penny they'd had, and left her choking on debt. Mary knew that in addition to teaching fifth grade, Leah waitressed evenings and cleaned houses on weekends just to keep the creditors at bay. But not for long. Mary was going to take care of all that with the money from Ronald's investments, with the money she made selling their home. She'd pay off her daughter's debts and tell her to take early retirement, because her Daddy—the man who'd been so imperfect and so deeply flawed, who'd messed up so bad with Ronnie and hurt Leah so much—had come through. Yes, he'd done wrong, but he had always loved her and her mother and her brother, and spent his life working and planning to make their lives as good as he could, and by God, he'd done it. He'd made them millionaires.

He'd made it so they could live easy.

So Mary had packed what needed packing, and thrown out and given away the things that needed throwing out and giving away, and she had gotten on that plane with her heart at peace.

Mary looked at her watch again: four-fifteen. Leah sang in the choir, too, had a voice like Ella Fitzgerald, if one would indulge a proud mother. They'd go out for dinner afterward, a nice restaurant with an ocean view.

Leah was working her way back, laughing more, looking less skeletal.

Mary smiled.

The last thing she'd done before she'd gone to bed on her last night in New York, other than brushing her teeth, was to seal the envelope she'd addressed to William Fairchild c/o Prosperitatis Absque Limitatione Eligi. She'd read about what his son had done in the paper, and given how important a man Fairchild was, and how awful the thing was that Christopher had done, she'd figured that Fairchild would be furious, and was probably thinking about laying down the law for his son. She wrote and told him her story, hers and Ronald's and Ronnie's and Leah's. She said she was just a simple woman without great understanding, but that she knew for a fact her husband had spent every minute of his life from the time he put Ronnie out of the house until his own death wishing that he could undo what he'd done.

Love is what matters, she'd told Fairchild, hokey as it sounds. If you don't have it, you don't have anything. And if you do have it, then you can overcome anything.

THE GIGGLE HOUSE

Now, as for Mr. White's style, there's so much to say, and so little time, so in the last few minutes we'll move on to the importance of ninja to surviving Black.

Ninja is all about the power of invisibility.

If we're going to survive Black, then we need to master the art of disguise and misdirection like the ninja did. They had their tools, and we have ours.

Ninjas dressed themselves as civilians to mask their presence.

We dress ourselves as wypipo.

CERA

—Let me kiss you, for your love is more delightful than wine.

—Of which you've had quite a lot.

—You smell so good.

—Aftershave.

—Take me to bed.

—Right this way. Watch the step.

—Do you think I'm beautiful?

—What kind of a question is that?

—I don't mind being Black—I'm proud of it—I just wish I wasn't Black, Black. Everyone stares at me.

—They stare at you because you're beautiful.

—You're just trying to get laid.

—Lights on or off?

—I'm just teasing.

—Let me help you with that zipper.

—Someone's in a hurry.

—Waste not, want not.

—Mmm, you taste like cinnamon.

—Altoids.

—I love it when you do that.

—I love doing it.

—I didn't know I was so tense. Up a little, right an inch—yes, there, right there.

—Your shoulders, oh most beautiful of women, are taut as steel.

Can I take your necklace off? Earrings?

—Please.

—Now where were we?

—Would you still find me attractive if I were white?

—What?

—Would you still be with me?

—How much did you have to drink?

—Lots.

—We don't have to do this.

—I know.

—Let me get you an aspirin and some water.

—Make love to me.

—Are you sure?

—But first tell me if you'd still love me if I were white.

—That's not even a real question.

—Yes it is. I'm asking it.

—It's like asking me if I'd like beef if it tasted like chicken.

—What?

—Beef tastes like beef, and you eat it because you like the way it tastes; if it started tasting like something else it wouldn't be beef.

—So, no.

—I didn't say that.

—No, you said I was a steak. Or a chicken. I can't remember which.

—Now you're just being ridiculous. I love every aspect of—well, most aspects of—

—Hey!

—You are what and who you are, and I can't imagine you any other way.

—So being Black...

—Is a part of you.

—A necessary part?

—Where is all this coming from?

—I don't know...let's just make love—better yet, let's fuck. Maybe a good fucking is what I need to clear my head.

—Now I know you're not okay.

—What? Men can swear, and women can't? Fuck that, I can talk however I want to.

—No one's disputing that.

—I know. It's just—can you please just make love to me? I don't want to talk anymore.

—Okay. I didn't mean to press.

—I know. Sorry. I'm just...I had more wine than I meant to.

—It happens.

—Kiss me.

—Of course.

—You love me.

—I do.

—I know you do. I don't know why I'm asking.

—You're drunk.

—No, it's not just that.

—Okay.

—I want you inside me.

—I—

—Now. I want to be close.

—Me, too.

—One of the partners said you had jungle fever.

—What? Which one? They said that to you?

—Doesn't matter, and no, I overheard him.

—But—

—No. Sit up and pull me to your chest. Now slow.

—Are you sure you—

—Very sure. Shush.

—I love you, Cera.

—She's gone white guy crazy, he's gone Black girl hazy, they got jungle fever...

—Stop it! You know that's not fair!

—Tell me it's not true.

—We've been together three years—I shouldn't have—

—Don't you dare pull out. Please. Look me in the eye and tell me you're not with me because you have some fetish.

—You're way out of line, Cera. You're being nasty and cruel, and I've done nothing to deserve this.

—I know.

—So why...

—Please just say it.

—I do not have jungle fever.

—So the fact that your ex-girlfriends...

—Yes, most of the women I've dated have been Black, but so what? What does it matter?

—I don't know.

—What's going on, Cera?

—I just keep thinking it'll all get clearer.

—What?

—That time will pass, and society will evolve, and eventually it won't be an issue.

—It? You mean us?

—That we'll go to a cocktail party and be able to eat and drink and enjoy each other.

—Don't we already?

—We try.

—I was under the impression that we succeeded.

—I think so sometimes.

—But...

—But then...

—I don't know what to say, Cera.

—What can you say?

—I don't know.

—Me either. I'm not even sure what we're talk—

—Lie back, I want to finish.

—You can't be serious.

—I am.

—Why? You're upset, neither of us is enjoying it. Why not draw yourself a bath, or let me massage your back?

—Because.

—That's not an answer.

—It's all I can give you right now.

—Then let me ask you a question.

—Go.

—Why is our relationship on trial every time some racist asshole shoots his mouth off?

—I need to know we're real—that we're possible.

—I don't—

—Imagine you saw people that look like me fucking over people that look like you, every day, and at every party they called you a slut or a bitch or a cock-hungry whore. After a while you start to wonder, and you look for a reason why they say what they say, but you can't find anything. But they keep saying it, and it gets stuck in your head, and you hear it over and over and over...

—I'm not understanding...

—I think that maybe we are impossible.

—That's absurd.

—Lie back.

—No.

—Lie back.

—I don't want to.

—I do.

—You're scaring me, Cera.

—I need this.

—Sex?

—Us. To know that we can do this. Make it.

—We can.

—You don't know that.

—But I believe it.

—How?

—Because I love you.

—Everyone loves the person they're with, right up until they don't.

—And because you love me too, and you know it.

—I...I do...I do know that.

—The fact of the matter is that it's down to a choice: do we face life together, or alone?

—But is it enough?

—Is what enough?

—Whatever it is we have.

—I want to find out.

—Yeah.

—Don't you?

—I want to fuck.

—Cera...

—No, I finally saw some of that video everyone was talking about, and it's making me horny as fuck.

—That's sick.

—Less talk, more cock.

—But—

—We'll figure it out.
—When.
—Whenever. Now fuck me.

THE GIGGLE HOUSE

Caucasian camouflage, write this down
- One pair boat shoes, leather.
- One pair Nantucket red pants—do not under any circumstance call them carmine, cerise, cranberry, fuschia, pink, or red—it will blow your cover quicker than Wu Tang.
- One Polo shirt, single color, Ralph Lauren or commensurate label, only—no off-brand shit. That will blow your cover quicker than NWA.
- One half-zip fleece.
- One pair sunglasses, preferably Oakley or Ray-Ban.
- One pair Croakies. They look as dumb as they sound, but wypipo love 'em.

Need to take stealth mode to the next level?

Cardigan, Oxford shirt, khakis, and loafers.

Wear that shit and you can jaywalk in front of a cop without getting the baton.

THE WRITER

She went to coffee shops to work, wore headphones without playing any music, and let her mind go, conversation saturating the air around her and sporadically slipping over and around her earbuds in ephemeral currents of clarity. She preferred local, independent coffee shops, but one day she found herself uptown in an unfamiliar part of the city with two and half hours to kill, and she saw a Starbucks and an opportunity to write, so she went in and took a small table near a window. A guy came in with an electric blue Mohawk spiked six or eight inches high and tattoos that twined around his neck like ivy creeping up over his throat, climbing over his jawline and up his face and higher onto his scalp to where his hair would be if he hadn't shaved all of it save for the inch-wide strip. His ears were stretched and gauged, and he had metal posts in each eyebrow and a ring in his nose and another in his septum and one through his lip. He took his place in line, moving closer to her table in increments as customers ordered and paid and the line dwindled, and eventually, for an interval of no more than a minute, he was close enough for her to make out the details of his tattoos: a hoard of writhing demons, horned and fanged and taloned and using their talons to punch through the man's flesh and make handholds of his muscles and tendons as they scaled his body. He wore eyeliner, and his skin was painted an eggshell white, and his nails ore-black, and she shuddered as he passed by.

She'd thought she was a poet right up through the first year of her MFA, but then a story had welled up without warning and spilled out of her and onto paper in a torrent that surged and churned for three feverish weeks, and she'd showed it to a friend, who said that if she didn't take the story to her advisor immediately, that he would, and so she did, unwashed and in sweats that were equally dirty and hallucinating for lack of sleep, and her advisor was so startled by her appearance that he took the story from her quad-shot-trembling hands and started reading it. And then he was talking to her, and though she had no sense of how much time had passed, she knew there was no way he could have finished the story, and she was so out of it that his words seemed wrapped in gauze and unable to fit into her ear, so she had no idea what he was saying, only that he was animated, and he kept on talking and eventually she was able to unwrap the layers of gauze from his words, and she understood that he was advising her to switch programs, to give up poetry for fiction, and to allow him to pass the story on to his friend at the *Atlantic*.

She assented, and he told her to go home and sleep, and put her in a cab himself, paying the driver much more than the trip should cost and telling him to keep the change, and to please not leave until he saw her close the door to her apartment building behind her.

Six weeks later her story appeared.

She was only twenty-four.

It all felt off somehow—not quite wrong, but not right either. She still thought—felt—in verse, though the truth was that she'd been a competent but unremarkable poet, and that even if she would admit it to no one, she agreed with the critic that had said her prose crackled and sparked, was at one and the same time promising and dangerous.

At first, Mohawk exuded a different kind of danger and none of the promise, but then he ordered a skinny decaf vanilla latte with extra whipped cream, paid with a bank card that had a bichon frise on it, and thanked the cashier as she handed him his receipt, which made him at once interesting and banal, and so she wrote a few words about him in the notebook she always carried before turning back to her computer.

Every time she sat down to write she started with poetry, seizing on an image or emotion and circling it again and again until she became entranced and words emerged from some deep, alien place for her to chase, from cocoons or burrows or somewhere else, and she was able to form and fix what she captured into a few lines of verse.

She was nearly there when Mohawk just about trucked her,

narrowly avoiding a full-on collision by throwing his weight sideways at the last moment, missing her, but catching his foot on her chair and spinning her so violently that her elbow slammed into the screen of her laptop and nearly knocked it from the table. Somehow, the latte was preserved.

"S-sorry," he said, picking himself up off the floor. "I didn't see you."

"It's fine."

"No, really, I'm—"

"Got it. You didn't see me. It's okay."

Mohawk fled.

Bicycles and *Wildcat Women* were sticking out of her messenger bag, both of them faded and dog-eared.

I didn't see you.

It was undoubtedly true, a 'Fuck you' carved ever-deeper into her face; into the bone of her forehead; into the pursed iron lips she jammed together to keep from screaming obscenities; into her irises. Fuck you freshly conjured, but aged and fermenting in a cask of individual and collective experience for twenty years and centuries more.

What was the image?

Black surfaces and white surfaces, absorbing light, refracting light.

No.

Assata Shakur.

Watoto wa Jua.

White cannot see Black because the brilliance of our mother's rays churning in our eyes and leaping from our lips and fingertips and charging the molecules of our flesh blinds them.

She felt her ears burn.

Perhaps her susceptibility to fits of ecstatic passion was what made her a marginal poet. Perhaps she was a literary Icarus whose emotions sent her too close to the sun.

Prose allowed her to diffuse her emotion over a greater mass of words.

And what of Mohawk and his metal and tattooed face? Could others see him, or did they run into him and cut in front of him in line and plead blind?

Had he made himself functionally Black?

Was that possible?

More notes in her notebook, the skeleton of a story and a few contours and many questions: Did he know what he'd done? Had he done it on purpose? If he had, why?

She called her friend to say that something had come up and she couldn't go to the party.

She wrote until closing time, and then she went to a nearby pub and took a booth in the back and ordered food and a drink she didn't touch and wrote some more.

It wasn't John Howard Griffin she was after—he had been a tourist, a voyeur. She wanted to raise the stakes, to make it permanent, or if that wasn't possible, to find out why not, and what one might do in the attempt, and how those around him would react to his efforts, and what they might do to prevent his becoming Black or reverse it if ever he managed.

Why a he?

She didn't really know. Not yet.

But she knew that the negotiation between Black and white was about power, and that a society that used women's bodies to sell everything from socks to cars to food, that set up cameras and made women fuck three men at a time and branded them sluts for doing so...

A society that did those things would never accept that a woman could be so powerful as to be capable of remaking herself as something other than what society told her she was.

So she wrote a man.

And since American society was predicated on the assumption that its citizens of color aspired to be white, she wrote a white man who sought to become Black, and set out to discover his motive, and she was still looking for it when the bartender announced last call, because despite what Steve Biko and Huey Newton and Malcolm X and Brother Farrakhan and Tupac and Kanye said, and despite all the Black-talking, culture-raping wiggers she'd met at college, she couldn't quite convince herself that a white man of sound mind would ever want to become Black.

She drank her beer, paid her tab, and asked for a box for her sandwich, which the waiter brought to her, and then she was out the door and heading for the subway, and just as she was walking down the steps to the turnstiles her cell phone chimed, and she saw that her mother had left her a message, and since her train wasn't due in for another seven minutes, she listened to it.

She deleted the message as she boarded her train. She'd watch the movie when she got home, but she was pretty sure she'd found the motive she'd been looking for.

THE GIGGLE HOUSE

Repeat after me:
"Living is easier when you look like the Beaver."
That is the realest shit you will say all day.

YOU

Imagine that you stepped into a pharmacy to refill your medications. There was a line, so you took a seat in the waiting area, which consisted of three chairs, a small coffee table, and a half-dozen magazines. Imagine that you picked a magazine at random and opened it to a page somewhere in the middle and saw your dead husband staring up at you. The industrial bulbs overhead reflected off the magazine pages, burning your eyes, and you squinted and turned and contorted yourself into various awkward positions in an attempt to shield the magazine from the jaundiced light, and when at last you found an angle that enabled you to see clearly, you discovered that there was smaller picture above your husband's, a picture of a bald white man with a ring through his nose like you'd see on a bull, and another piece of metal through his eyebrow, and a third through his lip.

He, you discovered, was a photographer, and your husband's face was among the images to be exhibited in his upcoming show at Gallery X.

Imagine that cancer and grief took your husband three months ago, and your son had died twenty-two months prior.

Imagine you heard the pharmacist call your name, and managed to collect your things, pocket your prescriptions, and pay without incident.

Imagine that you were on the subway before you realized you'd stolen the magazine, tucked it in your purse and left without thinking.

Imagine that you'd never stolen anything your entire life. This is how it was.

She laid the magazine on her kitchen table and sat, reached into her purse for her reading glasses. She'd had excellent sight her whole life, but now she was sixty and needed glasses to see anything up close, even to dial her phone.

She opened the magazine to her husband's picture, smoothed the page flat, set her hands in her lap, and stared. She expected to feel a surge of emotion, but none came, at least not immediately, and when she started to feel, the feelings came like a puddle of milk spilled on a poorly-planed tabletop, not surging or flowing or falling, but dragging themselves a quarter-inch at a time, unable to move forward until the rear had been hauled to the front, and the puddle's collected weight pushed it forward again.

Imagine that, confronted unexpectedly with an image of the man you loved for more than thirty years, you felt neither sorrow for his loss, nor anger at the vicissitudes that stole him away from you. You had buried and mourned and wept over so many you held dear: your son, your mother and father, your sisters and younger brother, your mother-in-law, cousins, friends.

Imagine that all you felt now was rage, and not at something abstract like God or fate, but at the photographer who had stolen your dead husband, reduced him to a face floating at the mouth of a chasm amidst the gloaming. Imagine that your husband's floating face was only barely connected to a head or a body, and that the photographer had been sure to convey that night was descending to finish the job.

Imagine you realized within a breath that the bald, thrice-stuck, goateed photographer whose picture sat above your husband's in that foolish magazine was every bit as abstract as God or fate, and that you only wanted him to be real so you could beat him with your fists and tear at his face with your fingernails.

Her eyes clamped down on the hand the photographer had allowed her husband as if it had some substance or depth she could bore into and unlock. The palm of the hand was turned and out of focus so that the fingers were in profile and stacked, falling in a cascade. Forefinger and thumb held a cigarette to his mouth, and you could tell he'd been inhaling by the flare at the end of the cigarette.

Imagine your husband had been an upright man, a deacon in the same church for more than forty years, a pillar of his community.

Imagine he'd always given God his tithe, no matter how tight the times got, or how lean his family had grown in the absence of food, or how ardently you implored him to do otherwise for his son's sake.

Imagine that the strength of his character and the soundness of his judgment had been like gravity, drawing people to him inexorably, for marriage counsel, direction on raising their children, spiritual wisdom, financial advice.

Imagine that people came to your door for food and money almost every week, and that he never turned a single one of them away, not even the drunks or cheats. And imagine that you sometimes gave him heck when he did so, and that he never once lectured you or scolded you, never once threw scripture at you, because he knew you knew the Bible backwards and forwards, and that you were a mother as well as a Christian, and only trying to protect your son.

Imagine your husband worked three jobs and sixteen-hour days in the hopes that he might make enough so that you didn't have to worry about your son's future, and that he never once missed a Sunday or the Sunday evening social at the church, even though he was exhausted and Sunday was his only day off.

Imagine that smoking had been his only vice, that you'd never once seen him take a drink or curse or gamble or run around. That the man you loved and at whose side you had stood for more than thirty years, in times of trial and privation, and in times of tranquility and joy, had been beyond reproach in every other way. That he'd been a devout man, a steadfast and loving father, and a devoted husband.

Now imagine, because of some narcissistic photographer, the last image people would see of your husband—and for most of the world, the only image they'd ever see—was of a gaunt, jaundiced, unshaven man smoking, a man who looked twenty years older than he was, a man who looked like he'd lived hard and godless and was paying for it.

Imagine the feelings had risen from somewhere deep inside you, risen in coils of wet rope that wrapped themselves around your lungs and throat and skull and eyes, and that they were tightening, tightening, tightening until you could barely breathe or see or think, and then a blade slashed through the ropes in an instant, and you were no longer sad, but seething, because you knew precisely where and when the picture was taken, because you had been right there beside him, your right arm intertwined with his left.

Imagine the photographer had cropped you out.

Now she remembered, too, why he looked so haggard.

He'd been up all night praying with their pastor.

Is everything okay? she asked.

Her husband shook his head.

What's wrong?

Pastor saw some kid being beaten.

In person?

Her husband shook his head again. On the internet.

So? she asked.

It was bad.

You watched it?

A few minutes. I made him shut it off, though; he was near hysterical.

The church reading group had been going through *The Cross and the Shroud*. She thought it was awful, but Pastor said they couldn't appreciate Christ's sacrifice until they understood all that it entailed. She shuddered even to think about it.

Words like 'hemorrhagia percutem,' 'plumbatae,' 'hypovolemic shock,' and 'pleural effusion.'

Imagine you believed in God. Not only believed in Him, but considered Him the cornerstone of your existence. Imagine that you believed God called people and gave them gifts and powers and touched lips with coals and spoke through those He called so that their words were His.

Now imagine your husband returned from the pastor's at four-thirty in the morning, and told you that your pastor was going to resign because he saw some white boy getting whipped and said it made him realize that's what Jesus had gone through, what God made him go through in order to atone for our sin.

Imagine you told your husband that didn't make any sense, that mankind's sin forced Jesus to die, not God.

Imagine your husband had nodded in agreement, sighed, and told you that your pastor said since man's debt was owed to God, God essentially sent his son to die a horrible death in order to pay himself back.

She moved to close the magazine, hesitated, allowed her hands to fall back into her lap. It was her husband's eyes that caught the photographer's attention. They were a Persian green, but with the sun rising behind him, were black orbs shimmering with golden sparks. His skin was more burnt sienna than dark, his beard pure white, and time and hardship had cut deep troughs into his face, and she was sure that the photographer saw all that and thought that he could transform her husband into a field of contrast, color against color and texture against texture, sharp details and blunted details and focus and no focus and light against dark.

So he severed her husband's face from his body, excised his arms, one hand, and his legs, erased her completely.

Imagine you were almost completely alone in the world, that you'd outlived your son and your husband, and most of the people you knew and were friendly with had moved away to be nearer children and grandchildren, and that most of those that hadn't moved away left the church after pastor Isaiah resigned.

Imagine that you went to the coffee shop near your brownstone every day, and that you brought a teabag from home and a mug because you couldn't afford to buy the tea that they sell, and you always approached that counter and asked the barista for hot water for your tea, and she always smiled and gave it to you because she'd figured out that you didn't really have anywhere else to go, and she knew that you'd take a seat in the back corner and alternate between reading and people-watching.

She sat at a table abutting a floor-to-ceiling, plate-glass window, cupping her tea in both hands. She checked her watch: three and a half hours until the soup kitchen. Her pen was set perfectly parallel to the Sudoku book she'd completed (her second this week), which sat atop *The New York Times* crossword puzzle, which she'd also finished. She had puttered about in her small garden that morning, weeded all there was to weed, and watered and trowelled all there was to water and trowel.

She was sinking; she'd better get ahold of something quick.

Imagine that you hurt so badly from moment to moment that you could barely breathe, that it felt like someone was standing on your chest and the very marrow of your bones boiled with sorrow, and that you believed that life was beautiful, nonetheless, and you still wanted to live, because every once in a while you felt something that you didn't have a word for, a surge of life or a spike of joy, a blunt steel rod that jerked you off your feet and ripped the breath from your lungs, and that it was somehow as exhilarating as it was excruciating.

She turned away from the magazine, away from her husband, felt something rising in her throat and tears like pin-pricks at the backs of her eyes. She looked out through a window and into the alley, steeling herself, smoothed a hand over her hair, and looked back down at the magazine. The moment pounced savagely, with fangs and claws and no temporal pivot. It swallowed her and she felt herself crushed and yanked down and down and down in spasms as the muscles of the moment's throat flexed and extended, and the moment was both an instant and eternal, and within it she saw that the photographer had failed. That the man had tried to make her husband into a thing he could hang on the wall of his gallery, had tried to turn him into an object, and failed. That her husband had defeated him.

Imagine the love that surged through you as you closed the magazine and took it out to the recycling bin, how it pulsed with each heartbeat so that, if only for a moment, you knew nothing of pain. You longed for your husband, but knew that he was in you and around you and waiting for you in Heaven.

214

Then Heaven's spear ripped through your ribs and buried itself in your heart, knocking you from your chair, sideways, onto the linoleum.

And lying on the ground, folded over in pain, with tears in your eyes, your thoughts ran to pastor Isaiah. The man was standing on your chest again, and you couldn't move your left arm or leg, and so you prayed, but your prayers were for pastor Isaiah. You begged God to forgive him and make Himself known to the pastor once more. You knew he'd sinned, that it was blasphemous and insulting to equate their Savior's suffering with that of a boy playing at being Jesus.

And to call God vicious and savage...to say He had a bloodlust...

Dearest God, you pleaded, Heavenly Father...Alpha and Omega...

You had been propping yourself up on your right arm, but now you let yourself slide down, lay your head on the cool floor.

You closed your eyes.

Forgive him, Father, you said. Forgive him, and restore him to the communion of saints, to the blessed children whose names are written in the blood of the Lamb, in Your Book of Life.

THE GIGGLE HOUSE

Navy blue, black, and charcoal gray suits, with or without pinstripes, often work similarly.

I once tricked a cab into stopping for me.

GEORGIANA FREDERICA FAIRCHILD, A.K.A. ALICE

A bell sounds beneath the heat lamp on the counter between the kitchen and the front of the house, and the proprietor calls out "Alice" in a voice that rises above the steady murmur of conversation emanating from the deli's half-dozen tables and the radio droning beside the cash register.

A woman trades her receipt for the sandwich and turns for the door, though she is not Alice, but Georgiana Frederica Fairchild, and in LA for less than forty-eight hours to visit her brother and see the premiere of an ex-lover's play.

Seven years older than Christopher, she has always looked after him, though it's harder now that she lives in Europe, curating the Fairchild Galleries in Barcelona and Rome. He never needed much in the way of care or supervision; it was just that he'd always been different, reticent, at one or two removes from those around him.

Alice was the name she and Christopher came up with one afternoon when he was twelve and she was nineteen, home on break between the first and second semester of her sophomore year. Her college friends called her Freddie, which was better than 'Georgie' or 'Georgiana,' but she had wanted to come up with the opposite of the pretentious, aristocratic name with which her parents had saddled her.

Christopher had been reading A.A. Milne.

They're changing guard at Buckingham Palace, he'd said.

What? she'd asked.

Christopher Robin went down with Alice, her brother had replied. *Alice is marrying one of the guard.*

He'd smiled at her.

A soldier's life is terrible hard, Says Alice.

That had always been his way. He was drawn to beauty and humor and joy, but he was extremely shy and skeptical of his abilities, so he was alone most of the time, reading and shared passages he liked with her.

We saw a guard in a sentry-box, he'd recited. *One of the sergeants looks after their socks, Says Alice.*

They'd laughed at Alice, at how perfectly plain and prosaic the name was, how deftly it conjured visions of a middle-aged woman in a denim jumper, her hair cut into the "I'm-too-old-to-wear-my-hair-long" angular chop that women over fifty inevitably don.

We looked for the King, but he never came.

Christopher had made himself theatrically solemn to recite that part.

Well, God take care of him, all the same, Says Alice.

It strikes her as odd that those lines remind her of Beckett, now, even though she still hears them in Christopher's voice.

Maybe the five years she's spent in Europe have changed her? It wouldn't necessarily be a bad thing.

They're changing guard at Buckingham Palace, she hears Christopher say again as she unlocks her car door, and then *Christopher Robin goes down with Alice*, again, as she turns her key in the ignition, and there's something about big parties as she backs out of her parking space, and something about not wanting to be king as she drives away.

Her father and mother had started Christopher at various sports, baseball and soccer and tennis. He'd been good at all of them, without ever really caring for any of it. He'd never complained, though, so she'd been the one to tell their parents to stop signing him up and to arrange for art classes, and piano lessons, and the like. She was the one who bought him a camera and took him to plays, the symphony. Operas.

Their parents really did love them both, it was just that they were very busy people, and, well, parents, and therefore clueless about their children in the way that parents have been since the beginning of time.

That was the thing about Christopher, though—he always kept things close to the vest. She knows they have something special between them, though, even if he doesn't tell her anything, and she hopes, and even prays, though she doesn't believe in God, that her brother will be alright.

A face looked out, but it wasn't the King's.

She's done with the poem and starting to get a little irked that it keeps coming, and in the little boy voice she'd been so relieved when Christopher outgrew.

He's much too busy a-signing things, Says Alice.

She can't wait to see him, to hear him say *I missed you so much, Alice.*

No one else calls her that.

Mother said that the plastic surgeons had been able to remove all the tattoos from his face, that Christopher looked like himself again, even if he wouldn't allow the surgeon to remove the ghastly thing on his back.

Those ghastly things.

Tom Shipp and Abram Smith, Christopher had told Alice. She'd looked up the story.

She has a theory about her brother. The reason he's so standoffish and aloof is that he literally absorbs people's thoughts and emotions, and feels them as if they were his own.

Christopher has to keep his distance from people in order to survive.

They're changing guard at Buckingham Palace, he'd said. *Christopher Robin went down on Alice.*

He'd been fifteen when he'd made that little edit. She'd rolled her eyes. *Don't be puerile*, she'd said.

Do you think the King knows all about me?

Then as now, the poem felt endless.

But he carried it to the end, as he always did:

Sure to, dear, but it's time for tea, Says Alice.

THE GIGGLE HOUSE

Finally, the ninja were never without tools. Now, I'm not saying we should all start carrying around shurikens, but there are a few situation-specific tools that can come in handy:

Is it between September and Christmas? Is a white woman being a little too friendly in view of white men? Toss a pumpkin latte at her and get your Black ass out of dodge.

Cops getting a bit too suspicious? Quick, grab your NPR tote bag, and tuck copies of the *New Yorker* and the *Economist* in your back pockets.

Will you be deep in enemy territory? At Bed Bath and Beyond? Ikea? The Pottery Barn? Throw a yoga mat in there, too.

5-0 be like, where'd that nigger go?

INCREDULOUS MIKE

—You're listening to WIND, Conservative Talk Radio. This is Incredulous Mike. Caller, you're on the air, now tell us what's on your mind.

—Ha. Very clever, Incredulous.

—You're not a regular listener, are you...

—Benton.

—Right. You're not a regular listener, are you, Benton?

—No, I'm not. What gave me away?

—'You're on the air, now tell us what's on your mind' is the show's tagline. I say it ten or fifteen times an hour.

—And it's clever every time. Don't sell yourself short.

—Um, great. So what's on your mind? You don't sound like our usual caller.

—A little too much bass in my voice?

—I didn't say—

—Ha ha. No worries, Incredulous. Ha ha.

—What's on your mind, Benton?

—I'm just wondering why no one's talking about the Fairchild kid anymore, you know?

—He's old news. Rich brat crying for attention, blah, blah, blah...nothing more to see.

—Son of a billionaire allows himself to be tortured for three days, films it, and puts it online—

—And there's your answer! He's a nutcase!

—He passed several independent psych evals...

—You're telling me you don't think he's crazy? Seriously?

—Seems a little strange that no one wants to even ask the question.

—He had himself chained to a cage. Naked. In the worst part of New York. In February. Asked, and answered.

—Hey, now...I'm from Mott.

—Jesus, that place is a war zone.

—Have you ever actually been there?

—Well...no, but—

—Right. Back to Fairchild...when a sane man who is, according to his college transcripts, exceptionally smart, chooses to—

—Benton! Benton. Let's call a spade a spade, okay?

—A spade.

—A spade. Let's call a spade, a spade—it means let's be honest.

—I'm familiar with the phrase.

—Well, I wasn't sure. You seemed a little...confused...

—I...never mind.

—Look, Benton, we're not going to get anywhere with this because there's nowhere to go. Fairchild was a nutcase with daddy issues, a camera, and an internet connection: end of story. The sooner he's forgotten, the better.

—I don't—

—I've got callers waiting on the line, and time's running out, so...

—Just one last thing. Won't be but a minute.

—You've got thirty seconds.

—You hear a lot about the freedom of speech in this country, and I've got to think that's because words have power.

—Fifteen seconds.

—So Fairchild uses this power to say something in a way that costs: blood, humiliation, agony.

—Five seconds.

—Given how much he has going for him, isn't it odd that no one is asking why he chose to do what he did?

—Three seconds.

—Like, maybe they're scared how he might respond?

—And you're done, Benton. Have a nice life.

THE GIGGLE HOUSE

I'm out of time folks, so let me leave you with this: wypipo's problem with us isn't really a problem with us.

That doesn't make it suck any less, but it might make it easier to love yourself.

I ain't a big reader, and I don't do hugs, but James Baldwin, y'all, all day, and all night, and in any weather.

A society that refuses to face its history is a society living in fear, brothers, sisters, in fear of Black people and Brown people, of anyone whose existence is evidence that it rests upon a foundation of violence.

What we do with that, I don't know.

I'm just a comedian.

And you don't see me headlining at the Apollo.

So claim your power, whatever that looks like.

Speak in love. To each other, and to yourself.

And live in peace, if you can, because ain't none of us in here that doesn't deserve it.

KAF

He has only the name he chose for himself and the scar that runs from the lowest crease of his forehead through his brow to the concave slope of his cheekbone. The man who put a roof over his head—the man who was not his father, but fed and clothed him—cut him with a straight razor.

***

The protester died the moment the SADF spotlight hit him, but his carcass ran on.

***

He'd been a boy at the time, somewhere between twelve and fifteen, felt blood falling the length of his face as he watched the man gather needle and thread, cotton swabs and rubbing alcohol. He'd been silent as the man cleaned the wound and stitched it shut.

***

Kaf's was a cash-only business; white or Black didn't matter, only green. He did hot shaves for twenty-five dollars and haircuts for thirty-five; for fifty he did both and threw in a five-minute shoulder massage.

***

This is so you'll never forget, the man said.

***

The Jeep chased the protester half a block before the mounted fifty-caliber punched a fist-sized hole in his back and detached one of his arms.

***

Man and boy; the man never gave him a name, nor told him his own. In the rare moments when one was required the man had called him 'Kaf,' and he called the man 'Baas.'

***

Baas drank a liter of whiskey the night he cut Kaf, but he wasn't drunk; Baas drank a liter every night.

***

Kaf kept to the shadows as the Jeep approached.

***

The man talked about the cities, sometimes. The view of the ocean in Cape Town, Table Mountain looming on the other side of a mythic fog; Durban, with its ocean views and the hunchbacked oddity of the Luthuli International Convention Centre; the severity of the Union Buildings and the Palace of Justice in Praetoria; the Constitutional Court in Johannesburg, its lush parks.

***

There were three soldiers, two in the cab and one on the gun and spotlight.

***

What little he knew about the man came from rumors and whispers, and Kaf's piecing together the scant details the man offered about his life and childhood.

***

Kaf locked the shop from 1:00–1:45 six days a week; bought *The Post*, a black coffee, and a croissant; and, weather permitting, ate and drank and read on a bench in Marcus Garvey.

***

Kaf knew that the man who kept him had been an interrogator for the South African Defense Force, and that now he worked for the police in the same capacity. He'd heard whispers that he was a member of the C10, the C1.

***

The man secured a pass granting Kaf dispensation to live in the city proper and walk the streets that led to and from the markets and the stores to which the man sent him on errands—never to the inner sanctum where people in larny clothes drove gleaming cars and bought kittes in pristine shops, before champagne and caviar in tony restaurants.

***

Sometimes he talks to those he might have loved, those growing or grown into a certain consciousness of a vast, vicious, and sometimes beautiful, world.

***

He is standing in line at Harlem Star, waiting to checkout and pay. A woman cuts in front of him. *Excuse me*, he says to her, *but I believe it's my turn, I've been waiting.*

* * *

Kaf knew that the man had hiked Platteklip Gorge and Table Mountain with his father at least twice, and he suspected the man's father was now dead, and that death had come crashing down on him swiftly and unexpectedly.

* * *

Hate and disgust, he knew, suspicion. The eyes that seized on you and didn't let go until you rounded a corner or got so far from them that there was no earthly way for them to maintain their grip. Even then, he knew they were waiting for him.

* * *

Things he didn't know: his age, his father's identity, his mother's, why the man kept him on, why the man had him read to him, why the man told him certain things, why he kept other things back.

* * *

Every movement of his monstrous body is an intended or unintended protest. He is a leviathan, an incubus; his every desire, every dream, a conspiracy. His every malevolent hope is a plan for insurrection, his every glance an act of aggression. His very existence is a crime.

* * *

Sorry, she says, stepping back from the counter, flustered. *I didn't see you.*

* * *

A door opened, and one of the soldiers got out of the vehicle, pointed at the spotlight and back to the corpse, approached the body and gave it a half-hearted kick. *Dooie*, he called back. *Ja*, the gunner answered, *Een minder Kaffer in die wêreld.*

***

The man's voice trailed off and he was staring into the distance, and the boy didn't know what the man was seeing, only that he'd gone somewhere, and that he'd expect him to be exactly as he was when he returned, sitting on the floor with his back against the warm metal of the oven, the handle jutting out into the shallow, vertical bowl of space created by the sweep of bone from his shoulder to his neck, flaring outward from his neck to the base of his skull.

***

The man never sent him to school or gave him any money unless it was to run an errand or buy food, but he let Kaf come and go as he pleased, and the proprietor of a Soweto shebeen had taught him to read.

***

1985: grand and petty apartheid, Pass laws, promises of reform, flaccid oaths to dismantle It betrayed by lust and resurrection, by a juridical Lazarus; Black Consciousness, boycotts, strikes, demonstrations; police, soldiers, guerillas and citizens long since scraped from the rolls, liminal, ululating creatures swarming from the space between human and animal, flooding South Africa-proper, unwilling to suffer beneath a malevolent taxonomy insistent upon their ontic disfigurement, refusing to be debased, yoked, and driven like the cows and goats and sheep their ancestors kept in the velds a century before Europe broke the serenity of their harbor, rowed ashore, and cast its pall over grass, tree, and rock.

***

Kaf came home from a reading lesson one night to find a note in Afrikaans telling him to be at such and such an address at eight-thirty the following morning.

***

228

Harlem had gentrified over the last decade and a half; just under half of Kaf's customers were white. White people and their corn-silk hair.

It stopped being an issue after a few months.

***

Kaf Biko: the name he gave himself when he immigrated, a name as good as any.

***

He hitched a ride to Sharpeville in the bed of dilapidated bakkies whenever he could, which was not often.

People didn't know him there.

***

Kaf arrived early and found himself standing outside a barbershop at the edge of Soweto that almost touched the white area on the outskirts of Jo'burg where he and the man lived.

***

Soweto. Night. Christmastime, 1985. South Africa well into the first of Botha's declarations of a State of Emergency, three days beyond the Amanzimtoti bombing, Operation Butterfly underway, reminiscent of Church Street in 1983, portentous of the Durban beach bombing in '86, an auger of the explosion that would rock a Johannesburg court in '87.

***

The boy knew the man would return, but not how long it might take, or if he'd finish the sentence he'd started.

***

Kaf was at the barbershop ten hours a day, six days a week. In the mornings before it got busy, or late in the afternoons when the lunch rush had died down and before the after-work crowd descended, the old coloured man who ran the shop taught him things. At first, it was just a clean and rinse—how to do the two-minute scalp massage. Next, it was a hot shave, and only after a year and a half, a haircut.

***

The man's father had been a colonel in the South African Defense Force, a man of few words, and probably as hard or harder than the man was.

***

Word had gotten around Soweto that he lived with a white man, so people called him a collaborator and glared death at him and threw rocks and cursed.

***

The man had a Bible he never read. Kaf read it because he wasn't allowed to do anything else.

***

Again, Kaf conceals himself in the shadows as flame torches the night, jumps and spits.

***

1985: machetes, fire, bullets, bombs, bullhorns, clubs, spears, rocks, broken glass, bulldozers, blood, the odor of rubber and meat refusing to ascend; a thousand dead and rotting in unmarked graves or reduced from cinder to ash in anonymous crematoriums; tens of thousands arrested or interred, beaten and electrocuted, sodomized with broomsticks; weeping and rage, terror and wailing, sorrow and surrender and pain upon pain upon pain.

***

Throw him in the back? Seis! The driver recoiled. *Are you bosbefok? There's no fucking way I'm putting that in my Ratel—let the skollie bleed where he fucking is.*

***

Yea, though I walk through the valley of the shadow of death, I will fear no evil: for thou art with me; thy rod and thy staff they comfort me.

***

Kaf didn't know how or why he'd come to live with the man, or why the man kept him on, but he couldn't remember living anywhere else.

***

Asking questions—any speech at all that wasn't reading—was rarely part of their routine.

***

He had many questions, most of them obvious.

***

Kaf's girlfriend gave birth to twins on December 30, 1999; he left their apartment on the fifth of January and never came back.

***

The man would drink and sometimes talk, and Kaf would listen, or the man would hand Kaf a book and have Kaf read to him. He was never voluble, but when he talked he did so for an hour or more in slow, truncated sentences separated by long intervals that made them seem deformed, somehow, as if they'd been maimed even before they were spoken.

Each sentence was a parade of the mutilated.

***

Buildings and shacks and people were burning, behind him and throughout South Africa. His Abaddon was Black, Zulu, a member of an IFP death squad matched by military death squads and police death squads and ANC terrorists and vigilante groups dealing in necrosis and ruination.

***

The policeman chased him even though he wasn't running. His heartbeat hammered in his ears.

***

My grandfather was a white man married an African before they made it illegal, and my mother was a white woman married my father against her parents' wishes, and I'd been barbering downtown for near thirty years before they made that illegal for a coloured man. The old man looked at Kaf and smiled thinly. *Point of pride that nearly all my customers followed me.*

The white ones and the Blacks and the coloureds.

***

They circled the scary man, lusus naturae. He—Lusus—was very large. A leviathan. Terrible. The policemen were not leviathans. They were good, very brave.

***

The alcohol sucked the moisture from his flesh, left him desiccated; his mind sputtered like an engine gone through its petrol, burnt out with a clang and a cloud of metallic char. He lost any sense of time or place, saw things he'd seen and been unable to locate in the whens and wheres of his unfurled life.

***

The Zulu struck the match; sparks leapt from its head, which didn't ignite. *Ima!* a woman yelled. Abaddon struck the strike strip again, breaking the match in half. He took another from the matchbox. *Shiya umfana yedwa!* the woman yelled. The man turned. It was Anele from the shebeen. *Ukuvala umlomo wakho*, the man sneered, *owesifazane sithutha! Muhle umhleli!* Anele shook her head. *Niyaphaphalaza, Siyanda. Ake umfana aye.*

***

Thou preparest a table before me in the presence of mine enemies: thou anointest my head with oil; my cup runneth over.

***

One of the brave men seized the incubus from behind, yanked his forearm against the demon's trachea; he had to crane his neck back to do it. The monstrosity bucked, roared. The policeman tightened his chokehold; he was very brave.

***

Kaf was careful not to fall into the chasm between the man's sentences, not to allow his thoughts to wander; if he did, and if he was caught, his nose or lip or face would disappear behind an eruption of blood and ash and the heavy crash and clatter of a wood-metal ashtray hitting the floor.

***

Sometimes the man would talk about the places he'd been and the things he'd seen, or about his father, who taught him both poetry and blade craft, to wield a knife like a conductor holds his baton.

***

Kaf was suffocating. The wreak of rubber and petrol were a pair of fists crushing his larynx; they'd poured petrol in the tire and over his head; it ran down his face with the blood flowing from his brow and nose and lip.

***

He'd only been caught a half-dozen times in the eleven years he'd lived with the man, and each time he'd seen the flicker of electric light leaping from the rim of the ashtray as the man raised his arm to throw it, but he never ducked or tried to shield himself.

***

Description rarely issued from the man's lips; when it did, the words fled his mouth like fugitives cutting themselves into the black of night. Litres of beer and handles of bourbon made their escape possible, trips that took him away for days, sometimes longer.

***

Almost no one spoke to Kaf Biko, and he spoke even less. He was a criminal, a refugee, a poor boyfriend, and a deadbeat dad, but no one accused him of any of it, so he offered no defense.

***

The Leviathan is recognized by the color of its eyes, which are large and incapable of focus, by the texture of its hair, which is coarse and dirty, by the unseemly flare of its nostrils, the exaggerated length and girth of the cock that drives and determines its brutish behavior. It is in such attributes that one sees the creature's indelible inhumanity.

***

He's not moving. No shit, I put him down. No, I mean HE'S NOT MOVING—check his breath. Shit! He's not breathing—check his pulse! Shit! Dispatch, this is Officer X we've got a 10-52! AMBULANCE NEEDED! I REPEAT: AMBULANCE NEEDED...

***

The man's father had taught him Lingchi, Clouts, and Butler, and sometimes the man would recite stanzas while holding a knife or a fork or a pen, delicately, almost effeminately, and moving it as a lover might caress a body, as a conductor directing his symphony to play adagio.

***

The important thing to remember with Lingchi is that you are the maestro, and the person on the table is your symphony, each distinct body part an instrument; the tonality is pain, and each has its own range and register.

***

The noiseless, gliding briskness of the straight blade is not ungraceful in its way.

***

The brave man stood over a corpse that had been a leviathan. It had shrunk in death. It was no longer scary. The brave man turned toward the other brave men.

***

From time to time he thought about the twins he'd left behind, but never about their mother. Fraternal twins: a boy and a girl. He wondered if he could have loved them if he'd stayed behind, if he could have learned to. He'd never loved anything that he knew of, didn't know if he'd been loved, either, or how one knew.

***

Kaf tried to struggle free, and a man hit him with the blunt side of a machete, baring the white of his skull to the night.

***

Kaf didn't know what Lingchi was, or have any way of finding out, but he remembered the poetry. Butler and Clouts were the man's favorites.

***

He was taught that the hone must be of Blackstone, and the strop of sheep's leather; that the brush must be of silvertip badger hair, never of best, and certainly not of pure; that boar brushes are for Philistines, horsehair brushes for the nouveau riche, and synthetic brushes are an abomination; that though shaving cream is presently en vogue, shaving soap is preferable; that a quality shaving soap contains a high level of tallow and glycerin, which lock water into the skin, soften the beard, and leave the skin smooth; that tallow is essential to a shaving soap because it provides the lubrication that allows the blade to shave without irritating the skin; he was taught that tradesmen use German blades, and artists, blades from France, and that, no matter what might be said, there is only one purveyor of blades in the whole of that country, and that purveyor is Thiers-Issard.

***

Kaf didn't know what he was, Xhosa or Zulu or Sotho or Tswana or Venda, only that he was about to die, to pass into nothing through agony and flame.

***

One less nigger to worry about, he said. The brave men nodded, save for one who turned away.

***

Though he cannot see it clearly enough to mark out the words, he sees that he is Black because of humanity's insatiable lust, not for money or sex or food—not even for power, but for divinity, the ability to call a creature into existence merely by naming it.

***

I have not found myself on Europe's maps...
I must go back with my simple slaves
To soil still savage, in a sense still pure...

***

He is six-foot-three, well over two hundred pounds, his arm is raised; the cab blows by.

***

It was April, and though it was still a little cold to be outside, cabin fever drove him to the park and his favorite bench. He was hungrier than he thought and made short work of his pastry, then peeled back the plastic tab on his coffee and took a sip, savoring the pungent steam and the pleasant half-scalding of his mouth. The Fairchild kid was back in the news; the paper had put it on page four just so they had an excuse to trot out one of the prurient stills from his internet movie, Fairchild naked and a Black man with a shovel frozen mid-swing, the scoop blotting out the boy's face.

***

Thiers-Issard, the old coloured man said, stropping his razor, *was founded in 1884 by Pierre Thiers. He spent his lifetime hammering away at a forge and had a barrel chest and iron arms, but make no mistake about it: he was an artist. A master razor maker. When he died, those who knew him mourned, but thankfully, he passed both his art and his business on to his son, who continued the family legacy.*

***

Kaf will never attend another braai—in South Africa or elsewhere—never forget the smell of cooking flesh and how it had made his mouth water even though his ears were choking on the collaborators shrieking as they turned to char, the collaborators, and the people that had necklaced them and been caught by a convoy of armored vehicles that arrived without warning like pale horses of death.

***

Kaf's one hundred and twenty-eighth shave had been a patron of the old coloured man's barbershop for twenty-seven years, and had a standing appointment for a hot shave at twelve-thirty every Monday and Friday, which, on at least one occasion, he failed to keep. The barbershop, popular as it was, was scheduled solid at that time Monday through Saturday, but the old coloured man told the regular that he could fit him in on Tuesday so long as he was okay with Kaf doing the shave. The man assented and arrived at the shop at the designated time. Kaf's stall was at the back of the shop, and as the regular headed toward his chair, the old coloured man grabbed his wrist. *Don't distract him,* he whispered, *this is only his third shave, and he cut the last two.*

***

There, he was a peacock, without even trying, a fanged, venom-spewing peacock with a rhinoceros horn and wolverine claws.

***

The clatter and clang of the shop bell were barely audible beneath the storm. Kaf looked up to see a white man in chinos and a high-end trench coat, dripping rain onto his floor. *Can I help you?* Kaf asked. The man opened his mouth to speak just as lightning cut the sky, and thunder shook the earth. *That's a storm if ever there was one.* The man gestured toward the outside. He and Kaf turned to the window just as another bolt of lightning burst, each staring himself blind as a white shroud obliterated the world.

***

No word is my dwelling place...
Listen, listen among the particles.
A vigil of the land as it appears.
Open, open.
Enter the quick grain: everything is first...
I am the method of the speck and fleck.

***

It is almost three in the afternoon, Kaf waiting at the bar in the shebeen for Anele to finish with the last of the lunch crowd so he can tell her that he's leaving South Africa at the end of the week. *For good?* she will ask, and Kaf will only nod, unable to meet her eye. *Why?* she'll ask, and he won't be able to give her an answer, save for that the man he lives with arranged it, and says he has to go.

***

Kaf was granted asylum in Canada in 1985 and moved to New York in 2000, by which time his never-quite-childish childhood had passed from his memory.

***

Kaf sent the old coloured man a postcard when he arrived in Canada, but he never heard back. A year went by, and a package arrived from a solicitor representing his estate.

***

He gave up meat out of necessity, love out of respect, and aspiration because it was unfamiliar.

***

Here, he phases from fanged, venom-spewing peacock with a rhinoceros horn and wolverine claws to invisibility and back. Sometimes he is both at once, depending on who's doing the looking.

***

How are you today, sir? Kaf asked as his customer lowered himself into his chair. The customer only nodded and allowed himself to be tipped backward in a reclining chair, to have steaming towels laid over his face and neck. The towels would remain in place for an additional three minutes in hopes that the tension would rise from the customer's face with the steam. But the customer's face was so pale and rigid and immobile that, after Kaf covered the lower portion of his head with lathered shaving soap, it resembled a carved bust of white marble, and Kaf, standing over him with his straight razor, the sculptor about to carve the lines and swells of the mouth and jaw that would complete his face.

***

Kaf was walking home from Anele's shebeen and came upon two policemen standing together on the perimeter of a crime scene. One man was Black, and the other was white, and they were smoking apart but together when a police helicopter flew overhead, hovered in place, and switched on a white-hot searchlight so bright you could smell the air burn. Kaf watched as it sucked the color from everything it touched; the Black man became nothing and the white man, more intensely nothing, and it was then that he understood that whiteness was not so much a color as the visible absence of color, and also, at the same time, the origin of all colors, and that was the reason for Van Riebeeck, Verwoerd, Vorster, Botha, apartheid, bombings, terrorists, torture chambers, assassinations, and all the rest, the reason that in the wide, violent landscape of human machinations, such dumb blankness can be full of meaning. No one is white. White is color turned inward, against itself, so that its existence collides with its non-existence.

***

1948-1989: 14,000

***

2015: 1,134

***

STOP!

***

He rarely drinks, but when he does, he drinks to annihilation.

***

Outside, it was cold, and the heat of the steamed towels Kaf lay on his customer's face, and later the shaving soap, and still later Kaf's ministrations upon the customer's shoulders and neck and skull caused the man to fall asleep, his mouth opening and his head tipping back and the electric light falling heavily on his pale forehead so that he appeared jaundiced. And since business was slow and there were other empty chairs in the shop Kaf could use were someone to wander in before the day was over, he let the man be, and tread softly as he swept hair trimmings and dirt into a dustpan. He'd learned that it's best not to wake them, that there are few things in the world as dangerous as sleepwalkers.

***

Woe to those who think they are white, for their blood turns to dust and their flesh consumes itself; they make of themselves a revenant and set a curse upon their own heads: they burn unto the tooth with an insatiable hunger, their throats parched and swollen with a thirst no amount of blood can quench. They set themselves apart.

***

Kaf closed the barbershop at the end of the day, locking the door and the external cage that protected it. The sky glowered above him, and he saw that it was still raining and realized that the jacket he was wearing was thin and not at all waterproof, and that he had left his umbrella at home. He set out through the rain, shielding himself with a copy of *The Post*. Fairchild dissolved between its fourth and fifth pages, black into white, white into gray, and all into nothing.

THE GIGGLE HOUSE

And that's it for me. Good night, Giggle House.

THE PRETZEL BAG

The pretzel bag slipped from the girl's hand into a breath of wind and was swept up over the rail and into the gray, free for the first time, plenary and riding the draughts westward above 33rd Street, gay and gyral, flit to scud and zephyr to zephyr.

Not five minutes ago the girl's mother had said it was too cold to go up, that they'd both freeze, but the girl begged and pleaded until her mother gave in, insisting, though, that they stop at a food cart first. The mother ordered two hot chocolates and a soft pretzel, and the vendor slid the pretzel into the pretzel bag before handing it to the girl, who was buoyant and giddy and delighted by the crinkling noise the wax paper made in her hands.

They entered the building and then the elevator, and the little girl startled as the elevator shot upward, clutched her pretzel so tightly the chunks of salt bit into the bag.

But that was over now.

The bag was about to cross 6th Avenue when the wind shifted, throwing it back toward Madison, and slantways towards 31st Street, and for a brief moment the bag thought it was going to swoop down along Broadway and twist and roll and leap over and around and through throngs of theater-goers and dog-walkers and smokers until it was blown through the door of a theater and went skidding between people's legs and came to rest beneath one of the seats.

For a moment the bag thought it was about to see its first show.

But, no.

It was okay, though, because another wind took the bag up, up, up and swung it by the Empire State Building, cartwheeling forward, higher and higher and higher.

The bag couldn't help but think of what would become of it when its flight came to an end: sunk down a storm drain, forgotten in an alley, buried beneath a shroud of dirt-marred snow.

But it was soaring now, so near the heavens that the people below looked like pushpins, and there wasn't a hand in the world that could reach up and catch it and crush it into a ball and throw it in a trash can full of dog offal and rotting food.

It would run, creep, flit, tumble, that's what it would do—a life on the lam!

Forgotten wasn't so bad, it thought, if you had your freedom—the bag would be a dashing fugitive, would sleep under cars and busses and beneath the trees in Washington Park.

Washington Park!

How far was it to Waverly?

Waverly!

How mellifluous! Like the song of a Malabar thrush at first light.

The bag would take up residence in Waverly and relish its beauty, marvel at all the comings and goings. It would do whatever it took to get there, even if it meant clinging to the bottoms of people's shoes.

Oh! Oh! Oh! And now it was snowing!

The bag felt like a god, a king surrounded by the wealth of Solomon, a million and one glittering jewels.

A king and a god, but the best of both, the kindest and most benevolent; it could have kept it all to itself, could have lived alone in a shimmering heaven and danced among its wealth for all eternity, but it didn't.

It was a good god and the best god and the kindest god, and so the bag allowed the gems to fall, and even though the world below had no use for the bag and would discard it, the bag commanded the jewels to become light as feathers, to flit and sway as they fell, to alight ever so gently on people's noses and tongues and outstretched hands. The bag spake, and thus it was, and it beamed as its riches poured forth upon the world below.

But CALAMITY CALAMITY CALAMITY! It hadn't thought its plan through—the cascade of diamonds fell and clung to the bag as an infant to its mother's breast, and the weight grew and grew and grew until it was borne to the ground, just outside Union Square, and it would have wept, except that bags have no tears, not even pretzel bags, which it regarded as the apex of its Genus.

There are feet, though, it thought, lots of feet.

But the bag was no god in the world of men, and just as bags have no tears, neither do they possess any means of locomotion, and so the bag languished in dwindling hope.

But lo and behold, there came a wind, and the bag was giddy and flush as it spun onto West 14th, only to be blown by 5th Avenue without pause, and by 6th and 7th too, and spat onto Washington Street, where it was left desolate in the shadow of the Whitney Museum.

The bag lay in place for some time, wetted against the sidewalk, inconsolable, wishing for tears to weep and teeth to gnash, and wondering if God was punishing its hubris.

But could God truly begrudge a pretzel bag a few evanescent moments?

No, it was unthinkable.

The bag had done no more than borrow a pair of feet so that it might dance one dance in the ballroom of heaven.

So little to ask for. A tiny quaff of celestial light.

People hurried by. The bag could not see them, but the steady flow of words was soothing, and though it had never slept, because pretzel bags don't, it imagined that the state and sensations it was now experiencing might be similar to sleep.

Another hour passed. All that was left was to wait and hope for wind.

But none came. Instead, it was a boy of eleven or twelve that ran at the bag and gave it a vicious kick five, six feet in the air, and a cab coming up Gansevoort hit the bag and dragged it left onto Washington, and then onto Horatio Street and Greenwich Avenue and 8th and Greene and—miracle of miracles—onto Waverly.

The man left his cab running, purchased something from a food cart, and, as an afterthought, flicked the bag off his windshield.

It fell softly, lilting to and fro like a pendulum. It landed face up so it could see the sky and watch the snowfall, and the lights and the people and the vendors.

It was glorious.

Then the lights were out, the candlewick once more between

God's fingers.

The bag didn't see where the boot came from, or who was wearing it, didn't even see the person's shadow.

People treat the planet like one giant landfill, the boy who stepped on him said. The planet's fucking dying—we're going to be seriously screwed if we don't make some major changes real soon.

Come on, man, someone replied, give the sermons a rest for a minute. I'm seriously worried about you.

Look, I missed one week, okay?

One week of what? the bag wondered.

The voices were getting too far away to hear.

Dammit, Chris.

One week...now...b...all g.

Things...not all...

Not–ick...I did what...not...

Never a...

...

Chris...

...olya...

Now.

...promise...

Somewhere in the eternity to follow the bag will remember this—the promise. It will find itself marveling at how gently the body's boot had landed upon it, and its anguish at losing Waverly will fall away and seep down through its bed of trash into whatever lies beneath it, and whatever lies beneath that.

Eternity is a promise, the bag will think.

We are given a part in an endless exchange of days, one day for the next, and each morning, the day offers itself as the day on which we can leave the rancorous, rotting bedding we have fashioned for ourselves, and make our way toward something better.

And if, on the cusp of nightfall, we realize that we have once again failed to accept its offer, the day, with its dying breath, reminds us that it will be renewed at the break of dawn.

THE END

ABOUT ATMOSPHERE PRESS

Atmosphere Press is an independent, full-service publisher for excellent books in all genres and for all audiences. Learn more about what we do at atmospherepress.com.

We encourage you to check out some of Atmosphere's latest releases, which are available at Amazon.com and via order from your local bookstore:

The Embers of Tradition, a novel by Chukwudum Okeke

Saints and Martyrs: A Novel, by Aaron Roe

When I Am Ashes, a novel by Amber Rose

Melancholy Vision: A Revolution Series Novel, by L.C. Hamilton

The Recoleta Stories, by Bryon Esmond Butler

Voodoo Hideaway, a novel by Vance Cariaga

Hart Street and Main, a novel by Tabitha Sprunger

The Weed Lady, a novel by Shea R. Embry

A Book of Life, a novel by David Ellis

It Was Called a Home, a novel by Brian Nisun

Grace, a novel by Nancy Allen

ABOUT THE AUTHOR

Ciahnan Darrell is committed to using his craft to help him engage the world in which he finds himself and those with whom he shares it. A writer and a scholar, he holds Masters degrees from the University of Chicago and Stony Brook University, and a PhD in Comparative Literature from the University at Buffalo. Both his creative work and his scholarly research explore systemic inequality and the ways in which discourse on race and gender shape the horizons of individual and social life.

Blood at the Root is Ciahnan's second novel. His debut, ***A Lifetime of Men,*** was released by Propertius Press in 2020 and received multiple honors in the 2020-2021 Reader Views Reviewer's Choice Awards.

To connect with Ciahnan on social media, sign up for his mailing list, or learn more about his writing, visit **https://www.ciahnandarrell.com**.

ABOUT ROCK YOUR WORLD

The author proudly donates 10% of the proceeds from sales of *Blood at the Root* to Rock Your World, a program of Creative Visions.

Creative Visions is inspired by the life of Dan Eldon, a 22-year-old Reuters photojournalist who was killed in Somalia in 1993. After his death, his mother and sister, Kathy and Amy Eldon, discovered 20 journals bursting with collages, reflecting his adventurous spirit and his life as a creative activist. Determined to capture Dan's life as an artist, adventurer, and activist, Kathy and Amy launched our foundation in 1998 to support other creative activists.

In the spirit of Dan Eldon, **Rock Your World** empowers youth to use their voices, innate talents, and the power of media to become changemakers in their communities and the world.

The Rock Your World curriculum is designed to inspire global citizenship while helping students develop 21st century skills. Starting with an understanding of the Universal Declaration of Human Rights and the Convention on the Rights of the Child, students research an issue of choice, then create a multimedia-based advocacy campaign to promote awareness and ignite positive change.

Originally created by teachers for teachers over a decade ago, the Rock Your World curriculum is standards aligned, flexible and free, complete with lessons and downloadable resources. To learn more about our educator trainings, course and curriculum design services, and virtual, global mentorship program, please contact:

Jessica Burnquist, Vice President of Education & Youth Empowerment **jessica.burnquist@creativevisions.org** or **rockyourworld@creativevisions.org**.

Inspiring Students to Change Their World
—— A program of Creative Visions ——

Made in the USA
Middletown, DE
07 November 2021